# PRAISE FOR THE VALENTIN ST. CYR SERIES

### CHASING THE DEVIL'S TAIL

"A beautifully constructed, elegantly presented time trip to a New Orleans of the very early 1900s. The characters are memorable and the period is brilliantly recaptured."

—*The Los Angeles Times*

### JASS

"Another voyeuristic tour of Storyville, New Orleans's red-light district during its heyday at the turn of the 20th century. Fulmer's dialogue adds its lyric voice to the gutbucket sounds and ragtime rhythms pouring out of the bars and up from the streets."

—*The New York Times*

### RAMPART STREET

"The sense of place is so palpable you can almost hear the music. Fulmer's writing is crisp and nuanced. Valentin is a hero for whom it's easy to cheer."

—*The Detroit Free Press*

### LOST RIVER

"David Fulmer's evocative prose captures the sights, sounds, and smells of 1913 Storyville in his superior Lost River."

—*USA Today*

# ECLIPSE ALLEY

**Also by David Fulmer**

THE VALENTIN ST. CYR MYSTERIES

*Chasing the Devil's Tail*

*Jass*

*Rampart Street*

*Lost River*

*The Iron Angel*

*Eclipse Alley*

&

*The Dying Crapshooter's Blues*

*The Blue Door*

*The Fall*

*The Night Before*

*Will You Meet Me in Heaven?*

*Anthracite*

# ECLIPSE ALLEY

## DAVID FULMER

New Orleans, LA

Crescent City Books is an imprint of Commonwealth Books, Inc. Distributed to the trade by NBN (National Book Network) throughout North America, Canada, and the U.K. Crescent City Books and its logo are registered trademarks of Commonwealth Books, Inc.

Joseph S. Phillips and Susan J. Wood, Ph.D., Publishers
www.blackwidowpress.com

Cover Design: Kerrie L. Kemperman
Text production: Geoff Munsterman

ISBN-13: 9780998643151

Printed in the United States of America

*To all those who have accompanied me on my fictional journeys, errant as it has been.*

*This is for Sansanee, my very real hero.*

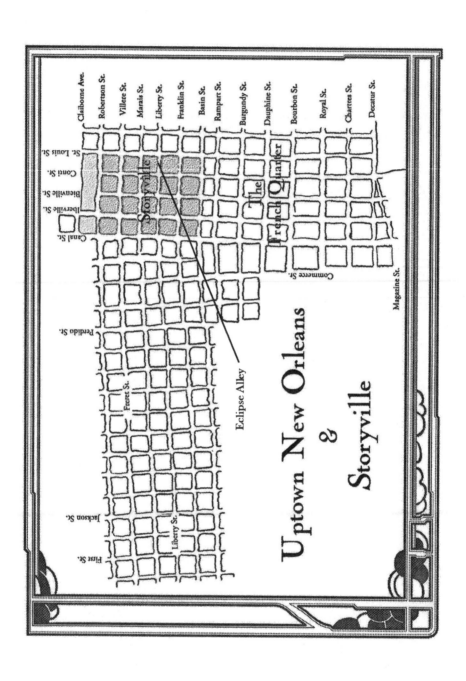

Uptown New Orleans & Storyville

# ECLIPSE ALLEY

# One

## March, 1900

The tall man walked into the back room of the Rampart Street dance-hall, his horn case with its frayed stitching and cracked finish tucked under one arm. He had dressed for the occasion as if for a performance, his suit pressed, hair razor-cut, and nails polished, a white silk scarf in a rakish drape over his shoulder. He was displaying the smile that too many women found too wicked to resist.

The four who had passed the time waiting for him with a bottle of Raleigh Rye varied in shades from pale tan to chocolate and had been making music for parades and cakewalks since they were kids. In the corner farthest from the door, a thin and nervous man hovered at a table where a device of brass and spun steel sat dominated by an ornate bell.

The establishment didn't open until dusk and so was quiet, save for a scraping of chairs and the clink of bottles being stocked in the big room. Once the sun went down, a crowd would ramble in off the street and the serious mayhem would commence. Then the tall man with the horn would become "Kid," as in Kid Bolden of the Kid Bolden Band. The moniker sounded a bit foolish and more than a little prideful inside those four walls. No one else, not even John Robicheaux, the best-known band leader in the city, was so brazen about using his own name.

Kid or not, to them he was Buddy, the nickname he had gone by since his childhood in the streets around First and Liberty in Uptown New Orleans. Buddy—the Kid—now took a quick swallow from the bottle Jeff Mumford offered and drew the silver cornet from the case. In the years to follow, his appetite for any substance that would derange him would become legendary. That would begin when the "Kid" became the "King" and was shaking New Orleans right down to its wet soul with music no one had ever heard before. At the end of that wild ride, he would be a dirty, broken, mad shadow of himself. But on this day, there was only the slightest glimmer of that fate and he was ready for whatever the afternoon and evening brought.

First was the business at hand. He paced the room, the tips of his long fingers dancing on the pearl buttons of the horn as he hummed a random batch of lines. Making a recording felt like the start of something; and at the beginning of a new century, no less. To his knowledge, they were the first jass band to take the step. Surely the first in New Orleans.

The recordist, a Frenchman who went by Mr. Cyril, stood proud at the machine, the most recent offering from the Edison company. The intricate and lovely assembly of moving parts and elegant curves was one of only a half-dozen in the entire city.

Mr. Cyril stole glances at the musicians, fretting, as they appeared to be in no hurry to begin. Watching the bottle of rye go empty, he decided to speak up before someone fetched another from the saloon. "Mr. Bolden?" he called. "I'm ready."

Buddy stopped his ambling to treat the little man to a cool slide of his dark eyes. "All right," he said and gestured with his free hand to the others. Willie Cornish on the bass fiddle, Will Warner with his clarinet, Pete Marcell on valve trombone, and Mumford on guitar stood up and flexed various joints. Buddy turned to the little man. "You tell us when," he said.

Mr. Cyril blinked. "You don't need to..."

"To what? Play some? Get warm?" Buddy's smile was easy. "If we ain't warm now, we won't never be." He raised his horn. "You just say when and we'll go."

Mr. Cyril took a moment to draw a handkerchief from his pocket, dry his sweating palms, and dab his forehead. Though the New Orleans spring had just arrived, the room was close. Laying the cloth aside, he opened the wooden box and drew out the wax cylinder as if it was made of delicate crystal. He placed it in the cradle, engaged the crank, and lifted the curved arm that held the stylus above the cylinder.

Now he looked up and said, "Ready, Mr. Bolden." With a steadying breath, he turned the rotor with one hand and lowered the stylus with the other.

Buddy mouthed a silent, "One, two, one-two-three-four," and in a sudden swoop, the bass fiddle thumped and the three horns and ten wound steel strings met in the air.

Whatever Mr. Cyril had been expecting, it was not the ragged burst of volume that was like a freight train hurtling from a tunnel, each instrument a part of an engine that seemed about to explode off its rails. But the horn was the loudest; indeed, the loudest he had ever heard.

He bent over his little machine, fearing that the volume of the horns would melt the wax and drive the stylus clean through the cylinder. The needle was vibrating along, close to bouncing, yet holding and he kept cranking. After all, whatever was happening couldn't last more than three minutes.

After one of them had gone by, he was surprised to find that he could pick out wild threads: Bolden's cornet ripping like a Gatling gun, the bass and trombone *whomping* at the bottom end, the clarinet looping over the top, and the guitar making a *chuck-chuck-chuck* rhythm, all of it so electric that he half-expected sparks to start flying. He had never heard anything like it; but then he did not venture out onto Rampart Street, where the same raw music—what they called *jass*—shouted and moaned deep into the night.

The musicians' ears and fingers were busy keeping pace with only a key, a beat, and the manic stream from the silver cornet racing ahead of them. By the time the needle passed halfway along the cylinder, Mr. Cyril decided he wanted to hear whatever happened next and leave with a good story to share at the saloon.

It was a shade under three minutes when the music stopped. The four players heeded the leader's raised hand and made a giddy spiral to their final note. After a beat of sudden silence, one long last C-sharp wailed from the bell of the horn and then evaporated. Mr. Cyril stood with his mouth hanging half-open until he caught a puzzled stare and remembered where he was and what he was doing. Just in time, he stopped turning the crank and lifted the stylus.

# Two

The two women, one in her middle years and the other young enough to be her daughter, had finished for the night and were settled at the kitchen table at Juanita Daly's house on Franklin Street, sipping small glasses of brandy. Both had talked too much for one evening and now sat listening to the faraway notes from the parlor piano, along with the voices of the men being entertained and the sporting women entertaining them.

Though Ida Clark was the older, she was at the moment the less weary. Her companion, Serena Tracy, had welcomed six gentlemen—or was it seven?—seeing the last one to the door not ten minutes earlier. She was sagging over her glass.

Miss Ida, taking pity, stood and helped her from the chair.

Serena felt aches in a half-dozen places. "I am sure wore out," she said.

"It's what the life does to you."

"Tell me again how long you've been at it," Serena said.

"Came in the year of oh-one," Miss Ida said. "So that's fifteen years now."

The younger woman gave a shake of her head, but didn't speak. She was wondering where she'd be in fifteen years. She hoped it wouldn't be in the New Orleans red-light district they called Storyville.

The jitneys, most of them Model T touring cars, congregated at the end of the line and all along St. Louis Street, converging at the walls that enclosed Cemetery No. 1, that venerable city of the dead. Their trade was a mixture of sporting women from the mansions, bartenders and waiters from the restaurants and saloons, and musicians from the dancehalls. The District's gentlemen visitors either owned automobiles or hired carriages. The rest walked or rode the streetcars.

Approaching along Liberty Street, Miss Ida and Serena Tracy spotted three of the machines and the glowing tips of the cigarettes the drivers smoked as they slouched on the fenders, waiting for fares. The women passed the end of the alley. A few steps along, Serena stopped, her tired eyes going wide. "Good Lord," she said. "Did you see that?"

Miss Ida said, "See what?"

Evangeline often woke in the small and dark hours. On this night, it was the pattering on the glass that had roused her. She loved the rain, whether in the city or back on the bayou, though it at times brought destruction. Indeed, most of the memories she held onto were awash under rainy skies.

Two of her three children had been born during soft morning drizzles, her husband had proposed to her in his broken English as fat drops from the leaves of a live oak dappled his black curls, and Valentin had come to rescue her in the midst of another storm. That had been in the spring. September brought a hurricane that ravaged the city, all but destroying much of what had stood for a hundred years. Valentin and Justine had closed the shutters and they moved inland to Baton Rouge while the storms raged. But the house on Lesseps Street had been flattened, most of their possessions lost. Most of the little library that Valentin had kept in the small sitting room had been blown to the winds.

New Orleans was recovering, one brick at a time. They claimed the work to be done would prevent another such deluge. Who could say? The world was a mad place. Across the sea, the terrible war dragged on, and thousands of Americans were now dying along with the rest. And yet for Evangeline, there was peace in the dark of this early April night. She thought a few sips of wine would suit her before she went back to bed. She had just taken the bottle from the cabinet when the telephone shrilled.

There had been other calls in the middle of other nights and they always meant the same thing. She stepped into the foyer, lifted the handset, and spoke a greeting. A moment later, she felt his presence in the doorway.

From the beginning, seeing him in certain combinations of light and shadow had given her pause. Did she know him? Or, more rightly, had she known him long ago? Such moments stilled her, as this one did.

Now he yawned and said, "Is it for me?"

Valentin slipped into the bedroom, hoping to change into his street clothes without waking his wife. His profession required stalking in cat-like silence along the city's back streets, a wisp in the night wind. Indeed, he could render himself nearly invisible. But not with Justine. Her sharp backwoods ears could sense him moving about at the far end of the house. Now she came awake, raised her head from the pillow, and said, "Where to this night?"

Valentin reached for his shirt. "Eclipse Alley."

The half-dozen police officers were standing around the body, smoking their cigarettes and cigarillos. One held a gas lamp.

The youngest of the lot, a new man named Casey, who had manned a desk for his first two years on the force and had yet to learn when it was permissible for a street "tad" to speak up—which was never—spoke up. "What the hell happened to him?" His voice was filled with awe. It was his first murder victim and a ghastly way to begin a career of viewing dead bodies.

This particular dead body lay face-down on the wet cobbles, the arms outstretched and palms flat. The middle fingers of both hands had been removed and all eyes fell on the stumps, cut just above the knuckles. The trousers had been pulled down to the ankles and bare white buttocks faced the night. It was a strange tableau that silenced the officers until Casey had the idea to cast the lamp about for the absent digits. They found none. There was nothing more they were permitted to do until a senior officer arrived on the scene. So they kept glancing at the wounds, shaking their heads and muttering curses.

———

Since the strange and abrupt departure of J. Picot seven months before, Lieutenant James McKinney had all but taken his place, at least as far as Storyville was concerned. There had been no promotion or assignment. Picot's replacement, Captain A.G. Warren, was a pious and fussy man who wanted nothing to do with the red-light district, and in fact was one of those who would prefer it be shuttered from one end to another. So the day-to-day responsibility for the twenty blocks fell to McKinney and it was he who was roused from the bed he shared with Mary Rose, the woman he had first met through Valentin St. Cyr's kindly wife Justine, who had known her years back at one of the grand Basin Street mansions.

At the sound of the telephone bell, she let out a groan. The lieutenant pushed back the covers and sat up. She said, "It'll still be there in the morning," her voice muffled by the blanket. They both knew what she was talking about.

The Creole detective arrived from the frame house on Bayou St. John. Lieutenant McKinney, having driven in from his cottage in Irish Channel, had already been on the scene for ten minutes. The alley was roped off and blocked by a police sedan and they met in the middle of Basin Street, each thinking how the other man had changed in the seven years since the case on Rampart Street first brought them together.

McKinney had been a young patrolman, a hard but fair street cop who accepted the graft that was a fact of a New Orleans policeman's life with a grudging hand. He was tall, with a rugged frame, a solid, freckled Irish face, and short ginger hair. Though a serious person, he kept a good store of humor in reserve.

For his part, Valentin's curling black locks showed strands of dark gray. His rare brew of African, Sicilian, Cherokee, and French bloodlines often caused him to appear as a different person from one moment to the next, depending on the light. In the dim glow of the streetlamps, his face was as pale as McKinney's even as its planes were carved from Creole clay. Time had passed for both of them, in other words.

It was a quiet pocket in the night and aside from the officers shuffling about, the only people in the vicinity were the jitney drivers standing on the running boards of their Model Ts, trying to catch sight of the carcass.

Valentin remembered when Eclipse Alley was bustling with little shops, a noisy dive or two, at least one gambling parlor, and a single hop den. Some nights it got so crowded it was hard to pass, meaning the pickpockets were working with both hands. Now it was another of those parts of Storyville that had fallen by the wayside, a dark tunnel that emptied out onto the last block of Liberty Street, with the only bustle these days produced by the rats that had surely scrambled for cover upon the policemen's arrival.

The lieutenant broke into these musings. "Sorry to drag you out like this," he said. "But it's a special circumstance. The patrolmen are saying that's no ordinary victim back there."

"I figured it was something like that," Valentin said. "Who found the body?"

"Two sporting girls out of Juanita Daly's were on their way to get a ride," McKinney said. "They saw the victim when they passed by. One of the drivers over there roused a patrolman."

"Where are they now?"

"I questioned them and sent them on. They just spotted him, is all."

Valentin let it pass. McKinney was a good detective and would have detained the two trollops if they'd known anything of value. "You have an identity?"

The lieutenant shook his head. "He's face down on the cobbles. And none of these beat coppers got close enough to see." After watching the uniforms mill about for another moment, he said, "You ready?"

Valentin hesitated. Every time he found himself standing over a murder victim, he swore it would be the last. But then this happened and that happened and this person or that called begging him to bring his skills to the investigation. In years past, the caller had been Tom Anderson. But Valentin hadn't heard from that gentleman in months and knew only from what others told him that the once-eminent figure known as "the King of Storyville" was even in the city.

Now it was city officials or police detectives who contacted him. And if the problem concerned Storyville, that meant Lieutenant James McKinney. The same James McKinney who was stepping toward the alley and gesturing for him to follow.

The patrolmen made way for the senior officer and the private detective. McKinney noticed the glances of recognition when St. Cyr stepped up. Some would have heard rumors about the Creole who had been a street copper working Storyville until he crossed a certain senior officer and found himself dismissed from the force, after which Tom Anderson hired him. He had been watching over the red-light district ever since. Most of the stories about him were true. There was no doubt that Storyville would have been a more lawless place had not St. Cyr kept his sharp eyes and hard hands on it.

Those hands were pocketed and the eyes looked neither left nor right, instead falling upon the hapless soul with his face plastered to the cobblestones.

He let McKinney do the talking and the lieutenant said. "No one's touched him, correct?" Three of the patrolman spoke up at once. He raised a palm for silence. "All right, stop. Who was first on the scene?"

"That would be me, sir." A short and slight uniform took a step forward. "Patrolman Second Grade Casey. I was a–"

"A clerk in the section," McKinney said. "I remember. Good. So no one touched him?"

"No, sir. No one," Casey said.

"Anything unusual?" McKinney said. "Other than..." He lifted his hands and wiggled his fingers. "And his trousers down like that?"

Casey was about to offer some bluster to impress the lieutenant. Then he caught himself and spoke simply. "There's the blood on the stones. That's all."

The Creole detective had not moved or spoken as he peered at the back of the corpse. McKinney said, "You want to turn him over now?"

St. Cyr came alert, bending close to the victim's head. He said, "Light, please?"

McKinney waved and Casey pushed the lamp over St. Cyr's shoulder. The lieutenant leaned in, his hands on his knees. "So?" he said.

"Not a mark," Valentin murmured. "Or nothing I can make out in this dark. Can we see his front side?" McKinney turned to order the patrolmen to help. "Wait." Valentin lowered his voice. "Get them back."

The lieutenant took Casey's lamp and in a few curt words ordered the coppers to wait on the street. The patrolmen turned away, only too happy to escape. Once they had exited the alley, the two detectives bent down, grabbed handfuls of the victim's long coat and turned him over.

What they beheld caused McKinney to bark out, "Jesus Christ!" He drew back, cursed under his breath, and crossed himself. Valentin caught a hard breath.

Something had happened to the mouth that had painted the chin and chest red. That was the less gruesome part. The front of the trousers were below the knees and had been slashed to shreds and the parts of body that made the victim male had been cut away. It was a bloody, galling mess, and the two men stared without moving, both biting down on the wrenching in their guts.

Once they were out of earshot, McKinney let out the breath he had been holding, and said, "Sonofa*bitch*." He lifted his chin to the gory tableau. "You know who this is?"

"Herbert Waltham," Valentin said. "The president of Crescent Cotton Exchange. And one important fellow in this city." He paused. "I mean, he was."

The lieutenant said, "Christ, what a fucking nightmare." He continued to stare at the ravaged body. "You ever see anything like this before?"

Valentin shook his head. "Can't say that I have."

McKinney said, "You think he was alive when it happened?"

"Could have been, I guess. I didn't notice any other wounds."

The policeman went into his pocket for a packet of Omars, shared one with Valentin, and lit both of them with a lucifer that he snapped on his thumbnail. "You believe we're standing here looking at this? What happened to good old-fashioned shootings and bludgeonings?"

Valentin allowed himself a grim smile. They both knew that within the past year, New Orleans had witnessed a dozen murders in broad daylight. One woman had mixed a poisoned tea that she served the husband who had been beating her black and blue, with the expected agonizing death. Three or four bodies had washed up on the banks of the Mississippi, each a victim of some brutal attack. Random violence claimed more lives. This was something else.

The two men stood smoking and thinking their own thoughts until they heard the grinding of wagon wheels coming their way from St. Louis Street. The city morgue had yet to give up horse-drawn hacks to transport the dead. There was no hurry and they needed something for the beasts still living in the stables to do.

Before the wagon pulled to a halt, Valentin said, "We can't have them seeing this."

"I'll have them give me a shroud," McKinney said. "And I'll tell Casey and the others to keep quiet about it."

"They won't."

"No, they won't. But it's the best I can do."

Valentin sensed something in the silence that followed and said, "What is it?"

"Are you willing to work this? I think I can get funds to pay you."

Valentin spent a moment considering. His wife wouldn't like it, but it was no time to say no to money. He was a private detective, after all.

"I can do that," he said. "This one case, though. Justine wouldn't abide me making it a habit."

"That's fair enough," McKinney said. Then, "Anything you can think of for the moment?"

"The doves," Valentin said. "The two who found him. They'll need to button their lips, too."

The lieutenant said, "Can you talk to them?" and before Valentin could answer, drew a leather-bound notebook from a pocket, opened the cover, and tore off a page.

Valentin squinted at the scribbled names. "I remember Miss Ida."

"The New Orleans Police Department appreciates your assistance," McKinney said. He flicked the butt of his Omar and turned for the street.

Valentin waited by the body, reflecting on his choice of career. There had been a half-dozen times that he could have walked away and once he had done just that, leaving New Orleans—and Justine—for the better part of a year, gambling when there was a game, laboring when there was work, and hoboing when there was neither. He came back to the city, to Storyville, and to her. Since then, he had lost count of the killings, the robberies, the beatings, and all the petty crimes that had fallen his way. He wondered if one day he might make a list.

This musing was interrupted by the lieutenant returning with a white sheet in hand. "They didn't even blink. Just tossed it to me."

"Because they're both drunk." Valentin was familiar with the parties on the wagon.

"That, and they're zeroes." McKinney handed Valentin a corner of the shroud.

After the detectives wrapped the body, McKinney summoned four of the coppers to carry it to the bed of the hack. The uniforms were sent off with another stern warning from the lieutenant to keep quiet. Even so, as he watched the last one stalk away, he knew they'd soon be chattering like Garden District matrons and before long every officer at Parish Precinct would know something gruesome had happened in Eclipse Alley. There was no way to stop it. The lieutenant was most interested in keeping the chatter out of the morning newspapers. That was as much as he could hope for.

He turned around to see the Creole detective standing over the bloody puddle the victim had left behind, his eyes fixed, as if the sight had hypnotized him. The policeman had seen that posture before: he was studying something only he could perceive, either on the cobbles or inside his brain. As before, he waited for him to snap out of it, spending the time with a second Omar and images of the woman asleep in the bed in the house off Tchoupitoulas Street.

Presently, he heard footsteps and St. Cyr appeared, wearing a quizzical smile. McKinney said, "What is it, Mr. Valentin?"

"She must be right fine," St. Cyr said.

"What's that?"

Valentin pointed. "The look on your face."

"Yes...I'm, uh..." The lieutenant felt his cheeks getting hot. "No, I meant what did you find in the alley."

"Back there?" Valentin cast an absent glance over his shoulder. Then he said, "Oh. Yes. What I found was nothing. It's too dark. Even with a lamp. We need to come back in the daylight." He now turned to peer into the shadows. "Can you still get an alley blocked without causing suspicion?"

"I can," McKinney said. "I'll have them get something up before morning."

Valentin said, "What's your plan?"

"I'll go in and write my report. You can join me at the morgue later."

The Creole detective sighed. "I was hoping I could skip over that part."

McKinney smiled and said, "If I have to go, you-"

"I know, I know," Valentin said.

"So I'll call you." The lieutenant waved a hand and turned to leave.

"Picot," Valentin said.

McKinney stopped, puzzled. "What about him?"

"He never came back?"

"No one's seen him. Why do you ask?"

"That was the last time we worked together. It's been a year."

McKinney shrugged. "I guess it was. Looks like he's gone."

"As long as he stays that way," Valentin said.

*Hiding here in the shadow of the cemetery wall, seeing policemen in their uniforms amble about. The two men who stay, standing over the place where the man who was carted away had gone down, are smoking their cigarettes and talking down low.*

*Oh, to hear what they were saying! To know what they thought about what had happened to him. To know if they had found any trace of anything that might lead to... But, no, they were too far away and the lonely horn from the freighter churning its way downriver was breaking into the night too loudly.*

*Waiting. Waiting. Now they shake hands and go their separate ways. From over the wall, the whisper of the wings of a night bird. And that's all.*

# THREE

Valentin leaned at the door to the back gallery sipping his coffee, the stark images crossing his mind in such raw detail that Justine had to snap her fingers to get his attention—and then after she had called his name twice.

She had been making breakfast when he walked into the kitchen and she waited for him to pour his cup full to ask what had been so important to beckon him in the middle of the night. He took a moment to listen for Evangeline running water for her morning bath before describing the body in the alley and telling her the victim's name.

She stopped what she was doing. "Herbert Waltham? I just saw him."

"Saw him where?"

"Not him. His picture. It was with another piece about that yellow fever committee."

He didn't recall anything of the kind and said, "Where was this?"

"Sunday. *The Times-Picayune.* On the Society page."

That explained why he hadn't seen the piece. "Do we still have it?"

"Next to the sofa."

He left and was back in a half-minute with the paper in hand. He paged through and stopped. The headline read "Tom Anderson to Head Charity at St. Ignatius." The story had been written by Rebecca Marcus.

> Mr. Tom Anderson is adding further renown to his good name with the announcement that he will chair the Yellow Fever Fund, a charity directed at collecting private donations that

will be dedicated to eradicating the dread disease. Former state senator and successful businessman Anderson adds the title to a growing list of endeavors directed to enhancing the public good, two of which are the Spanish-American War Veterans Foundation and the...

He stopped reading to examine the photograph of thirteen serious men in suits that carried the caption "City Leaders Join Forces to Combat Yellow Fever." Among them was Herbert Waltham. He recognized most of the other names: George LeMond, the president of First National Bank; Father O'Brien from St. Rocco's; Raymond Villiers, chief officer at Mercy Hospital; Bartlett Barry, the former City Attorney; Dr. John Green, the dean of Xavier University; Captain A.G. Warren of the NOPD. The others were luminaries of one stripe or another.

"Waltham." Valentin tapped the image. "It was him, all right. Lying in that alley."

Justine said, "And they called you."

"That was James's doing." He laid the newspaper aside. She was waiting for the rest, so he said, "He asked me to work it with him."

"And you said yes."

"I won't do it if you don't want me to."

She didn't reply to that, instead saying, "So you're getting paid?"

"I will be."

She digested the news as she cracked eggs into the frying pan. "Do you have any idea why he was murdered? And why there?"

"We don't. It's just starting."

"Well." She scrambled the eggs in an absent way. "Now what happens?"

"I'll go to meet McKinney at the morgue," he said. "Later this morning. And we'll have another look at the scene in daylight. Today or tomorrow. Then go from there."

She slid the eggs, boudin, and half a brioche onto a plate. "You, working for the police department again after all these years. Who would have imagined?"

"They need the help." He kissed her cheek. "And we need the money." He carried his breakfast to the table.

"What do you think your friends on St. Charles will think?" she said. "They didn't like it the last time, as I recall."

"I don't think they'll care much," he said. She heard the note of doubt in his voice.

He returned to the newspaper. "There's Mr. Tom, right at the center. No mention of a certain red-light district." He picked up his fork.

Justine said, "You think he knows about Waltham?"

"I'm sure he does."

"You don't need to call him?"

"I'm not in his employ anymore." He didn't remind her that this was partly due to her wishes.

Justine said, "When was the last time you spoke to him?"

"It must be eight or nine months now," Valentin said. "Just before he turned over the Café and walked away."

It felt odd saying that. Tom Anderson had run the twenty-block square since before it had been made legitimate by Sidney Story's 1897 ordinance and had been so successful at managing the economy of sin that people called him the "King of Storyville" and the red-light district was sometimes dubbed "Anderson County." He amassed power beyond the city limits, getting elected as state senator with influence to spare. Three of his four wives had been madams of fine sporting houses. In short, Tom Anderson *was* Storyville. Or had been. He had given it all up, most importantly the Café and Annex that had been the District's anchor, and where Valentin had first entered the old man's employ. So it was now history to him, too. He hadn't set foot there in over a year.

Justine began humming a soft melody and he raised his head to gaze at her, a welcome distraction. How had she had changed over the years and yet stayed so lovely that it still surprised him? The young sporting girl, a Creole-of-Color from deep in the bayou, had become a woman of rare substance. Her high cheekbones, eyes with a slight slant, and gentle curve of a nose announced the Houma on one side, while her full lips and latte skin professed other blood. He had always loved her ample curves. They had grown more ample, delighting him.

They had traveled down a road both blissful and harsh. He had left her and she had left him before they found each other again. He had made her his wife in hopes that he would not lose her a second time. And now she stood bathed in the morning light through the window in the kitchen in the house. Their house. He was watching her and musing on their winding trail, when the telephone bell jangled. She turned in time to catch a hint of a dreamy look in his eyes. "You'd better get that," she said.

Lieutenant McKinney had arrived at Parish Precinct while it was barely light and spent a half hour writing up his report on Eclipse Alley. He had just penned the last entry when a clerk called to inform him that both Captain Warren and the precinct commander Major Delphine were waiting for him. The lieutenant climbed the stairs to the commander's office to share the basic facts of the savage murder.

When he had finished, Captain Warren, who looked more wan than usual, spoke up to explain about the newspaper piece and the photograph that included him and the victim. He said, "It's just..." He didn't finish the sentence.

The commander muttered something before dismissing the two officers with instructions that the details of the crime were to remain inside the building. It was no use. By ten o'clock, the identity of the victim had leaked to the ranks and within another hour, went tumbling out onto the streets to greet Storyville's earliest rising madams and sporting girls. Yes, a body had been discovered and yes, the victim had a name: Herbert Waltham.

The morning papers had missed getting to the story before deadline, but when word reached the newsrooms of *The Times-Picayune* and *The Sun*, the editors came alert. The crime beat reporters for the former daily were nowhere to be found. Someone recalled seeing Barney Goings on St. Claude in the early morning hours. Elmo Miller's whereabouts were unknown. A copyboy was sent out to scour the saloons.

Rolf Kassel, the city editor, began yelling from his office door. "Find them! We need someone on this, goddamnit."

It was loud enough for Rebecca Marcus to hear as she crossed the newsroom. She stopped for a startled second, then turned around and charged the editor's office.

She had spent her brief career at the paper writing for the Society pages and every now and then a bland news item or obituary. There were whispers that she earned her way in the door by bestowing favors on the some higher-ups at the paper, but this was untrue. She in fact divided her amours between certain men who intrigued her and women who offered French arts at houses dedicated to that specialty. The final curiosity that dogged her was the rumor that she was a niece of Josephine Marcus, the common-law wife of Wyatt Earp. She chose to neither confirm nor deny this gossip, hoping that it might draw more readers to her bylines.

Niece or not, she was, like that famous woman, of Jewish extraction, and presented a handsome Levantine face and figure, the flesh olive and the curves pronounced, all driven by a generous dose of forward motion that propelled her to the decision that she didn't want to spend her career writing candy cotton about wealthy matrons and their spoiled daughters. And so she stepped up to Kassel's office with the intention of leaving with the assignment or not leaving at all.

She found Reynard Vernel there, in conference with his superior. Before his recent promotion to junior editor, he had been a crime reporter who knew Storyville. A thin, bespectacled, and studious sort, he reminded Rebecca of a young college professor, and had always treated her well. Her hopes rose.

In a few breathless sentences, she laid out her plea for the Eclipse Alley assignment. She had the skills. Both crime reporters were missing. She knew the family from working the Society page and had already visited them a half-dozen times. And so on, all in less than a rushed minute.

When she finished, the two editors exchanged a look she couldn't read. She was afraid they were about to start laughing. Then Kassel said, "I've been wondering when you were going to get to this."

Rebecca said, "Excuse me? To what?"

"To asking for something with some meat on the bone."

She glanced at Vernel and detected a smile lurking.

"I'm well aware of your talents," Kassel continued. "I know you can handle more. And I know you've been chafing upstairs. But I'm not sure that the murder of a prominent citizen in the red-light district is a good place to start."

"I can do it," Rebecca said.

Kassel blinked at her cheek. "I've got some damn good reporters on this paper."

"Well, where are they?" Before he could respond, she said, "And I can do better than good. I just need the chance."

Kassel looked at Vernel, shaking his head in wonder. "You hear this?" he said. Reynard shrugged, enjoying the show.

The editor opened his mouth to speak, but Rebecca again jumped in ahead of him. "You let me take this. Reynard can watch me. And if I don't deliver, pull me off. I won't ever ask again. Can we agree to that?"

The editor stared at her for a tortuous moment before shifting his attention to Reynard. "What do you have to say?"

Rebecca said, "Please, Reynard."

Vernel addressed the senior editor. "Well, knowing the family will certainly help," he said. "I think she can handle it. And I'll keep up with her." He guessed that he and Kassel were sharing the notion that a female name attached to a story would draw more eyeballs. It was also true that it would draw the ire of the beat reporters.

Kassel pondered for few more seconds before saying, "All right, Miss Marcus. Take it. We'll see what happens. But remember, there's a witness to what you promised." He turned to Vernel. "Get her set up at a desk down here."

The junior editor hoisted a vague thumb toward the back corner of the newsroom. "All we have is the..."

"That's it, then," Kassel said. "Put her there."

Rebecca didn't know what they were talking about and didn't care. She dug out her notebook and pen to scribble what details were available, then rushed out of the office before either man could change his mind.

———

Lieutenant McKinney spent an hour filling out reports on his ongoing cases and tending to other police business. When he finished, he picked up the telephone and asked the operator to dial St. Cyr's number.

He wished the Creole detective a good morning, then told him that Mr. Waltham was laid out on a cooling board at the city morgue, with instructions that no one was to as much as peek at the body.

"I'll be down there right around noon," he said.

"All right," Valentin said. "I'll see you then."

He dropped the phone in the cradle as a clerk stepped up to explain with an odd smirk that there was someone from the newspaper waiting in the lobby.


Eyebrows and whispers were raised when the young woman all but burst through the doors of Parish Precinct. The sergeant at the desk listened in astonishment to her request and then asked her to wait while he summoned someone.

Lieutenant McKinney appeared a few minutes later and in a gentlemanly manner guided her to a quiet corner. Miss Marcus offered her name and said she was from the *Times-Picayune,* then pushed her sunhat off her curls, reached into her canvas bag, and produced a notebook and pen.

"So," she began, the pen poised. "I understand that you were on the scene in Eclipse Alley this morning."

Confounded by her pleasant looks and eager attentions, he said, "I was, yes. But—"

"Will you verify that Herbert Waltham was the victim?"

"Excuse me," the lieutenant said. "You're covering this for the paper?"

"Yes. *The Times-Picayune,*" she repeated. "You can call my editor and he'll—"

"No, no. It's all right." He was still trying to settle his thoughts. "I'm sorry, what were you asking?"

"If Herbert Waltham was the victim."

The lieutenant considered, then said, "We're not prepared to confirm that as yet."

"It's already all over the street."

He wasn't sure whether to be amused or annoyed at the way she was challenging him. So he simply shrugged and said, "It's out of respect for the family."

"I know them," Rebecca said. "Quite well, in fact."

"You wrote the story. The one with Mr. Waltham in the photograph."

She smiled. "Do you follow the society news, lieutenant?"

He returned her stare, cool for cool. "Someone pointed it out."

She moved on. "Do you have any suspects?"

"No. But it's very early."

"What can you tell me about the crime?"

McKinney took a few seconds to choose his words. "It appears that the victim bled to death."

"Was he shot? Stabbed?"

The officer hedged. "He was cut."

"Cut?" Rebecca said. "What does that mean?" She caught something in McKinney's expression. "Wait. Was he mutilated in some fashion?"

The lieutenant wondered if word of that aspect of the crime had spread, too. "I'm not prepared to discuss the particulars," he said.

"Because there are things only the killer would know."

"Among other reasons." He glanced over her shoulder at the clock on the wall. "We'll be going to the morgue later to examine the body. I might have more after that."

"Will Mr..." She glanced at her notebook. "St. Cyr be there?"

McKinney hid his further surprise. "Yes, he will."

"I'd like to join you," she said.

The lieutenant took another moment before saying, "I'm sorry. You wouldn't be permitted inside."

Her black eyes flashed. "Why, because I'm a Jew?"

"What?" This time, he laughed. "No. Because you're not an official."

She said, "I'll just wait by the door, then. What time?"

Herbert Waltham was no ordinary citizen and so it was Chief of Police Reynolds himself, accompanied by two other command-level aides, who arrived in their dress blues at the house on Esplanade Avenue to deliver the terrible news to the victim's wife. Joseph Waltham, Herbert's younger brother by a year, had driven himself directly from the morgue.

The Chief had thought to contact Father John O'Brien of St. Rocco's, where the deceased had worshipped, and the priest was waiting in his black Pierce-Arrow and pondering God's mysteries when the police sedans pulled up.

The somber procession passed inside with the brother leading the way. The maid's eyes widened when she greeted them. They filed into the living room. Waltham's wife—now his widow—looked up from the book she was reading and said, "Joseph, what's..." She saw who was behind him and said, "Chief...? What do you...Oh, no. Oh, no..."

Her brother-in-law sat down on her right side and the priest on her left. The Chief took a chair and related what had happened in as gentle a tone as that gruff man could muster. In the next moments, screams echoed through the house, causing the maid to come running. The mad moans and weeping had barely subsided when first her son and then her daughter arrived. A new round of heartbroken wails followed.

With the Father consoling the mother and daughter, the Chief requested that Joseph and his nephew and the victim's son, Herbert Waltham, Jr., join him and the other two officers in the kitchen. Once the door was closed, one of the Chief's aides delivered a sanitized description of the murder.

"And you're sure it's him?" The young man's voice was trembling.

Joseph Waltham said, "I made the identification, Herbert." He did not share the sickening details about his brother's ravaged body. The officers couldn't omit all the facts, however, and the aide sketched out the location of the murder.

"Eclipse Alley," the younger Waltham half-gasped out the words. "Where is that?"

"It's at the end of Liberty Street," Joseph said. "Near St. Louis."

"Liberty Street?" Herbert, Jr. said. "What in God's name was he doing down there?"

The aide explained the investigation was underway but still in the preliminary stages, and the pertinent information would be forthcoming. Detectives would be paying a visit. The son shook his head in a numb way, then said something about his mother needing him. He and his uncle returned to the living room. The policemen followed them, stopping to murmur their condolences before making a relieved exit. Father O'Brien remained behind to pastor to the grieving family.

Valentin puttered about the house through the morning, busying himself with chores, and hoping in a vague way for something to come along that would divert him from what was waiting a few miles to the south. It was no use; he had taken on the job. He was expected to deliver. So just before noon, he offered Justine and Evangeline reluctant good-byes and left out the front door.

Justine took her second cup of coffee onto the back gallery and sipped while she watched the birds flutter through branches that were plump with new leaves.

How many times over the last eight years had she been greeted by the news of a dead body in Storyville, which was followed by her husband running off to get his fingers into the crime? The answer was too many. She puzzled regularly over the strange life they led. They had almost escaped the District on at least three occasions. But then something happened to pull him back. And she had followed along, even though it incensed her. His work seemed to take him to such dark places; and to her dismay, she tended to get swept up in it. She had to admit, though, she preferred it to the lot of a bored homemaker.

It wasn't that what came before him had been tranquil. Far from it. Coming out of a brutal childhood on the bayou, she had gone on the road as a dancer in a traveling show and then ended up in the red-light district. Though she had never served as a common whore; her looks and her figure and sharp mind saved her from that. Then she met Valentin St. Cyr and after some years of turmoil that came and went, found herself settled as his wife in their little house on Bayou St. John.

And maybe it would have been enough, had she not gotten caught up in his last serious case, the one that ended with the murderer who called himself "Gregory" disappearing into a Terrebonne Parish bayou and Evangeline moving into their home. She was a mystery, a woman who had lost the remembrance of most of her past. Valentin never said it, but she knew that he spent part of every waking day wondering if she was in fact the mother who had vanished when he was still a boy—after he had lost a brother and a sister to yellow fever and his father to a murderous mob. Justine had doubts, but kept them to herself. She suspected that the truth would come out in time. For now, Evangeline brought a certain peace to the household.

She now heard that kind soul moving about. Soon she would appear and they would spend a pleasant hour in the cool of the morning, talking about nothing. No matter what Valentin thought, she sensed in the older woman a need for family. Whoever Evangeline was, she had been a mother to someone.

Justine knew that she should be pleased with her lot. How many one-time Storyville harlots had found themselves with a good husband and a nice home that were likely to last for life? Every now and then, she ran into a sporting girl she had known from those times and saw the envy in the eyes as she related her story. And yet, she found herself staring at Valentin's empty chair, thinking about the noise swirling around the murder of the wealthy gentleman that had taken place in the narrow byway they called Eclipse Alley and admitting to herself that wherever her husband was at the moment, she longed to be there, too.

# FOUR

Valentin left the Model T on his favorite lot by the Mint and began walking along Esplanade. It was such a pleasant morning, with a cooling breeze from the northwest, and as he passed the fine homes along that boulevard, he saw citizens strolling and children playing in the sun. It wouldn't be long before the world would turn, the heat would rise, and New Orleans would bake.

He arrived at the corner of Claiborne Avenue and for the first time in a year or more, began a tour of the red-light district from the bottom up. Claiborne and Robertson, the next street over, were the worst that Storyville had to offer. Cribs lined the four blocks of each, with a few women in attendance even at this early hour, raw-looking harlots in filthy Mother Hubbards, smiling with bleary eyes and mouths missing teeth as they called crude invitations to the ill-advised men wandering by.

"Ten cents. Come get it. Ten cents."

"Bring that thing over here. I'll suck it dry."

"'Round the world for a quarter. One quarter. Come on, now. I know you wan' it."

Valentin had been hearing the same cries for a decade or more and they always sounded the same to him: weary, joyless, empty, as if coming from the throats of crippled animals. He passed on. Villere and Marais marked a step up. The houses, while small, were mostly tidy. The sporting women were cleaner and when they posed at windows, offered their enticements with a degree of modesty. Roughnecks were employed to handle the unruly.

Crossing Marais Street, he gazed west. A few blocks down, Frank Mangetta, his "uncle" in all but blood, ran his busy little grocery and saloon, on the one side catering groceries to the Italian community during the mornings and afternoons and come evening, serving up food, drinks, and music on the other. He would have to stop there on his way back. There would be a price to pay if the proprietor found out he had been in the District and hadn't visited.

At Franklin Street, the Storyville renowned far and wide began in earnest and the houses began a shift in the direction of grand. The gentlemen who patronized them were citizens of means rather than rowdies. The women wore gowns and the madams contracted with doctors to make weekly visits to examine them. Most addresses offered a parlor for entertainments, with a professor at the piano and ten-dollar bottles of champagne.

He arrived at the end of Liberty Street. He took quick notice that McKinney had done as promised and a barricade had been placed at the mouth of Eclipse Alley. Across the street, a patrolman strolled up and down. Before him, in the light of a March day with the mule-drawn water wagon having passed through and washed the gutters and facades in repose, the street all but sparkled.

Come sundown, it would all change. The street would be a sight to behold, still dazzling as the only legally-sanctioned red-light district the nation had ever known. Block by block, it offered a carnival of wicked pleasures and for the better part of ten years, Valentin had worked its seams and edges and shadows to make sure the show played on.

That had come to an end. Now that he was married, working as a private detective in the daylight hours for St. Charles Avenue law firms and then roaming the District half the night was too much, even if his wife would have put up wih him, crossing the tracks into the French Quarter, nodding to the Negroes unloading wagons piled high with produce from the market and toting sacks into this restaurant or that. At the corner of Dauphine, he saw two coppers standing over a drunkard who had tumbled into a gutter and decided to spend the night there. One was poking the poor sot with his nightstick and saying, "Up, Ernest. Up." They paused long enough to treat Valentin to glances that were cool but not hard, recognizing him still as Tom Anderson's former private copper.

A breeze blew off the river and up Conti Street, sweetening the air. Valentin sighed at the thought that in a few short blocks, he would be stepping into a dark, chilly warehouse of the dead. But as he passed Bienville Street, he cheered himself with the notion that once the visit was finished he could step back into the sun. Unlike those who occupied the cellar. He walked on.

*One of the fingers is a good choice for a first step. The blood is dry now and even though all the parts are in the icebox, this piece is already showing taints of gray. Going bad. Rotting away. Like the rest of Mr. Herbert Waltham. But a tight wrap of waxed paper sealed with paraffin and a package that is glued and tied shut will work just fine. It's not going far.*

Rebecca had two hours before her deadline. Once she had cleaned off the top of the desk and emptied the dust and general grime into the trash bin, she checked the typewriter to make sure it was usable. Glancing around the newsroom, it occurred to her that Barney Goings and Elmo Miller, the two crime beat reporters, would be appearing soon. She mulled that over, then hurried to Reynard Vernel's desk to inform him that she was heading out to work on her story. The editor wasn't around, so on her way out, she asked one of the copyboys to pass the word.

Valentin was standing at one of the two small front windows, smoking a cigarillo, when McKinney descended the steps with a young woman wearing a dark blue walking dress following behind. A sun hat was held in place with a bow tied beneath her chin and her dark hair was lanced in back with two chopsticks, a trick that only fast girls used to employ. As she drew closer, he took in her features: olive skin a shade or two lighter than his own, round, dark eyes, a nose neither narrow nor broad. She made an appearance that was more than pleasant and he felt he had seen that pretty face somewhere before.

She stopped when the lieutenant reached the bottom steps and crossed her arms as he passed inside.

"Who's your friend?" Valentin said when McKinney closed the door behind him.

"She's from the *Times-Picayune*. Rebecca Marcus."

"The one who writes for the Society pages?"

"Not at the moment," McKinney said. "They put her on this murder."

"She wrote a piece about Tom Anderson," Valentin said. "There was a photograph. And Waltham was in it."

"I guess that's how she got the assignment," the lieutenant said. "Things sure are changing, aren't they? But maybe she'll come to her senses and go away."

Valentin peered out at Miss Marcus, who was now staring at the door as if she could bang it open with her glinting eyes. "I wouldn't count on that," he said.

They walked along the corridor, feeling a chill that went beyond the temperature maintained to preserve the bodies. Some four dozen late residents were warehoused in that dank cellar. The Creole detective always imagined some haint drifting along the hall and in and out of the examination rooms and lockers. Whatever the case, the morgue never failed to make him uneasy, an irrational fear that he one day might not be able to escape it.

This unease was not shared by the staff. McKinney stopped at the lobby desk to sign the book. Valentin walked on to the main examination room to find an attendant who, having already been at the bottle, was as jolly as could be. He let out a whoop when the detective entered. His name was Howard and he had been a fixture there for the better part of ten years.

"Mister St. Cyr!" he spoke the name the French way, *sawn-seer.* "Ain't see you since... since..." His brow stitched in a comic wave.

"Last April," Valentin said. "That fellow, what was his name? Walked in front of a train."

"That would be right." McKinney stepped into the doorway. Howard shot him a nervous glance, and said, "Lieutenant."

"You been staying out of trouble, Howard?" McKinney said. "Keeping your hands off the belongings of our recently deceased?"

"Don't have no problems with that anymore, no, sir." The voice was hushed with shame.

Valentin rescued him. "We'd like to see the body brought in from Storyville this morning."

McKinney produced the release form from the coroner and handed it to the attendant. "Has the coroner been in?"

"Yes, sir," the attendant said. "He had the fellow's brother with him."

"Did he make a positive identification?"

"Yes, sir, he sure did." He paused, peering at one detective and then the other. "So where was it they found him?"

"Eclipse Alley," McKinney said.

Howard returned in a few minutes, pushing a gurney that held a body covered with a sheet splotched with faint reddish stains. The two detectives stared at the draped corpse for a somber few seconds. McKinney said, "We'll call when we need you." The attendant's mouth dipped in disappointment, but he made his exit without a further word.

The door closed behind him. Valentin said, "How did we ever get into this business?" The lieutenant shook his head, stepped to the gurney, and pulled the sheet from the body.

The sight was all the more gruesome under the hard lights. Valentin peered at the butchered crotch and the severed digits and found his stomach churning. He turned his attention to the face that he had not been able to examine in the shadowy alley. The victim was in his fifties, his round face blank and pale, his hair thin and blond going to white. The body was thick, with little tone of muscle; a man who spent his life behind desks and at dining tables laden with rich food. Though slender had become stylish, men like Herbert Waltham still carried their bulk as a sign of their prominence.

Valentin raised one of the lids and looked upon a dead eye of muddy green. He let it close and began a survey of the skull that found no wounds other than bruises that had resulted from the head striking the cobblestones.

McKinney had lit a cigarette while he had been finishing his examination.

He now plucked a shred of tobacco from his lip and said, "Well?"

"Nothing to go on." Valentin covered the body with a sigh of relief. "So now, what?"

"I have a photographer coming directly." McKinney said, looking abashed. "I wasn't thinking about that in the alley. My mistake."

Valentin said, "I don't think having pictures would have gotten us anywhere."

They waited for a quiet quarter hour. At which point, Valentin said, "You think your reporter friend is still out there?"

"No telling." With a glance at his pocket watch, the lieutenant straightened and left the room.

Valentin had been alone with dead bodies too many times to count. And yet, the thought of the cadaver with those parts missing under a sheet just a few feet away was making his skin crawl. He was relieved to hear footsteps in the corridor.

McKinney stepped inside, holding the door open for a photographer Valentin didn't recognize. He said, "Miss Marcus is gone."

"Well, I suspect she'll be back," Valentin said.

Rebecca had barely settled in, leaning on the railing at the top of the steps, when the same copyboy she had seen as she left the newsroom came racing across the street. Of course, copyboys were always racing somewhere. Though it was true it had never been for her and his shout of "Miss Marcus!" sounded like music. The pink-faced, sweating kid stopped at the top of the steps, all out of breath. "Miss Marcus, ma'am? Mr. Vernel says for you to come back in right away. He says it's important."

After breakfast, Justine and Evangeline took their cups to the back gallery and sat in the wicker chairs to enjoy the start of the day. New Orleans was brutal at the height of summer and mostly drab over the winter months, but the early springs and late autumns were heavenly. And so it was at this hour, with a cool breeze making the jacaranda leaves and the oleanders dance on their stalks.

They were quiet for several minutes. Then the older woman said, "I know you've told me where you come from. It was... Indian Bayou?"

"Yes, ma'am. Beyond Lafayette." She smiled. "Way out in the woods."

Justine sensed another question hanging. Though she had provided bits and pieces of her background, she couldn't tell Evangeline the whole story. How she had been the product of a brutal, drunken father and the woman he broke apart. How they had survived his reign of terror until they did something to end it. She escaped, first as a dancer in a traveling show and later as a sporting girl in the Basin Street mansion where she had met Valentin St. Cyr.

Instead of these details, she had made up little stories to gloss over the rough parts. Even so, she could never get past the suspicion that Evangeline saw beneath her fictions with the same gimlet gaze in her eyes watching her at this moment. How much did she understand? There was no telling.

Now the older woman interrupted her thoughts, this time saying, "So Valentin is off on an adventure."

Justine was perplexed. "Yes, he is. Did he tell you?"

"No," Evangeline said. "It was the call so early. And now he's gone." The older woman was regarding Justine with an expression she couldn't read. "When can we expect him home?" she said at last.

Rebecca and the copyboy made a hurried walk back to "Press Row," the Tulane Avenue block where *The Times-Picayune*, *The Sun*, and the half-dozen smaller city newspapers huddled. The elevator ride to the third floor gave her time to catch her breath and she stepped out and into a jumble of clacking typewriter keys, ringing telephones, and the random shouts of "Copy!" The day shift was in full tilt.

She saw Reynard Vernel waving to her from his desk. His expression was giddy and his cheeks pink. Leaning close, she caught a whiff of whiskey on his breath. "You've been out doing research," she said.

The editor laughed, his flushed cheeks flushing more. "And too early."

"How did you know where I'd be?"

"The victim was carried to City Morgue. So…"

Her brow stitched. "Did you have someone following me?"

The editor drew back. "Of course not. I wouldn't do that. I just figured that's where you'd be."

Rebecca caught another breath, realizing she had been flattered. "I'm sorry. So?"

Vernel bent his head and lowered his voice, drawing her in. "I talked to a copper friend of mine who worked the overnight shift," he said. "I bought him a couple glasses at Fewclothes. And he had a tale to tell."

"Reynard..."

"All right, all right. The victim was mutilated."

"I know that. Mutilated how?"

"Both his middle fingers were sliced off. His tongue, too. And..."

Rebecca said, "Yes? And?" Vernel swept a quick hand below his belt. She gave a start and let out a fierce whisper. "His *cock*?"

The editor choked. "What the sporting girls call-"

"His *yancy*. I know the language. And was it Herbert Waltham?"

"It was," Vernel said. "His brother made the identification."

Rebecca stood without moving, as if frozen in place, her gaze fixed on something invisible. The editor thought he saw a trace of a smile cross her features. He said, "Rebecca?" She blinked, coming out of her daze. "When can you have your story?"

Now there was no doubt of a smile, taut as it was. "Give me a half-hour."

The two detectives were happy to exit the cellar and they stepped into a morning that even the high gray clouds couldn't dim.

Valentin looked over the intersection. "I was wrong. She disappeared on you."

"I guess she did," McKinney said.

"Where are you off to now?" Valentin said after they had spent another half-minute watching the busy foot traffic.

"Back to the precinct," the policeman said with a sour smile. "It will be my pleasure to report to Captain Warren."

"That sounds like great fun," Valentin said.

McKinney snickered in a grim way. "What about you?"

"I'll get some lunch. And then meet you in Eclipse Alley."

"Tell Frank I said hello."

"No, not there. I'd spend half the afternoon."

The lieutenant offered Valentin his hand and said, "Three o'clock?"

*Nobody notices the little people, the thousands who scurried this way and that, up and down the streets, all but invisible. They were mostly after-thoughts. Some did jobs that helped the city live and some did nothing at all but drift. There to be used, they went unnoticed, some practically from the cradle to the grave. Only now and then was one of them thrown into public notice and that was most often when that citizen was the cause or the result of some terrible tragedy.*

*This time, it will be different. Wasn't it already? The police were rushing this way and that. The gossip was swirling. Who was murdered? My God! Soon the newspapers would be all over it. All the while, not one of them would see the person moving among them like a breath of air.*

Standing with a hand on the gallery railing, Miss Lulu White knew that if she closed her eyes, she'd see Basin Street as it had been a dozen years before, a busy tableau of grand mansions filled with lovely women, fine drinking and dining establishments, and elegant gambling parlors, all set to the sound of the happy jass music, a *demimonde* created to serve gentlemen of means from every corner of the globe. That was when Tom Anderson stood firm as its king and she presumed the mantle of queen.

Though there were many who said she was queen only of snooping and gossip, she and her spies swept up all the information that mattered in that twenty-block square and pushed solutions when things went wrong. The removal of the vile witch French Emma Johnson and the closing of the hellhole known as the Circus some eight years before counted among her proudest victories. With that, it seemed the District could truly shine.

That was then. Time had passed and with his health failing, his head full of fears of damnation, and his foolish eyes turning toward heaven, Tom Anderson allowed the District's glory to dim and then turned his back and walked away, holding on only to a piece of the café that still bore his name.

Now moral crusaders on one side and criminal gangs on the other were snatching off bloody bites at Storyville's edges, as if feasting on a dying beast. This, even as the wealthy families and churches that secretly owned real estate there demanded their rents, every month without pause, and no excuses, thank you.

A maid stepped onto the gallery carrying a cup of coffee, breaking into these musings. Miss Lulu offered a nod of thanks and sipped, tasting the pleasant hint of bitter chicory as she turned once again to her own history in that place. She had risen, a common sporting girl, to become the crafty fox who had created Mahogany Hall, the grandest mansion on the line, known around the world as a palace of earthly delights. That didn't stop Uptown's envious bitches and bastards from laughing behind her back every time Anderson shamed her by choosing other women for his wives and consorts and young, pretty doves for his mistresses.

A year before, she had embarked on a scheme to make a last stab at tracking down George Killshaw, the fancy man who had disappeared some seven years before that with over sixty–thousand dollars of her money. The mission to California failed, right along with her dream of becoming part of the motion picture business that was going wild there. And so she came back, beaten but not finished, and resumed her former place on Basin Street.

She stopped to sip her coffee and catch her breath. The time for her reward had come at last and so she had all the more reason to keep an even closer eye on the most notorious red-light district in the country. On this day, that included news of the body found in the little byway at the end of Liberty Street.

She had wakened to her girls whispering something about a man mutilated in some horrible way in Eclipse Alley, not three blocks away. Within another hour came the shocking news that the victim was the former State Senator Herbert Waltham. She knew the gentleman as a once-a-week visitor who always selected one of her youngest ladies after he had made his discreet way inside and up the stairs through her private entrance. He was a large, jolly, free-spending type who treated the girls well. He had a dark secret here and there, but who didn't? And now he was dead; butchered, in fact.

She also heard that Valentin St. Cyr had been summoned to the investigation, which meant she could expect a visit. She pondered all this for a few minutes more, then carried her coffee into the house, just in time to miss that individual rounding the corner from Conti Street.

Without ever having seen him before, Rebecca picked St. Cyr out of the crowd. She trailed him across a busy Canal Street into the shadows of Dauphine before calling, "Excuse me, please, Mr. Valentin?" The detective stopped and made a startled turn. "My name is Rebecca Marcus. Did Lieutenant McKinney tell you? I'm reporting on Mr. Waltham's murder."

Valentin found himself thrown a bit as she bore down on him. "He did tell me, yes."

"Do you have a few moments for me?" she said.

Her chest heaved prettily. If she caught his glance, she gave no clue. He said, "I can spare some time." He tilted his head in the direction of the next corner. "The Paradise Café is on Iberville. Will that be all right?"

"Yes, yes, thank you," she said.

He took her elbow to steer her along the banquette, a gesture she accepted with a sly shift of her eyes. Valentin felt an odd tingle of danger, a small electric shock up his spine.

As they walked on, he asked how she had come to be assigned to the story. She explained and he considered that most men would laugh out of hand at the idea of a woman as a news reporter. It would take backbone for her to charge ahead in that male world. Good for her. But she had caught one horrendous crime to cover and he wondered if she had any idea what she had walked into.

He held her chair and she sat, removed her hat, and placed it on the table. When the waiter appeared, she asked for a café latte. Valentin requested a black coffee, along with an order of the café's almond biscuits. He waited for her to get settled before saying, "So how can I help you?"

"I don't know if you can," she said. "But I'd like to find out."

He was used to news scribblers who were pushy and demanding at best, worse when they had been tippling, which was much of the time. Her voice was even and he sensed something quieter, deeper, not so easy to dismiss in her. By the way she was studying him, she was ready to reach across the table and remove a hunk of his flesh.

He looked away to break the gaze. "You understand I have no official role. That's Detective McKinney."

"I do understand," she said. "I asked him about you. I asked Reynard Vernel, too."

"How is he?" Valentin said. Vernel had trailed along on three of his murder cases.

"Doing well," she said. "He spoke kindly of you. You know he's an editor now."

"I didn't know."

"If it wasn't for him, I wouldn't have the assignment. It helped that I'm familiar with the Walthams. From the Society pages." She leaned a few inches in his direction. "That means you could use me."

Valentin didn't dare meet her eyes, so he feigned a thoughtful look.

"I know the victim's identity," she went on. "And the details of his murder. What was done to his body."

"I see."

"It's a big story, Mr. Valentin."

"I'd say so. But I still don't understand—"

"What you can give me?"

Valentin said, "Yes. That you can't get from the police."

Before she could respond, the coffees and plate of biscuits arrived. She added a cube of sugar to her cup and stirred, her eyes on the swirling liquid.

"It's important that I earn your trust," she said, her voice still low. "Yours and the lieutenant's." She stopped, raised her head, and fixed him with her black stare. "I have to make this work. To prove myself. That means be at least as good as any of the men. Better would be..."

"Even better?"

She smiled, white teeth flashing. "Yes. Even better. So I need whatever you can offer. That you might not share otherwise."

He broke off a piece of a biscuit and nibbled it, wondering if everything that came out of her mouth suggested more than was said. Or maybe his imagination was running—

"Are you willing?" she said. "To answer some questions, I mean."

He mused for another moment, then said, "Ask. But you don't use my name as your source."

"Agreed." Her notebook and pen appeared in a quick instant. "Have you ever seen a crime like this one?"

"No two are ever the same."

"But you've seen all sorts, is that correct?" She plunged on before he could answer. "Reynard told me about the Black Rose Killer. And those jazz musicians. And what started on Rampart Street. And—"

"And there were others, yes." He smiled. "You've been diligent."

Her pen was poised like a weapon. "What does the way the murder was committed tell you?"

"It was a savage attack," Valentin said. "That suggests rage. Maybe at Mr. Waltham in particular. Or he could have simply got in the way of a madman who wanted to slaughter someone. His very unlucky night."

"But you don't know which it was."

"I don't. And we won't unless—"

"Another body turns up."

Her gaze was intense and he took a moment to sip his coffee and wonder if she was thinking how that happenstance could help her career. "So if he was targeted, it's another kind of investigation," he said.

She had started scribbling again. Now she stopped and looked up. "Either way, there's still the question of why. Correct?"

"Yes, that's true," he said. "But if it was an insane person, 'why' might not matter."

"Is that the reason you're on the case? To find that out?"

"I think it's because I know Storyville."

One eyebrow dipped as if she found the reply wanting. A moment passed. "You said 'madman.' You don't believe the attacker could have been a woman?"

"I suppose."

"I mean, the way he was cut up."

"That would be guesswork at this point."

"Tell me something, please. Do you believe that anyone could commit a murder?"

"Yes," Valentin said. "And quicker than you'd think."

She pondered for a few seconds, then sat back, put her pen down, reached for her cup, and lifted it in gesture of thanks. "You've been a great help," she said.

She made it back to the newsroom and finished her story with time to spare before deadline. She ripped the sheet from the machine and for the first time ever, shouted, "Copyboy!" A moment of surprised silence at the feminine lilt followed. Then the clattering of keys and chatter resumed. A few seconds later, a boy ran up to snatch the pages from her raised hand.

*It was worth the trouble to take the time and spend the money to make sure that such a special package would carry the correct number of stamps. And worth walking all the way to the box at the corner of Fulton and Notre Dame to drop it. It was a long way, but lovely under the wisps of high clouds that hung like rags on the afternoon sky.*

It was after three when Valentin arrived at Eclipse Alley, ducking past the police barrier before anyone could notice him, but taking enough time to scan the intersection for any parties who appeared too interested. He saw only a lone copper strolling the banquette opposite, no doubt placed there by McKinney to keep any nosy citizens away.

The lieutenant was waiting, puffing on an Omar. He tossed the cigarette aside and they both got busy with an inspection of the spot where the body had been discovered.

"I spoke to the coroner," the lieutenant said. "He said Waltham was probably drugged. Our friend Mr. Finn."

"So it's possible he got here on his own power."

"Especially if he had help."

They pondered in silence and reached the same conclusion at the same moment. Valentin said, "He knew whoever attacked him."

They returned to their work. A minute passed and Valentin stopped and bent down.

"What?" McKinney said.

"This," Valentin said and reached his fingers into the gap between two cobbles. He straightened and held it out for the lieutenant's inspection.

"Damn," McKinney said. "There it is."

Rebecca had paced and fidgeted through the afternoon, waiting for the evening edition to come rolling off the presses. When the first copies appeared, she carried one outside and held her hands stiff to keep them from trembling.

SEARCH ON FOR
TENDERLOIN MURDERER
by
REBECCA MARCUS

> New Orleans police are mounting an intense search for the murderer of Herbert Waltham, whose mutilated body was found in Eclipse Alley on Wednesday morning.
>
> Captain Warren of Parish Precinct promised quick action. "We will spare no effort in apprehending the person who committed this ghastly assault on a respected citizen," the captain stated. "We can assure the public that a capture will be swift."
>
> The investigation is being led by Lt. James McKinney.
>
> An announcement of funeral services will be forthcoming.

*Yes,* she told herself, *it was a crime story, yes, it was on the front page of a major city newspaper,* and, *yes, that's my name in the byline.*

She bit down on an urge to shake the page in the air and shout out to anyone who might hear that *she* was Rebecca Marcus and the story you have read or will read was written by *me.* Instead, she steadied herself and perused the piece one more time before folding it and slipping it into her bag. They'd all know who she was soon enough.

*The ink on the soft paper is a mighty sight, committing the deed to history, like the blood on the stones, only it won't be washed away. And the woman's name at the top; how strange. What sort of woman would write about a bloody murder in particular? One who might see the world in a different way than the others? One who might understand?*

Valentin pulled to the curb to find Justine standing on the banquette, chatting with the ancient Miss Annette Neville from across the street. Miss Annette scowled at the machine until the four cylinders rattled into silence.

He climbed out and said, "Miss Annette. Good afternoon."

"Not with that racket, it ain't, no." The crone delivered the comment from beneath her headscarf without any particular rancor, more a general observation. Valentin offered a slight bow before climbing the steps to the gallery. After a few more words to the old Frenchwoman, Justine followed him.

In the kitchen, he was greeted by the sight of Miss Evangeline at the cast-iron stove and the smells of filé spices wafting from the pot she was stirring. She glanced over her shoulder and smiled and the light caught her features in a way that held him in place. The questions that had been circling his brain for the past year made another orbit and again he wondered why, if he was so skilled a detective that he earned the trust of the New Orleans Police Department, he was unable to solve the mystery of this woman. Perhaps, he mused, because he wasn't yet ready.

Justine joined them, depositing a bunch of sassafras in the bowl next to the sink, Miss Evangeline said, "This'll be ready in ten minutes or so."

Valentin said, "I'm sorry to be so late."

"You didn't eat, did you?"

"Just a little something with my coffee," he said.

She treated him to another of her curious smiles. Justine pushed open the screen door to the back gallery and tilted her head for him to join her.

They walked to the end of the garden. Valentin knew the questions were coming, so he didn't wait for her to ask. "It's Waltham. The brother identified him. We visited the scene again."

She digested the news. "Any clues?"

"We found the broken tip of a hypodermic between the stones," he said, "No telling how long it was lying there. Could have been used on him. Or not." He paused to pluck a plum from one of the trees and spent a thoughtful moment enjoying the fruit.

Justine said, "Have you seen the evening paper?"

Valentin's thoughtful moment ended. "No, yet," he said.

"The first story about the murder is out."

"Well, it's—"

"It was written by Rebecca Marcus. From the Society page."

"Oh, yes." He looked about for a path of escape, found none. "I spoke to her."

Justine stopped and turned his way. "You spoke to her when?"

Valentin said, "It was... today. Earlier."

"Why?"

"Well, she's assigned to the story. It wasn't for publication. Just..." He gave a pitiful shrug.

"And you're just telling me now?" Justine said.

"Well, I was going to."

"What did you give her?"

"Nothing much. General information. She's not going to use my name."

"I see." Her eyes were on him. "And what did Miss Rebecca Marcus have to say?"

"Well... she wondered if it could be a woman who did the murder."

Justine said, "I thought about that as soon as you told me. Because of him being cut up like that."

"Yes," Valentin said, relieved to have some place to run. "He wasn't a small fellow, though. A good bit over two hundred pounds. It would take some kind of woman to handle a man that size. That needle tells me he was likely drugged."

"Do you think whoever it had help?"

"Possible. But usually these crimes are the work of one person."

"Then she lured him."

"Or he did."

"A man wouldn't have the charms," she said.

It was a crossing of swords that they both secretly enjoyed. Still, he could tell she was not pleased about the Rebecca Marcus business. The moment brightened when they heard Evangeline in the house, singing a quiet tune. They spoke of trivial matters until she called them to the table.

# FIVE

Valentin woke up Thursday morning, grateful that his wife could not read his thoughts. Because among the first of those was a rumination on Rebecca Marcus.

She was hungry; and the fact that she could barely find her way wasn't stopping her as she used her good looks and pretty figure and the signals she cast that she was open to anything that would help her along. All that, and then not telling Justine about meeting her right away. He had seen the look in those eyes, cool and sharp, and he cursed his stupidity. She could all but smell another woman on him.

New Orleans was nothing if not a roiling sea of temptations. Before Justine had appeared, he had been quite the rounder, hopping his way from one bed to the next and only on occasion returning for second visits. Sweet fruit hung low on the branches and he had plucked it at his will. For all the pleasure, he had also dealt with women so infatuated that he wondered if they might kill him if they didn't get what they wanted.

Those were younger days. He had been with Justine for nine years, broken only by the two periods of several months each. They had been married for three and neither had strayed. Why, then, did he find himself so affected by a few short minutes with a young lady who had talked her way into covering a bloody murder for the city's largest daily newspaper? It was true that he had been struck by the forward motion in her eyes, like those of a predator on a chase. He was not shaken, but she had unsettled him and he wasn't sure why.

Justine shifted and whispered something low and sweet and he swung his guilty self out of the bed so he could get a bath and dress for his return to the District and the case and have coffee waiting for when she woke. It was a weak ploy, but all he'd have time to do, and better than nothing.

Detective McKinney spent the morning tending to two other investigations and arrived back at the precinct just before noon. When he reached his desk, a clerk stepped up to tell him that Captain Warren wanted him upstairs; and not in his office, but in the room set aside for conferences. He wondered if he was already in some kind of trouble. A thumb raised to the floors above was a time-worn signal around the detectives' section, often delivered with a ghastly smile of doom. Now and then an officer would never come back and a clerk would be tasked with cleaning out his desk.

The detective arrived on the third floor to find Warren waiting at the long table with two visitors from police headquarters: Deputy Police Commissioner Elvin Garrett and Chief of Detectives John Leroux. They were an odd couple, the commissioner as round as a beer barrel with lazy eyes and the chief a short and intense man. The contrast would have been comical, save for the stern expressions both policemen displayed. It was matched by Captain Warren's—or at least his attempt at it. That crooked beanpole could not manage the hard cop face that was all but a requirement for the job.

After curt introductions, the captain waved McKinney to a chair. "Before we begin, I want you to know that the Chief and I will be speaking to the newspapers. That will be downstairs in a half-hour and you'll join us."

The lieutenant said, "Yes, sir," even as he was thinking, *Please, no....* He paused to consider that Miss Marcus would likely make an appearance. At least that would be interesting and he felt compelled to mention it.

"The *Times-Picayune* has a woman reporter on the story. Rebecca Marcus. She wrote a story about Tom Anderson and some campaign about yellow fever."

The commissioner said, "Yes, her editor called to tell me." He shrugged his thick shoulders. "It was going to happen sooner or later."

Captain Warren had chosen not to speak up about the photograph in which he and the victim had appeared or anything else, for that matter. But now he said, "She's a Jew."

The other three men turned at the sudden utterance. The commissioner stared at him, Chief Leroux gave a baffled shake of his head, and McKinney looked away. The captain's pale cheeks flushed. He straightened in his chair and said, "We'd like a report on your investigation of the murder, please."

The lieutenant now took pains to conceal his dismay. It had been only thirty hours since the body had been discovered and with little in the way of clues. But he kept his face passive as he began. "We have a positive identification. The coroner brought Mr. Waltham's brother Joseph to the morgue yesterday morning. He confirmed it."

"I don't suppose we could have spared him that," the captain said.

McKinney saw the chief of detectives' eyebrow hike. It was not a comment an officer with any sense would make. Who else would identify the victim? He continued. "I viewed the body a few hours later."

The chief spoke up. "Please describe Mr. Waltham's wounds," he said. "Because we're hearing wild reports."

McKinney kept it brief—and clinical. When he finished, he heard the commissioner mutter under his breath and saw that Captain Warren looked like he was about to be ill. The man was not made for the street. With a pronounced sigh, the chief said, "And there's no history of other attacks of this nature in the city?"

McKinney allowed a moment in case the captain wanted to respond. Then he said, "No, sir. I'll be putting in calls to some departments around this part of the country to see if they've seen anything similar."

Chief Leroux folded thin hands before him. "Has Mr. St. Cyr agreed to assist you in the investigation?"

"Who?" The commissioner spoke up for the first time. "St. Cyr?"

The Chief of Detectives turned his way. "Valentin St. Cyr. He was Tom Anderson's man in the District, going back, what, nearly ten years."

"Oh, yes. I remember him."

Leroux said, "The lieutenant asked that he be brought in on this one because he knows the streets down there." He fixed on McKinney. "Correct, Lieutenant?"

"He does. Very well. And, yes, sir, he has agreed to help us."

The chief said, "I guess that's all, then. Please report to Captain Warren twice daily. Everything you have until this is resolved. Understood?"

"Yes, sir. Understood." He offered the captain a perfunctory glance and stood up.

"One more thing," the commissioner said. "This is a police matter. You're in charge. Not Mr..."

"St. Cyr," McKinney said. "Valentin St. Cyr."

Rebecca arrived at the newsroom to find Reynard Vernel fretting. He beckoned her with a sharp wave then directed her back out to the lobby.

"Where have you been?" he said. "Chief Reynolds is having Captain Warren address the press in twenty minutes. We couldn't find you. Kassel was just about to send me."

"Where is it?"

"First floor of Parish Precinct."

"Tell him I'm already there." She spun around and headed for the stairwell.

When she walked into the precinct and was directed by the puzzled desk sergeant to the room off the lobby, she found what appeared to be most of the New Orleans newsmen on hand. The chatter ebbed as she made her way through the crowd and she thought she heard nasty words muttered under whiskey-scented breaths. She knew she heard snickers.

She was wondering exactly how mean it was going to get when the door on the back wall opened and four men entered. The first two she recognized as the Chief of Police Reynolds and Chief of Detectives Leroux. Behind him came the officer she assumed was Captain Warren, though he looked more like a clerk than a policeman. Last in line was Lieutenant McKinney.

They mounted a low platform, the mob pressed forward, and the shouts began ringing out.

"Captain, what were the extent of the wounds?"

"What was he doing in Eclipse Alley?"

"Captain? A question?"

"Do you have any suspects?"

"Captain, please!"

Captain Warren was frozen in place, his mouth half-open. Chief Reynolds shot a look at Leroux, who rolled his eyes in disgust, stepped forward, and barked, "All right, that's enough!"

The yells subsided into murmurs and then into silence. The chief gestured for Warren to commence. "All right, gentlemen," the captain said.

Rebecca had just managed to push her way to the front, accompanied by a pattering of laughter. Chief Leroux said, "And lady." He spoke the title in a way that did not invite mockery and the snickers ebbed.

"What?" the captain said, still trying to catch up. He spied Rebecca. "Oh, yes, of course." He got past his moment of confusion and wasted everyone's time identifying the two senior officers and himself and then McKinney as the detective leading the investigation.

What followed was an exercise in foolishness. The police had little to offer other than the name of the victim and the location of the crime. The questions that were hurled from the mob of reporters were deflected with repeated replies of "no comment" or "the investigation is proceeding" from Captain Warren, who was to Rebecca about as bland a human as she had ever encountered. She caught McKinney's eye at one point and he looked her way for only a moment before his eyes shifted to something over her head. The policeman looked like that room was the last place he wanted to be.

And so it was with a visible sigh of relief that he greeted the end of the charade, following the three officers out the way they had come in. He treated her to a last glance over his shoulder as the door closed behind him. She scurried out before the esteemed gentlemen of the New Orleans press could notice she was gone.

She raced back to the newsroom, paid a quick visit to her editor, and crossed to her desk to begin pounding the keys of the Underwood.

Mangetta's Grocery and Saloon occupied two storefronts in the center of the block between Conti and Bienville streets. The door on the right opened onto a grocery that lured even the most pious Italians to the red-light district. Because no other location had the selection of imported meats, cheeses, bread, and canned goods, along with the special produce that no self-respecting native of the *mezzogiorno* or the island would do without. "American" citizens who paid a visit were often overtaken by the smells. To all the rest, it was perfume blown from across the Atlantic.

The door on the left welcomed the local crowd to the saloon, a room twenty feet wide and forty deep. A bar occupied most of the common wall and six booths its opposite, with ten tables placed about the middle of the floor.

Valentin found the proprietor at his usual post behind the grocery counter and also as usual in the midst of an operatic spiel delivered half in Sicilian dialect and half in his broken English, this one about the flooding of the Carondolet Canal in the year of '01 and of Grand Isle in 1909. When he spied Valentin, he winked and jerked his head in the direction of the other side without missing a beat.

The detective passed through the connecting hallway, crossed to the corner booth, and slid in. The barkeep was a few steps behind with a bottle and two short *piquetta* glasses, pouring one full before returning to his station. Valentin sipped until Frank Mangetta, short, dark, with a grand mustache that was showing ever more streaks of gray arrived. The olive-black and sparkling eyes were the same as always. In a curious twist, the Sicilian, who was also his godfather, spoke fine English, but had drifted more and more to his mother tongue as the years progressed. He always said he would return one day.

He now sat, poured, and quaffed half his brandy in the glass. "*Ciao bello*," he said. Valentin returned the greeting. "You're back." The detective nodded.

"*L'omicidio?*" Frank whispered. "*Tutti vero?*" A murder?

"He lost four parts, if that's what you heard."

The older man gave a little shudder, drank off his brandy, and poured again. Frank switched back to English. "Who does this?"

"Someone sick." He touched his temple. "*Pazzo.*"

The bartender returned with a cutting board laid out with cheese, olives, and Italian bread. Valentin helped himself, nibbling while Frank watched. "He was an important man, eh?"

"He was," Valentin said. "Powerful. And rich."

"So what was he doing down that alley?"

"I don't know."

"They want you to catch who did that to him?"

"They want my help."

"*Ancora.*"

"*Si.* Yes, again." Maybe it was the brandy and the quiet of the room that caused Valentin to feel the sudden weight of his situation. Why had he let himself be drawn into the middle of another bloody Storyville mess? Had they selected him only to have a–

"Bolden."

Valentin blinked, coming out of his daze. Though he spent a moment or two almost every day thinking about his lost friend, it had been a long time since he had heard the name spoken. He cleared his throat and tried out more of his rusty Italian. "*Che mi dici di lui?*" *What about him?*

Frank drew out the moment with another sip of brandy and smiled in an odd way. "It was Saturday. Sunday, I mean. Early in the morning. Last customer." He waved a hand. "Sitting at the back table over there. I never seen him before." He mimed tipping a bottle. "*Un unbriacone.* A drunk. But he seemed like a good sort. I was ready to send him on and lock the doors when he said Buddy's name. So I stayed. He said he remembered when he played here. The last time was…"

"About ten years ago," Valentin said.

"*Si, certo.* So then he starts about did I know about the record that he made back before that. You remember? It was a…" He spun a finger.

"A cylinder," Valentin said, musing. "That was while I was away in Chicago. Around, what, ninety-nine? I remember him telling me about that. I never heard it, though."

"This fellow said he was the one made it."

Valentin had been raising his glass. Now he put it down again. "He what?"

"He made that record. So he said."

"Did he tell you his name?"

The brow stitched. "It was... *Signore*... Mr. Cecil. That's it." The saloonkeeper was enjoying his godson's surprise. "Oh, yes, and he said something else. He said he still has it."

Valentin had left the saloon and meandered across the tracks, making his slow way to the lot by the Mint. His bewilderment over the reporter had been washed away by the startling news about the recording.

He and Buddy Bolden—real name Charles—had grown up together in the neighborhood around First and Liberty streets. Buddy began taking horn lessons around the same time Valentin left the city and was soon playing his cornet for cakewalks, Sunday concerts in the park, and the occasional funeral, sedate extra work to supplement his work as a plasterer. He was an astute musician, but not remarkable. He married a church-going girl from the neighborhood and fathered a daughter.

But by the time Valentin returned to New Orleans, he had undergone a crazy transformation and was now blowing wild with that same horn, drinking like a maniac, smoking hop and whiffing cocaine when he could get it, chasing every skirt in sight, and in the meantime making a new music that they started calling "jass."

It was near the beginning of his run to the top that he and his band made the recording that went missing. When his mad life began to catch up with him, Valentin was helpless to stop his jagged descent. In the end, it was heart-breaking story that he never quite got over, even as Bolden faded into invisibility. And the wax cylinder had simply disappeared.

Now Frank Mangetta had delivered the news that one piece of Buddy had been left behind, at least according to a drunkard who promised to come back at the same time on the Saturday night to follow. The detective couldn't decide what he wanted to do about it. He was saved from making up his mind when he heard a whistle from across the street.

———

Emile Carter had gone by "Beansoup" until he got older and thought the moniker too silly, tried out "E.C," and settled finally on "Each." He had been on the loose from the Waif's Home when Valentin had first met him, a street rat who somehow endeared himself to Justine. There was no getting rid of him, even if the detective had wanted to. He spent half his nights on their living room couch. As time passed and he reached his twenties, he had proven himself an able consort with sharp eyes and ears for Storyville on the street level.

As Beansoup, he had come off clownish and he hadn't completely lost it when he grew to be a man. As hard as he tried to pass for a sharp, there was always something of the oaf in his posture and his face was simply too sweet for the hard stares that struck fear.

A former sporting woman named Betsy had broken his poor heart into a dozen pieces and Justine had nursed him through that, shushing Valentin's dismissals of the harpy who had done the damage. Each had done his best to come off as a tough customer, one whom no woman could take down.

In other words, he tried to put on the rounder, as he now did crossing Franklin Street to intercept Valentin. The detective offered his hand and a smile, glad for the distraction. "Are you looking for me or just passing?" he said.

Each tugged his lapels and adjusted his derby, a gawkier version of Charlie Chaplin from the moving pictures. "On my way over to..." he gestured to the east, but did not complete the details of his travels. Valentin didn't ask.

"Did I hear you're back?" Each said. "Working that deal down Eclipse Alley?"

Between Miss Marcus and the news of the Bolden recording, Valentin had almost forgotten what had brought him there in the first place. "They just need a little extra help, that's all."

"Help. Ha! You'll be the one finds him. Won't you?"

"As long as he leaves a trail. And they usually do."

"Or she."

The detective cocked an eyebrow. So Beansoup—E.C.—Each had learned some things from him. "That's right. Or she." Watching Each's face, he got a message. "You keep alert, in case there's any talk in any of the saloons. You might hear something."

Now the odd eyes shifted in a cunning way and Valentin sensed that he was about to say something. Whatever it was, he thought better of it, and looked into the distance. "I might, that's true."

"You know where to find me." Valentin turned with a wave and started off.

"How's Miss Justine?" Each called out.

"Doing well," the detective said. "I'll tell her you asked."

Evangeline had insisted on washing their cups and the breakfast dishes and Justine carried the basket of laundry to the back gallery. As she began folding it, she found herself getting lost in a stir of resentment. There she was, doing wife's work, while he was on a chase. Him and his partner James McKinney, in the middle of things. She knew that much of what he did was boring: waiting, watching, digging into papers. She also knew that she could do it, too. Maybe there was no place for her. But maybe there was and he just didn't want her there.

She stopped with one of Valentin's shirts half folded in her hands and sat down in the wicker chair. A female was writing crime stories for the newspaper. Women would get the right to vote. She spent an idle moment imagining herself taking Valentin's place, tracking and nabbing a miscreant. When she came out of the little fantasy, she studied the mussed shirt for a moment, then tossed it back into the basket.

*Now that it has started, there is work to do. Plans to make. A path to walk that will leave bodies but no traces. It's a story. One that began a long time ago, carried on, and now comes to an end. And then the silence that will last for years and that will not change until it's too late for anyone to do anything except remember. Then all they will be able to do is shake their heads in wonder. Who would have known?*

After the sideshow for the local press, Lieutenant McKinney ran out to grab a ham biscuit from a cart and then spent an early afternoon hour calling around to police departments within a 500-mile radius to find out if any had investigated any similar assaults. News of the murder had come across the wires and most everyone had heard about it. But the departments had not seen matching crimes to report and he found himself giving out rather than gathering details.

There were no detectives available in Dallas and Vicksburg, so he left messages. He wasn't expecting much in the way of responses in any case. Departments had their own crimes to solve and extra work was pushed to the bottom of the stack. He told the clerk at the front desk to watch for return calls and headed out the door to meet St. Cyr.

The police sedan sat idling at the curb with a detective named Huey Riley at the wheel. Riley was the last partner the lieutenant would want along on an investigation, but it hadn't been his choice. The captain had insisted on him bringing the decrepit officer, likely to keep an eye on St. Cyr, who was climbing into the back seat as he settled in the front. On the bright side, Riley would be happy to stay in the machine and doze while McKinney and Valentin went into the Waltham's house.

Which is what they did, after a quiet ride north. By the time they reached the gallery of the grand home, Riley was already asleep, no doubt dreaming of the day when he could begin drinking his pension away.

McKinney gave the door a light tap and a mulatto maid appeared, her face drawn with distress. He stated his business and she stood back. As they passed inside, Valentin caught a glance of recognition from the girl. After a moment, he placed her as one of Bettina Galen's ladies; formerly, that was. He couldn't recall her name. So she had moved from a scarlet mansion on Basin Street to one of a different sort on Esplanade Ridge. And just like that, he had someone inside.

She escorted them into a dining room, where the family was gathered around a long mahogany table. A thin stalk of man rose to introduce himself as Herbert, Jr. The matron was at the head of the table and the young woman at her side her daughter. Mrs. Waltham's eyes were red from weeping, while the daughter sat near-paralyzed with shock and grief. The man standing in the corner with the stricken stare was introduced as the victim's brother Joseph—the one who had viewed and identified the ravaged corpse earlier in the day.

McKinney began by offering condolences. Then he tilted his head and said, "This is Mr. St. Cyr. He's a private detective and he's been hired by the department to assist the investigation. He's worked in Storyville for years." Mrs. Waltham winced at the mention of the District. Herbert, Jr. kept his eyes on the far wall. The two women studied Valentin for a moment, then looked away.

McKinney took a chair and gestured for Valentin to sit down. "I know this is a difficult time," he said. "We won't stay long." He looked between from mother to daughter. "Is there any information you can share regarding this terrible crime?"

"No!" Mrs. Waltham half-shouted, startling everyone. "Nothing. My husband was a successful man. He provided for his family. He was *important*. There is no reason for... for..." She wept into the handkerchief that was balled in her fist.

Valentin knew that he and the lieutenant were thinking the same thought: most times, *important* was not enough. But they kept their bland faces in place. McKinney said, "I want you to know that we will do everything we can to close this case and bring your husband some justice."

The mother sobbed into a flowering handkerchief and nodded a teary thanks. "Please contact me if anything that might be of value comes to mind." He laid one of his cards on the table. Valentin was watching the faces in the room for any flicker and saw none. He made a small sound in this throat and he and the lieutenant stood up and replaced their chairs.

"Thank you for your time," McKinney said.

The maid was waiting by the front door. Valentin studied her for a moment. "It's Dolly, isn't it?" he said.

"Dolores now, Mr. Valentin," she said. "That's what I go by." Her distress had been replaced by eyes batting with concern, which told him that the family had no idea of her former life.

"Sorry, my mistake," Valentin said. "It looks like you have a nice situation here."

"Yes, sir. I do," she said.

"I might need a few minutes of your time," Valentin said. Tomorrow, if that's possible."

"Well, all right, if you like." She tensed again.

"Nothing to worry about." He patted her arm, treated her to a small smile, and followed McKinney out the door.

Rebecca bent her head over the typewriter, her fingers resting on the keys and straining to hear voices from inside Rolf Kassel's office. Now, it was Barney Goings; a half-hour earlier, Elmo Miller. By her count, the two crime reporters had visited the editor no less than a half-dozen times and it was only the second day. She hadn't caught much save the occasional words that were spat loud enough to carry. Among them "fake," "amateur," and of course, "bitch." There was no way to tally the hard glares that they and the other male reporters had been shooting her way, though it was also true that a couple showed sympathy. They didn't say anything, of course; it was all in their pitying smiles.

As she sat neither typing nor talking on the phone, she felt like a spotlight was shining on her. Who knew when Reynard Vernel would appear to say the words: "I'm sorry, Rebecca, but we've decided to..."

She had to stay ahead of them. Simply running into the police department's stone walls would only get her sent down. Those drunken beat reporters had the contacts, the special people they could reach to ferret out information. And they weren't about to share. Now she needed something. A line they couldn't follow. Something they couldn't get. Or someone.

Her head was swimming, so she stood, snatched up her bag, threw her shawl over her shoulders, and headed out of the newsroom.

Valentin had the officers leave him at the corner of Franklin and Iberville streets so he could stop by Juanita Daly's modest house. Miss Juanita settled him at her kitchen table and fetched the two women who had discovered the body. Ida Clark, the older of the pair, displayed the worn, craggy look of a strumpet who had been at it for too many hard years, her eyes a dull blue, her flesh a liverish yellow, and her thin frame barely holding up her clothes. By contrast, Serena Tracy, while tending toward plain, was sturdy and bright-eyed and wearing a curious smile. Valentin knew that she could transform into a copy of the woman sitting next to her in a very short time.

As he expected, they had little of value to share. They had spied the body as they passed the alley and hurried to call the coppers. That was all.

Miss Ida said, "Is it true what I heard? His yancy was cut off?"

"That's correct," Valentin said.

"And his tongue?" Serena said.

"He was a mess," the detective said with a sigh.

"It was Mr. Waltham from the cotton exchange?" Miss Ida said.

"It was," Valentin said. "Have either of you ever entertained him?"

The younger woman shook her head and said, "No, sir."

"Not me," Miss Ida said. "Fellow like that would spend his time at Lulu White's and Willie Barrera's. Places like that. And I ain't ever been." These last words were wistful.

The detective had learned what he thought he would: nothing. He thanked them for their time and stood up.

"You think there's going to be more like this?" Serena said.

"We won't know that until it happens," Valentin said.

As he left the room, he saw Miss Ida pull her shawl over her shoulders as if feeling a chill.

# Six

Tom Anderson stood befuddled at the window facing Fourth Street. As stunned as he had been to learn that the man he knew—and with whom he had stood for a photograph just a week before—had been murdered in the most hideous fashion, he was doubly disturbed that no one had thought to share the news before it hit the streets. Instead, he'd heard about it by accident.

He had been dawdling over his breakfast when his handyman George come into the pantry to tell his wife and Mr. Tom's maid Lucy, about an awful killing in Storyville. Too embarrassed to call to George to ask for an accounting, he rose from the table and crept to the dining room doorway like some naughty little boy. What he heard was ghastly. Once George and Lucy had gone off, he made a quiet call to a friend in the police department and confirmed that the victim had indeed been Herbert Waltham. The renewed shock sent him back into the dining room and down into his chair.

Now he saw gray clouds through the branches, suiting his mood. He had also learned that St. Cyr had been brought in to investigate and wondered why the Creole detective hadn't contacted him. Because he had assumed that Tom Anderson would already know? True, he had walked away, but he was still privy to most of the District's secrets.

The brooding moment was interrupted by footsteps from behind. Lucy entered the room, her row stitched with concern, and said, "You feeling all right, Mr. Tom? You ain't ate much today."

He turned and smiled. "I've been better, Lucy. Thank you for asking. I believe I'll survive."

The maid said, "I believe you will, sir. I believe you gon' outlast me and everyone else, too."

Anderson spent a wistful few seconds appraising her. She was the kind of woman he had always enjoyed most, a good face, dazzling eyes, and a Junoesque figure that stretched the seams of her cotton uniform. A younger Tom Anderson would have dodged his wife so he could plot and maneuver and flirt until he had her in his bed, stripped naked and sweating as she flailed beneath him. This would be sweetened by various gifts and George, that kind fellow, would have no knowledge of any of it.

Nowadays, there was no wife to dodge. His last, the once-famous madam Gertrude Dix, had taken a nice bag of his money and retired to some other domicile. Even so, just the daydream of such an erotic interlude tired him to the bone. He had to conserve his energies, in any case. Who knew how longer it would be before his God called him home? And he was still part of Storyville and its calamities, no matter how thin the thread had drawn.

Rebecca asked, and then cajoled, until Reynard Vernel agreed to take one of the Fords reserved for staff use to carry her to Esplanade Ridge. He did not ask Kassel for permission, as it was midafternoon and the editor was well into the bottle of Raleigh Rye that he kept in his desk drawer.

As they drove north on the boulevard, Reynard asked what she had learned so far.

"From what I can tell, we haven't had a murder like this in New Orleans. At least, none that have been detected."

"And the point is to be detected."

Rebecca drew her gaze from the mansions they were passing. "Is that something you learned from Mr. St. Cyr?"

The editor smiled and said, "I guess it is." He thought back to the three murder sprees that he had covered that had been investigated—and solved—by Mr. Valentin. The Creole detective had told him more than once that killers were often brought down by the craving of attention for their vile acts.

"So you met him already?" he said before he realized the words were out.

"I did." She smiled as if tasting something that pleased her. "I cornered him yesterday. We went to a café on Conti. He's an interesting fellow. What's his background?"

Reynard caught something in her voice; she was just a little bit too intrigued. So he kept the story to a minimum. The Creole detective had been a street copper until he was pushed out for crossing the wrong superior. At which point Tom Anderson hired him to work the District. Which he had done as a full-time occupation until time and his wife drew him away. Now he only appeared in Storyville when something happened that required his special skills—like the murder of Herbert Waltham.

Rebecca considered the information. "And his wife?"

Reynard decided he wasn't going to discuss that part of Mr. Valentin's life at all. So he said, "Her name is Justine. I don't know her really. Met her just the one time." He was saved from any more prying by their arrival at the corner of Prieur Street.

Rebecca sat forward. "It's the third house down."

He pulled to the curb and shut off the engine. "I can go in with you."

She shook her head, explaining again that she knew Mrs. Waltham from the Society pages and that the widow would prefer her alone. Reynard suspected that in fact she didn't want anyone else from the newspaper getting in her way.

"I won't be but fifteen minutes," she said and opened the door and stepped out before he could say another word.

The postman who emptied his bag of the envelopes and small packages that had been left in the box at Carondelet and Julia took bare notice of one of the packets showing a small stain. He passed it on to the sorters at the Lafayette Station without a second thought. Citizens regularly sent poorly-wrapped sausages, andouille, boudin, and even shrimp and catfish, and the like through mail. Sometimes the fat soaked through so that it was near impossible to read the addresses. Such it was working for the United States Postal Service in New Orleans.

The deceased's eldest son Herbert, Jr. met Rebecca at the door. He was a tall, drab-looking young man who was unremarkable save for mournful eyes that twitched when she announced herself. She heard sobbing and the murmuring of voices from another room. Herbert, Jr. asked her to wait and disappeared through the doorway.

Rebecca surveyed the foyer she had seen not six months before when she had interviewed Clarice Waltham about a society function she was chairing. She had then covered several dreadful committee meetings and recalled that Mrs. Waltham took her foolish self and her silly position with utmost gravity. Simple questions brought spiels that went on so long that Rebecca had to restrain the urge to grasp the woman by the throat and squeeze.

She pushed those thoughts aside just in time for Herbert, Jr. to reappear and beckon her. With a steadying breath, she followed him into the dining room, where she found Mrs. Waltham at the end of a mahogany table and her daughter seated next to her, ghost-pale. Rebecca had covered the girl's coming out soiree. A man in his fifties was hunkered in a corner. From his features, she guessed that he was Joseph Waltham, the victim's only brother—and a vice-president at the Cotton Exchange.

The widow saw her and began to wail. "Oh, Rebecca. My dear Rebecca. It was so kind of you to come. Herbert's dead! What will I do?" She sounded like a child repeating words from memory.

Rebecca sat down and grasped the widow's trembling hands. "I'm so sorry," she whispered. "He was a fine man." She in fact had only met him three times and he had leered at her.

Mrs. Waltham dabbed her cheeks with a lace handkerchief. "But the Society page?" At a time like this? It will just have to wait. I'm sorry."

So they hadn't seen her story. She said, "No, ma'am. I've been taken off that section."

"Oh, is that so?" the older woman said in the matter-of-fact tone that Rebecca had heard from others in the midst of tragedies. She blinked and more tears welled. "Oh, my dear. You came all this way to–"

"No, ma'am." She interrupted before the visit grew more tangled. "I'm here for the paper."

Clarice Waltham blinked. "You are?"

"I'm reporting on your husband's murder."

The room quieted. The widow drew back. "You?"

She felt eyes on her. A tense moment passed. The son stepped up to say, "Excuse me, Miss Marcus. Could I have a moment of your time?"

She followed him out of the dining room and down a short hallway to the kitchen. He held the door until she passed through, then closed and leaned against it, his arms crossed, studying her. She waited.

He said, "How did you end up reporting on this story?"

She made a vague gesture. "They decided to give me a chance."

Herbert, Jr. thought about this, then shrugged it off. "The family is devastated," he said. "My poor father. What he meant to the city. His enormous success in business. And what this is going to do to all of us."

Rebecca discerned something behind the words and in the glance he threw at her before looking away again. "I can assure you that I'll give all of you every consideration," she said and paused to let the comment sink in. "That's not something you could expect from every reporter. You know what they're like."

Now it was the son's turn to sense something more and he fixed his stare on her. She went on, "The only way to control what people read is for you to keep what you say to the other papers to a minimum."

Herbert, Jr. didn't flinch and she worried that she had lost him. Then he said, "All right. I can agree to that. And I'll tell the others." He unfolded his arms, turned around, and opened the door for her.

She spent another few minutes at the dining room table, consoling the widow, who kept glancing through her tears at her son for signals of reassurance. When the older woman gave her hand a final grasp before releasing it, she guessed that she had passed the test.

As she readied to leave, she caught the victim's brother watching her from the corner where he had been lurking. She made a point of passing close by him and bowing her head to murmur, "Perhaps we can speak?" He did not respond. She stopped when she reached the front door and turned to find his cool, absent eyes sending a message that it was not going to happen.

# SEVEN

Valentin finished his early dinner and sat listening with half an ear to the women talking in lazy rounds. At one point, he became aware of Justine casting her eyes on him in a strange way, even as she paid heed to Evangeline sharing her list for market. Had he missed something? It passed. His thoughts wandered away until the telephone chirped. With a yawn, he rose from the table.

He was surprised to hear the voice of Tom Anderson, though in truth it sounded so craggy that it took a few seconds for him to identify the speaker. He asked after his health and received a brief litany of ailments in return. Once that subject was exhausted, and Anderson sounding nearly so, they got to the point of the call.

"I knew him," the King of Storyville said.

"How well?"

"Fairly." Anderson said, always parsing. "He visited the Café perhaps once a week."

"And?"

"And he spent time down the line. Mahogany Hall, I believe. Countess Piazza's."

Valentin stored that bit of information.

"I saw him a week ago," Anderson said. "We stood for a photograph."

"Yes, I know," Valentin said. "Do you have any idea at all why someone would want to do this? And in that place?"

"Lord, no," Anderson said.

"You know of any enemies?"

Anderson said, "He was in business, so he had rivals, of course. But someone who would..." He produced a shaky sigh. "No, nothing like that. I don't recall anything suspect about him. A rich man who enjoyed his pleasures. That's all." He was quiet for a moment. "Have you found anything?"

Valentin told him there had been nothing of substance so far. "But it's still early."

"Yes, yes," Anderson wheezed. "It's just so strange. And ugly." Valentin chose not to point out that they had seen strange and ugly before. Finally, the older man said, "I'd like you to come pay me a visit. Tomorrow after breakfast, if that's possible." Valentin told him he would wait to see how his morning progressed and call back. Anderson's "Thank you," sounded like it required a large effort.

The Creole detective placed the handset in the cradle and made his absent way back to the kitchen, wondering if after all the years, Storyville was witnessing the final chapter of its king's long story. And what would New Orleans be then?

It had already been a long day and it took all the effort James McKinney could muster to climb the stairs to Captain Warren's office. He found the captain frowning out the window at the city below, looking like a man who would rather be in some other place. Any other place. McKinney knew that certain such individuals went into police work for the security, only to realize that they didn't like it much after all. Too bad for him.

"Captain?" McKinney said.

"That was some kind of mess, wasn't it?" Warren spoke without turning.

"You mean the murder? Yes, it's a—"

"I mean that press announcement. Those people..." He shook his head. "And that woman? What are they thinking?" McKinney didn't comment. The captain pulled his eyes off the streets and offered a reluctant, "What else do you have for me? Are we on the way to wrapping it up?"

The lieutenant hid his astonishment. Did this bookkeeper with bars on his shoulders really think that the investigation had advanced since the morning meeting with the commissioner and the Chief of Detectives and then the press gaggle? But the captain was watching him, so he repeated that there were no similar crimes in the region; no leads yet as to suspects; no madmen reported on the loose; the family in shock and of no help whatsoever. He was about to mention the one piece of evidence from the alley, then decided against it.

"You know the papers are going to crucify us if we don't get this put away," the captain opined. McKinney understood that by "us" he meant himself. Had it been any other officer, he might have felt some sympathy. "So what's next?"

They both knew the answer was more of the same for the time being, but the lieutenant ran it down anyway. When he finished, the captain said, "Very well, then."

McKinney left him standing at the window wearing the same forlorn visage. When he arrived back at his desk, the clerk passed him a sheet of note paper. He glanced at it, then stopped and stared.

Valentin put his dish in the sink and announced that he was ready for a nap. Worn as he was, he wished that his wife could join him for a frolic, but that was not possible during the day anymore. The house was small and the bedsprings noisy. So he cast a longing look her way as he exited the kitchen.

Justine understood the look and smiled. Nine years and he still desired her. Good. She spent some minutes at the table while Evangeline tended to the washing. She had almost dozed off herself when she heard the slap of the afternoon newspaper landing on the perron.

The lieutenant exited the building and walked the blocks to Magazine Street and the café located next to Gaspare's Tobacco Shop. He stood by the door until he saw her come round the corner. When she drew close, he touched the brim of his hat and said, "How is it you chose Martin's?"

She stopped. "It's popular with the newsroom folks. Those who don't relax in saloons, I mean."

The lieutenant had a snide response to the explanation that he kept to himself. He also didn't reply when she asked why, instead busying himself with ushering her inside and to a table by the window. The "why?" was the curious coincidence that St. Cyr had kept an apartment over Gaspare's store for years.

Mr. Martín looked up out from behind his brass register and gestured that he was on his way.

"Thank you for meeting with me," Rebecca said. "I hope I didn't take you away from anything."

"I needed to get out of the building." He didn't want her getting any ideas about her import. Before she could continue, Mr. Martín arrived, greeting McKinney with a pat on the shoulder. He knew what the lieutenant would order, so he turned to Rebecca to inquire, "And for the lady?"

"A jasmine tea, please." The proprietor bowed and retreated. She settled her dark eyes on the policeman's. "I'm going to share with you what I've learned so far," she said. McKinney shifted in his chair, the smallest sign of interest he could muster. "I called eight different newspapers in cities around the South," she went on. "There have been no crimes similar to this one that anyone could recall."

"And they would," the lieutenant said. He kept his face passive as he considered that she had gotten a better response than he had from contacting police departments.

He said only, "We're finding nothing from police departments, either." This was true—in a way.

She went on to tell him that she had visited the Waltham's house. The family hadn't offered her any information of consequence. Yet. She said she had not been inclined to push them—a statement he found faintly humorous—but she expected much more.

"You've been a busy woman," he said when she finished.

"I want to make the most of my opportunity," she said. "And so I'm hoping we can work together."

He raised an eyebrow. "And how would that be?"

"I'm covering the story. It's mine. I'm going to find out things. Maybe some that you don't know. I'll share what I learn. And if I do that, I—" She stopped as Mr. Martín arrived with her tea, the lieutenant's coffee, and an order of the *petit beurres* that were the specialty of the house. He stepped away again.

Rebecca barely sipped her tea. "So I would like to be privy to your investigation. As much as that's possible."

McKinney said, "You already have what's possible. We give all the reporters–"

"I'm speaking of something a bit more confidential," she said and offered a smile that her eyes didn't join.

McKinney sat back. "Special treatment?" he said. Now her eyes brightened and remained that way until he said, "That's something you'll have to arrange with Captain Warren."

The smile faded. She placed the cup in the saucer, looking petulant. "I'm offering something you can't get from anyone else," she said.

"And what would that be?"

She replied with a taint of impatience. "I told you. I know the family. They trust me. I have someone in the house who will keep me informed. It's been agreed."

The lieutenant spent a moment wondering if it was the maid that St. Cyr knew and decided not. He guessed it was the victim's son or brother and he and Mr. Valentin could shake loose anything they were hiding.

Before he could speak, she said, "You can't get that from any of those..." She waved a dismissive hand. "...others."

The officer decided that he didn't want to have the discussion. She was already wearing him down. "Thank you for the offer," he said. "But we don't need additional assistance at this time."

"Oh?" She selected one of the beurres from the plate with fingers that were too sharp. "I thought you could use all the help you could get."

"That's true, we do," he said. "And we depend on the press and the public to do its part. Such as when they have information that's critical to a case." He sipped his coffee to hide his annoyance over walking into a trap. "We expect it," he went on. "And the department doesn't take kindly to anyone withholding evidence. For whatever reason. So if you come upon information, from the family or anyplace else, we'll expect you to share it."

She tilted her head and her face composed into a darker mask as she bit down on the beurre. She took another sip of her tea and her eyes shifted away from him. "Please excuse me. I have a deadline." Ten seconds later, she was out the door, leaving her cup still steaming.

Mr. Martin heard the little bell over the door and crossed to the table. "Something wrong?" he said.

"Everything's fine." McKinney said. "She had something better to do." It was then that he noticed that she had left a calling card on the table.

Justine carried the newspaper back to the kitchen table. The brief item about the Storyville murder was just above the front page fold. She hadn't gotten past the headline when the byline caught her eye. *Rebecca Marcus.* There it was. The woman who had not a few days ago been writing sugary stories about the daughters of New Orleans' wealthiest families and puffery like the piece with the photograph was now writing about the murder that her husband had been hired to investigate.

She laid the paper aside and stared out the window, pondering this. From the back of the house, the mattress springs squeaked as he shifted on the bed.

The sun was fading like a dying fire over the corner of First and Liberty. From the last licking flames a figure appeared, tall, angular, an ink drawing come to life. One hand was raised in a wave. In the other, a horn dangled. The features were not clear, but there was no doubt it was Buddy. And coming his way. The voice was the same as when they were kids running those streets. *Do you hear, Tino? Do you hear?* Only Buddy heard, as always. The sounds of the music of the city exploded around him and he drank it all in.

The figure was slowing in a painful mime and the arms and legs began to jerk about. Was he dancing? No, the sounds he was making were not joyous but anguished. He drew just close enough for his face to become clear. In the next second, it faded, as invisible hands dragged him away, carrying him to that place where he would live in stillness and silence, leaving his one true friend to stand on the now-empty street. Valentin tried to follow. His feet wouldn't move.

Now he heard his name called. "Valentin? Valentin!"

He opened his eyes and his body heaved in a sharp jolt. She was standing in the doorway, watching him. "Are you all right? You were thrashing so much I thought you had another woman in here."

He laid a hand on his brow. "It was..."

She crossed to stand by the bed. "What?"

"A dream. Just a dream." A moment passed and his face changed. He reached for her. She mouthed a scolding, *No!* and moved away, gesturing toward the kitchen and the woman who was sitting within earshot.

He said, "All right," and laid back. Outside the window, the light was waning, just like in his dream.

Rebecca slowed her steps just as she reached the doors of the *Times-Picayune* building, assailed by a notion that someone was watching her. She stopped just inside the lobby and turned to peer outward. Pedestrians and street traffic eddied this way and that, but she saw no one suspicious.

She crossed to the elevator and resumed her fuming over the way the lieutenant had treated her. It was all the more galling that he hadn't fallen for her raising the temperature of her charm. She wondered if it would have helped to lay a caressing hand on his, a promise of a reward for his cooperation. No, he wouldn't have given in. She sensed she'd have better luck with St. Cyr. St. Cyr might; but then she'd be at risk of that sweet danger that he radiated.

By the time she stepped off the elevator, she had decided that she was not about to accept either of them brushing her away like some pesky insect. She would just go past them; above, in fact. She needed to speak to a superior officer anyway.

When she reached her desk, she shoved the end of the roll of yellow paper into the Underwood and reached for the telephone. She spoke to Captain Warren, who had again offered a meaningless quote. Ten minutes later, she called for the copyboy and turned over her second story on the murder of Herbert Waltham. He took the pages and handed her an envelope, explaining that it had been left at the lobby desk before walking away.

Rebecca studied the envelope, puzzled. She had received missives all the time she was on the Society pages, most of them from mothers or wives promoting their daughters' or husbands' importance among the city's upper crust. The penmanship was always the most florid possible, replete with curves and curls. What she saw in her hand were plain block letters, not severe but simple, like the careful work of a child.

Perhaps it was a note from an admirer, some young woman who had seen her byline and was inspired. It could also be an attack, deriding her for doing a man's job. But what if it was a tip of some sort?

She held her breath as she opened the flap and drew out a single sheet of paper. *Dear Rebecca Marcus,* it read in that same neat hand, "I saw the news that you wrote. So you know, there will be more to come. More to fall. Wait for me."

Her first instinct was to rush to find Reynard Vernel and show it to him. She turned in her chair, prepared to do just that. Then she stopped to read over the words another half-dozen times.

She read the note again and was convinced that it was more likely the former. Her flesh prickled, a shiver ran up her spine, and after a few seconds, she felt the wetness of arousal between her legs. She looked around again to see if anyone had noticed anything. The men were all pounding keys, talking noise, or snoozing.

It was fantastic. A person involved in the murder of Mr. Herbert Waltham had sent a message to her desk. If it was real and not some someone playing a cruel joke.

She peered across the newsroom and caught sight of Vernel standing in Rolf Kassel's doorway with a sheaf of pages in his hand. Taking her time, she folded the note, rose from her chair, and began winding around the other desks toward the editor's office. Reynard noticed her and was waiting with an eyebrow raised. She was halfway to the office when she stopped, made a gesture of absent-minded dismissal, and turned back for her corner desk.

The night breeze passed through the branches of the trees, carrying the scents of the flowers that were just beginning to bloom about the grounds of St. Rocco's and fading hints of the acrid odors of the city. All else was still, as befitted holy ground.

A dozen penitents had passed in and out of the heavy doors. Only one remained inside. Someone with a heavy burden to lay down, or else why stay so long? Perhaps something other than the activity that took place within the booth of polished walnut. This would not be a surprise.

But, no. When the door creaked opened the supplicant who exited and drew near was an old woman, her back bent and head draped in a kerchief, edging along on slow steps. So that was the delay. A lock clacked in the silence that followed. There would be no sanctuary for lost souls this night. The wind rose again, then fell.

Father Patrick O'Brien had finished the last confession with great relief. He had received a terrible early call about the tragic murder of one of his parishioners, Mr. Walthams. He had summoned a lay pastor, who pulled the car around to the Sycamore Street doors, then spent a good part of his morning at the house on Esplanade Ridge, comforting the bereaved family.

He had returned to his parish and busied himself with church matters until dinner time. Upon his desk were a small stack of letters and packages that the mailman had delivered, along with the afternoon *Times-Picayune*, with the story about poor Mr. Waltham staring him in the face. A tormenting memory came and went about that gentleman—was it something scurrilous?—but he could not recall the details. In any case, he had appetite for neither the newspaper nor the tedium of the mail, so he decided to attend to them in the morning.

He made it through three hours of confessions without hearing the words, *I have sinned, I committed a murder* from the other side of the screen. It had happened once before and had haunted him ever since. Though he had suspected the identity of the confessor, he hadn't known for sure. That individual was still walking the streets of New Orleans.

He was ready to retire to his bed and after bending his knee before the cross and asking that God shed His grace on the Waltham family, he made his way through the chancellery to the side door. He was halfway along the flagstone path when he heard footsteps and caught a shadow moving on the edge of his vision.

What came next was a hard blow and a blinding shock of pain that sent stars through his brain. Something thick and wet was flowing down his chest. He staggered and went again to his knees. There was not time for him to clutch his rosary before he pitched forward and down into a pit of darkness.

# EIGHT

Evangeline was awake first, as she was every morning, and like every morning, she brewed coffee and carried a cup onto the back gallery. The garden was all blue shadows and she could smell the perfumes of oleander, jacaranda, and dark soil. The rain that had passed through during the night had left tiny diamonds on the leaves. She stood very still and let the remainder of the night drape her.

It was at such moments that some of the many broken places in her memory were repaired and she might see a face, hear a voice, recall a name. At those times, still in darkness but with the light of day approaching, she viewed small pieces of another world, with the dawn inside her brain coming earlier over the weeks of the past year. She wondered if she ever would arrive at a place where her thoughts would bask in sunlight rather than hide in shadows and she would remember all that she had forgotten.

For now, the peace that enveloped her was a balm. She hoped that Justine, who was usually second to appear, would be on this morning wearied enough by the brisk midnight frolicking that she had heard through the wall to stay in bed. She had covered her mouth to keep from giggling at the gasps and moans she heard, even as she was sure Justine was covering *her* mouth. From her fog of remembrance had come moving pictures of her flesh entwined with another's, his olive against her pale latte. That was a blur, too; but she dreamed that those images would too become clearer as more days and weeks had gone by. This was her hope.

———

Valentin was curled around his wife, feeling the heat of her through her thin slip. Her head was turned so that he could just make out her profile and the way her braids had come all undone. He had an urge to wrap her tighter and let himself get hard. She'd be willing, of course; hadn't she always thrown herself into the passions of their bed with abandon, at times so wildly that it sometimes startled him? But he decided to let her sleep. She had put in enough work after the lights had gone out.

His thoughts drifted from her and in the direction of Eclipse Alley and from there to Rebecca Marcus and the trouble he had barely skirted. To put a stop to that, he closed his eyes and invited himself into another hour of sleep. Then he and his wife could see what happened.

He was gone only a few minutes in that direction when the telephone began squawking. He rolled over to peer at the clock on the night table; a few minutes before six. He slipped from the bed just as the ringing ceased. Justine muttered and dug deeper into the sheets.

Evangeline was coming down the hall. She pointed over her shoulder. "He says it's important."

Valentin yawned as he followed her to the foyer.

The caretaker, an aging mulatto named Henry, had arrived at St. Rocco's at the same time he had for the past forty-odd years: five a.m. sharp. At seventy-six, he still had memories of slavery. Then came the War and when it ended he had wandered for ten years, landing in New Orleans and coming into the employ of the church. He was a small, bent-backed, and sinewy man, medium brown and white-haired. Though he attended mass daily, two nights a week he slipped into Sign of the Covenant Baptist on Eve Street for the rowdy praise of God. He was, in other words, a pious man of varied tastes.

But all his churchgoing combined could not prepare him for what he happened upon after he had checked the furnace and stepped out to attend to the rectory. The shadows were gray and deep along the flagstone pathway and he saw what he guessed was one of the branches of the drooping satsuma trees that had finally broken off and dropped onto the stones.

When he bent to pull it away, he let out a wail that echoed against the wall of the church.

Valentin laid the handset in the cradle and turned to find his wife standing in the doorway.

"Another one," she said.

"Yes," Valentin said. "Another one."

"You only signed on for Waltham's case."

He caught the faintest scolding hint in her tone. "I know," he said. "We just need to make sure that this is not the same one." He attempted a dismissive hand. "If it's not, I'll be back in an hour."

"And if it is?"

She made him wait a long few seconds before stepping aside. He met her eyes as he passed and found along with spikes of anger an odd kind of pity there.

He was pulling on his vest when she returned to the bedroom. "I had a feeling this was going to happen."

"I was hoping it wouldn't," he said as he opened the closet door.

"Where this time?"

"St. Rocco's."

"In the *church*?"

"Outside, is what James said."

"Who was it?" He didn't answer and she said, "Valentin?"

"It was the priest," Valentin said. "Father O'Brien." He read her expression. "And, yes, he was in the photograph with Waltham."

She pondered this for a few seconds. "How was he killed?"

"McKinney said cut."

"In the same way?"

"I think he would have told me." He sat on the edge of the mattress to button his cuffs. "I hope not." He stood up and took his jacket down from the hook on the door. "I'll call if I can."

He kissed her on her forehead before he left. She turned around, nursing an urge to ask to go along, but she didn't speak.

Lieutenant McKinney had the card Rebecca Marcus had left behind tucked in his billfold. He hesitated only a moment before deciding to let her find out what happened along with everyone else. Which would be soon enough. The church would be swarmed once the news started swirling. His gut told him that it was what he and St. Cyr had been fearing: that Herbert Waltham's killing hadn't been an isolated event.

At that hour, with dawn just breaking, the streets were mostly empty and he steered his Dodge the seven short blocks along St. Charles to Carrollton and then to Jeannette Street, where he pulled to the curb. Three sedans, a touring car, and a runabout, all bearing NOPD shields on their doors, were parked outside the church.

Uniformed officers were standing posts and moving about the banquette in front of the church, a few still carrying lanterns. McKinney stepped up, showed his badge, and was directed to the walkway that connected the side entrance of the building to the rectory, where he came upon a detective from Parish Precinct named Grady and one from the fifth precinct named Capet. They were standing over the body of a silver-haired man in a cassock, his blue eyes staring at the sky. Or perhaps heaven, McKinney considered. The gaping wound in his neck had been made by a blade that had passed through his white collar. Only after he had studied the body head to toe did he look at the other two detectives. "Father O'Brien?" he said.

"Father O'Brien," Grady said. He was holding a note pad in one hand and a pen in the other.

"Who found him?"

"The caretaker, up early." He nodded to a colored man sitting on a nearby stone bench, gaping at his clasped hands in private horror. "Name's..." He glanced at his pad. "Henry."

"Any witnesses?" McKinney said.

"None have come forward."

"Murder weapon?"

"Not yet," Grady said. "We've got patrolmen covering the grounds." He pointed to the modest brick house opposite the back of the church.

"Church deacon was here, but he's back in the rectory. I told him to wait for you."

"What's his name?"

"Terrell. First name Ross. Man's a mess."

"I can imagine," the lieutenant said.

Capet spoke up for the first time. "Where's St. Cyr?"

McKinney eyed him. The question had come out with an edge. "On his way," he said. "Why do you ask?"

The detective said, "Just wondering, is all." Then: "I'll go check on the search." He hitched his suspenders and ambled off.

The lieutenant looked at Grady, who shrugged. "You think it's the same as the other one?" He asked after a moment.

"No telling," McKinney said.

"Two men slashed in, what, twenty-four hours?"

"Could be a coincidence."

"Oh, yeah?" Grady's eyes shifted to something over the lieutenant's shoulder. "What do you think?"

Valentin stepped up on McKinney's left. "About what?" he said.

"Just saying we got two fellows cut up, one after the other." He produced a smirk and said, "I'm sure you'll figure it all out." He turned around and walked away and they heard him call out, "Good morning, Chief," in a voice louder than was necessary.

Chief of Detectives Leroux stepped up, accompanied by one of his aides, who hung back. Neither detective was surprised that Captain Warren was not in attendance.

"Let's have it," the chief said.

McKinney shared what little had been gathered about the murder as the chief glared at the body and muttered. "No parts missing?" he said when the lieutenant finished.

"No, sir," McKinney said.

*Except for his windpipe*, Valentin reflected.

"Goddamn, Lieutenant," Leroux said. "A priest?"

"Yes, sir. And..." He glanced at Valentin.

"And what?"

"The Father was in that photograph with Waltham. And Chief Warren."

"And eleven other men," Valentin said. The captain stared, reading his meaning.

"I hope it's not," McKinney said. "But we're on it."

Leroux cursed some more. Before he left the scene, he bent his head to whisper something. The lieutenant watched him walk off.

"What was that about?" Valentin said.

"He wants me to report directly to him. To keep what I tell Warren to the basic facts. And that's all."

Valentin said, "You know he'll figure it out."

"I know. He's not stupid. Just a poor excuse for a police officer." He shrugged. "I don't know that he'll care."

It wasn't the hack from the morgue that arrived for the body this time, but an ambulance from Charity. The two attendants, both in hospital white and both sober, went about placing the priest on a gurney and hustling his remains into the back of the vehicle with a minimum of fuss. They fairly leaped into the front seat and within seconds, the ambulance was pulling into the morning traffic.

The lieutenant asked one of the patrolmen to fetch the caretaker. The copper walked off and returned with a mulatto who stood quivering in his shoes, his sweaty palms locked together and eyes swimming about. Valentin could not remember the last time he had seen someone more in need of a drink.

That would have to wait. He listened as McKinney had Henry describe coming upon the body. In the end, he was no more help than the strumpets out of Juanita Daly's had been. All three were the victims of terrible timing. Now the images of what they had seen would stick in their minds for the rest of their lives.

The lieutenant thanked the caretaker and told him to wait with one of the officers. He turned to Valentin and said, "All right, let's have a look around and then go talk to the deacon."

———

It was her third day on Waltham's murder and Rebecca woke early, washed and dressed in the bathroom at the end of the hall, then hurried outside to find a jitney waiting to carry her downtown. The guard let her into the lobby and she snatched a fresh morning paper off the counter before crossing to the elevator. She scanned the headlines as she rode up, finding to her delight that not only was the story with her byline above the fold, Reynard had barely cut a word.

When she walked into the newsroom, she found it mostly dark, with only a few lamps casting yellow cones on heads resting on desks. She fidgeted and scribbled notes, wondering what the day would bring. On her list were separate contacts with Lieutenant McKinney and Mr. St. Cyr, hoping that one or the other would fold before her charms.

Reynard Vernel appeared a little after seven, stopped, and peered across the room. She could read his puzzlement even at that distance. He called, "Rebecca?" as he approached her. "What are you...?"

"What am I what?" she said, sensing something.

"You haven't heard?"

She was on her feet and gathering her things before he could say another word.

A young nun in a habit ushered them into the rectory. The front room was austere with walnut moldings and only a couch and two chairs for furniture. Lieutenant McKinney removed his hat and they waited until the gentleman appeared from the dimly-lit dining room.

Ross Terrell was a short and thin man in his forties, balding, his eyes wide behind the thick lenses of his spectacles. He was wearing a suit and every stitch was in place, right to the perfect knot of his tie. A spike of a nose and a pronounced Adam's apple protruded. His odd, stiff posture struck Valentin as military, but more like a boarding school than the army. With all that, he was broadcasting his distress from every pore.

The lieutenant spoke up. "Mr. Terrell? I'm James McKinney, New Orleans Police. This is Mr. St. Cyr. He's assisting in the investigation."

Terrell stared at the officer, gave the barest nod of his head, and waved a limp hand in the direction of the nun. Valentin barely caught the name, "Sister Marie."

"I know this is a shocking event," McKinney said. "But before things get too busy, I'd like to ask you some questions. All right?"

"Yes, all right." The deacon's voice was high and tense.

"First of all, do you have any idea who might have committed the crime? Anyone among the congregation who would be capable of–"

"No!" Terrell fairly cried. "I can't imagine any one of the Father's flock doing such a horrible thing." He sniffed and trembled, as if on the verge of breaking down and weeping. "He was kind. A man of God. His parishioners loved–"

"If you would, please..." The lieutenant cut him off, pulling out his pad and pen before he went on a flight of reverence, testifying to the priest's holy perfection. "Can you tell me what the Father did yesterday and last night?"

"The whole day?" McKinney nodded. The deacon's brow stitched and he began recounting O'Brien's comings and goings.

Valentin listened for a minute, then let his attentions drift. He knew the lieutenant would fill him in on anything important. His gaze settled on the nun, who was standing to the left and five paces behind the deacon, her eyes cast downward and her mouth in a tight line. Her face was pleasant in a simple way and he could picture her as the Virgin Mary or even the Magdalene. Who knew about these things? He could name a half-dozen women who had come out of Storyville bordellos to land in the arms of Christ. So went his idle thoughts as the deacon droned on in a low voice about the Father's last day on earth.

The sister turned her head in his direction as she sensed him studying her. A moment passed, she faced him more fully, and he noticed along with her grief an intensity in her eyes that transmitted a message. She held his stare for a few seconds, then lowered her head once more.

Valentin returned his attention to McKinney and Terrell in time to hear the deacon say, "I left at six o'clock. My normal time. I told the Father that I'd..." He swallowed. "That I'd see him in the morning."

The lieutenant said, "And once more, you can't think of anyone who held bad feelings toward Father O'Brien?"

"No I cannot," Terrell said. "There were always little spats within the congregation, but nothing that would suggest..." He shook his head in numb woe and swallowed again, his eyes blinking like fans.

McKinney drew a card from his pocket. "Please call me if you think of anything more."

Terrell's hand jerked forward to accept the card.

The lieutenant and Valentin passed outside, where morning was rising in a pleasing way for such a gruesome tableau. They stood watching the officers milling about and holding back the crowd that was assembling on the street, even though the word was barely out.

"You'll be making another run at him?" Valentin said.

"Yes, he needs to give up what he's hiding." He pointed to the church. All right, let's go see what the good Father left us in his office."

"Wait," Valentin said and started down the steps. "Give me a couple minutes." The lieutenant watched him begin a slow stroll around the side of the house, then dug into his pocket for his Omars.

Sister Marie was in the garden at the back of the house, idly plucking dead leaves from among the blooms on the branches of a cherry tree. Valentin stood by in silence until she turned to face him.

"It's Mr. St. Cyr?"

"It is, yes."

"About what happened to the Father and Herbert Waltham. I over-heard something. Mr. Waltham was here Sunday evening. The Father heard his confession." The detective waited. "Afterward, they were walking by and I heard Mr. Waltham say, 'Am I truly forgiven for this? Can I ever be?' He was very upset."

"And what did the Father say?" Valentin asked.

"I couldn't hear that part," she said. "I'm sure it was something to comfort him."

"That's all?"

"That's all," the nun said. "They walked to the rectory and the Father went inside. Mr. Waltham started down the path. He was always quite nice to me. This time he said, 'Sister,' and just brushed past. Afterward, I asked the Father if something was wrong and he just patted my shoulder and said there was nothing to worry about. And now...." She sighed and shook her head.

"You did the right thing speaking to me," Valentin said.

She offered him a quiet smile before moving away.

Lulu White learned about Father O'Brien from her morning maid, who said she was "friendly" with one of the coppers who had been on the scene at St. Rocco's. She had not come close to getting over her shock over Herbert Waltham's murder; now this, something worse, if that was possible. The only less than horrible detail that the policeman had shared was that the priest had not been mutilated in the same awful way.

She ordered the maid not to tell anyone else for the time being. The young girl, an Ethiopian with her hair cut short and nappy, frowned at having to keep mum about something so delicious, but then nodded. She was happier when Miss Lulu slipped her a gold dollar.

Once the girl had left her office, the madam paced, getting her thoughts in order. A priest murdered? Was it possible? Who would be so mad as to commit such an outrage? She paced, working through the angles. At least he hadn't been killed in Storyville. Though someone would surely find a way to blame the murder on the District and its inequities.

With that thought, she returned to her desk and went about calling around to get the information that wasn't yet public.

Henry opened the heavy wooden doors and led the two detectives around the rows of pews. Sanctified spaces had never been a balm to Valentin's spirit. So while his wife attended mass most Sunday mornings, he stayed away. Now he kept his eyes averted from the altar and sacristy and tall gold cross bearing a suffering Jesus. Lieutenant McKinney's piety was shared by others in the department who saw too much evil and he stopped to bend a knee and genuflect.

The morning light was beginning to touch the panes of stained glass and they passed through red and orange swatches out of the chapel and along the corridor to Father O'Brien's office. When Henry's hands shook so that he couldn't insert the key, Valentin took over and unlocked the door. McKinney told the old man he could wait outside.

Valentin took the opportunity to repeat what the nun had told him. "Well, we figured there was a connection," McKinney said when he finished. "What does it tell you?"

"There's some business from the past. And maybe someone is back to settle a score."

"Like this?"

"It's happened before."

"Though, no, not quite like this. So then the question becomes who else is in the sights," McKinney said. "Unless the two of them are the end of it." He looked at Valentin, who gave a slight shake of his head. "I don't think so, either." He pondered for a few moments more, then said, "All right, let's see what we have here."

They scoured the room, the lieutenant covering the perimeter and all the cabinets and Valentin the desk at its center. The only art was a portrait of the Pope near the door and a cross behind the desk chair. The late father had been a meticulous man, tidy in his workplace. The pile of mail on one side of the desk offered the only disorder. Valentin sifted through the envelopes and examined a half-dozen packages.

He was almost to the bottom of the stack when he came upon a stained parcel of two by five inches and sealed with glue in a rough way, as if put together by a child. And yet the hand that had printed the address was precise, a string of careful block letters. Something about it gave the detective pause; the only item he'd come across that was out of place.

He said, "James? Look at this."

McKinney joined him at the desk and Valentin handed him the package. They studied it for a long moment. Then the lieutenant said, "Oh, hell..." He picked up the silver letter opener that was embossed with a cross, slit the seal, pulled the wrapping loose, and cut through the waxed paper.

After a few seconds, the lieutenant said, "We have a repeat killer."

"At least it was just a finger," Valentin said.

Lucy had just put Mr. Tom's breakfast and coffee before him when the telephone chattered. She disappeared into the foyer, then stepped back into the doorway to say, "It's Miss Lulu White."

Anderson said, "Oh, Good Lord, what does she want?" He spent a moment debating whether to take the call. Then he tossed his napkin aside and pushed himself out of his chair. "All right," he said. "I'll speak to her."

The maid was placing a cover over his plate when she heard him shout, "What? Jesus Christ!" From that point, she heard only odd curses and random mutterings. Though she was done at the table, she decided to wait.

It was well that she did, for when the King of Storyville appeared in the doorway, his face ashen and his body was one large tremble. He barely shuffled to the table, where he laid a hand for support. He gasped, "Lucy... I... I'm..." before dropping to his knees, the hand now grasping the arm of the chair so that he wouldn't topple to the floor. His chest heaved as he struggled to catch his breath.

Lucy backed away and ran out of the room, shouting, "George! George!"

Justine took her bath and put on one of her cotton day dresses. Thursday was their day to make market and she wanted to be ready to be on her way as soon as Valentin got back with the Ford.

In the kitchen, she poured coffee, selected a pear from the bowl, and watched Evangeline roaming the back garden in the same patient way, or so her husband had recalled, that she had traversed the grounds of Our Lady of Sorrows, the convent where she had been taken in and where he had found her. Justine thought she looked like a saint, her head bowed and hands folded before her as she moved with gentle steps to the back of the garden, where the shade from the new leaves was the deepest.

She carried her coffee to where the morning newspaper lay folded. Settling in a chair, her eye was caught by a headline above the fold. Before she read the first sentence, a name jumped out at her.

POLICE INVESTIGATION
OF THE BRUTAL MURDER
OF HERBERT WALTHAM CONTINUES
by
REBECCA MARCUS

The New Orleans Police Department has not yet discovered the perpetrator of or the motive for the brutal slaying early Wednesday morning of former State Senator and president of Crescent Cotton Exchange Mr. Herbert Waltham.

"We have dedicated all available manpower to apprehending the person who committed this terrible crime," said Captain Bob Warren of Parish Precinct. "We are hoping for developments in the case very soon."

Waltham's body was discovered early Wednesday in Eclipse Alley, a narrow passageway near where Liberty Street intersects with St. Louis. The police are working to learn why the victim was in that location at that time.

Mr. Waltham was a prominent figure in New Orleans. In addition to his business and political endeavors, he was a deacon at St. Rocco's Catholic Church and active in various charitable groups. He is survived by his wife, a son, a daughter, and three grandchildren.

Lieutenant James McKinney is heading the NOPD investigation. He is being assisted by the detective squad at Parish Precinct and Valentin St. Cyr, a private investigator who had a long career securing Storyville on behalf of Mr. Tom Anderson.

The police are asking that anyone with any knowledge of the incident contact Lt. McKinney or any detective at the Parish precinct.

This reporter will be providing new information from these and other sources in the morning and afternoon editions of the *Times-Picayune* until the case is resolved.

Services for Herbert Waltham will be on Saturday beginning at noon at St. Rocco's. Visitation will begin at ten o'clock at the Gasquet Funeral Home on Carrolton Avenue.

She laid the paper on the table with the byline staring up at her. There it was: his name in view for anyone in New Orleans to see. He wasn't going to like it; he had always avoided the spotlight. And hadn't Rebecca Marcus promised she wouldn't use his name?

She read the article, then sat back, her thoughts shifting. She had seen photographs of Miss Marcus on the Society page. The woman was attractive in the way that Valentin liked: dark eyes, skin that appeared closer to brown than white, with flesh on the bone and not a stick—like his wife.

She perused the article a second time. The Waltham killing had been startling. But it was about to get swept aside by an even more dreadful crime: the murder of a priest. By late afternoon, the city would be a riot of wagging tongues and officials bellowing for action.

She sat turning it over, then rose from the table to prepare a simple breakfast for Evangeline and herself. After starting a fresh pot of coffee, she cut slices of French bread and placed them on an oven rack to toast. They kept a tray of cold meats and cheeses in the icebox and she slid it out and began cutting slices. When she finished, she called to Evangeline, who offered a soft wave of her hand.

As she set the table, she wondered how long she would have to wait for her husband to return. And what he would have to say about Miss Rebecca Marcus.

The sun was climbing over the trees and Valentin and McKinney had to shield their eyes on the way back to the street.

"We'll need someone watching the mailboxes around that post office," Valentin said. "I can get Each."

"I'll request some cash for him and you can— " He stopped as an apparition wavered out of the morning's red light. "Oh, my," he muttered. "I think we're in trouble."

Rebecca hiked the hem of her gray moire skirt as she bore down on them, coming to a halt a few feet away. McKinney touched the brim of his fedora. Valentin offered a bland smile.

"You know I can be reached by the telephone," she said by way of greeting. "The number is on the card I gave you." Her cheeks were flushed and her eyes shooting out little beams of hard light. "Neither of you could alert me? I thought we had an understanding."

Valentin could tell by the quizzical way the lieutenant tilted his head that the policeman didn't know any more about an "understanding" than he did. Even so, they were both amused—and daunted—by the way the reporter had charged them.

She didn't wait for either detective to speak up and forged ahead. "All right, never mind," she said. "Another stabbing victim? And a priest?" She fastened her eyes on the lieutenant. "Don't tell me you can't comment. You know I'll get nothing from your captain. You won't be quoted."

McKinney thought it over, then said, "Yes, the victim was stabbed to death. One deep cut to the throat."

"This was Father O'Brien?"

"It was," the officer said.

"Were there any witnesses to the crime?"

"We haven't found any. We're working on it."

"Do you believe the perpetrator was the same one who murdered Mr. Waltham?"

"We have no way to know right now," McKinney said. "And we don't want to... uh..."

"Speculate," Valentin said.

'Oh?' Rebecca Marcus said. "I see." She looked between them. "Did you know that Mr. Waltham was a lay deacon here?"

Valentin stood still as the lieutenant responded, hardening his expression along with his tone. "We want to work with our press, but reaching conclusions without more evidence would be a mistake," he said. "And I'm sure you don't want to do that."

The reporter got the message and leaned back a bit, even as the ends of her mouth curled upward. "I do not, Lieutenant." She glanced at Valentin, then returned her attention to the policeman. "When will you have more you can share?" she said in a voice that had gone gentle.

"After I make my report," McKinney said. "You can reach me at the precinct at, say, nine-thirty."

"Good," she said. "You can expect my call."

The lieutenant touched the brim of his hat once more and began moving off. Valentin felt the reporter's heated stare on him as he followed behind. Walking away, he had to admit that he hadn't seen many women do the look better.

They reached the street and stopped to scan the dozen or so souls who had assembled, drawn by the early police presence. They both knew that the murderer could be in their number, though what they saw were working men and women, off to their jobs around the city. There didn't appear to be a depraved monster among them. Not that it was ever that easy.

"Did you know about Waltham being a deacon here?" McKinney said.

"I did not," Valentin said.

"Terrell didn't mention it. I wonder why." The lieutenant looked back to where Rebecca Marcus stood scribbling notes on a pad. "She's a clever one, isn't she?"

"That she is," Valentin said. With a wave, he moved off.

# NINE

George and Lucy managed to maneuver Mr. Tom onto the couch in the sitting room and the maid ordered her husband to fetch the brandy bottle while she dabbed the old man's forehead with a wet cloth.

"Do you want me to call Doctor Calvert?" she asked. "Sir?"

"Yes, go ahead." The words came out each with its own little gasp. "And call Mr. Valentin again. I need to speak to him."

Lucy stood and whispered to her husband to stay there while she tried to locate the Creole detective. Though she wondered seriously if Mr. Tom would be alive when she got back.

Valentin knew Justine would be waiting for him to return and drive her to market. He could avoid the downtown traffic by making a simple loop north on Carrollton to City Park and turning onto Dumaine. That would be the easiest route. Instead, he steered back to St. Charles, heading east.

As soon as he arrived at Mahogany Hall, he told Miss Lulu he needed to make a call. The madam left him in her office while she went to direct her maid to fetch coffee.

"Where are you?" Justine said.

"At Miss Lulu's."

After a pause, she said, "What are you doing there?"

"Waltham was one of her regular visitors."

"And what about Father O'Brien?"

He explained what he could before the madam returned, including the severed finger someone had sent to the priest.

"It wasn't *someone*," she said.

"Yes, I know." The door opened and Miss Lulu stepped in, followed by one of her house girls carrying a silver tray.

"We can talk some more when I get there," he said.

"When will that be? You know I need—"

"To make market. I know. An hour. Maybe less."

"Wait," she said. "Have you seen the paper this morning?"

He heard something in her tone. "No, not yet. I'm sure Miss Lulu has a copy."

"You'll want to have a look at it," she said, and before he could reply added, "Please don't be long," and clicked off.

The madam had caught the tail end of the conversation. Valentin replaced the phone in the cradle and turned to see her holding up the *Times-Picayune*.

"You made the front page," she said.


Miss Lulu shooed the maid and served the coffee herself, after which she sat back in her leather tufted chair to sip from her cup. Valentin was fuming over the mention of his name in her article. But it was his own damned fault.

After some more thought, he decided to put it away until he got to Dumaine Street. He hadn't stopped moving since he was awakened in the dark and now took a few moments to gather himself.

The madam was studying him in return, wearing one of the bizarre red wigs that she believed somehow made a case for her imagined youth and white blood. She had in fact been born in an Alabama sharecropper's cabin and yet spent years trying to convince New Orleans and the world that she was the daughter of a white Jamaican and his Creole mistress. She possessed the talents to rise from common trollop to the grandest madam in the city. Men of wealth around the globe knew the address of Mahogany Hall. She was in some ways Tom Anderson's mirror reflection —if that mirror changed images from black to white as well. Valentin had known her all the time he'd been in Storyville and their dealings had swung from gratifying to maddening and every degree in-between. With all this, he had always found her a kind-hearted woman, loyal, and a great ally.

His great ally now placed her cup in its saucer. "Valentin, my dear. Have I seen you since I got back to New Orleans?"

He said, "I don't believe so, Miss Lulu." He was not about to mention her recent foolishness.

"What in God's name is happening? Two murders in two days? The president of a huge company? A priest? What is this insanity?"

Valentin knew he could speak freely with her, that she would not betray his confidence. "I think the same person committed both murders. That's the easy part." He waited for the madam to draw a brandy bottle from a drawer and pour a slug into both their cups. "Did you happen to see Sunday's paper?"

"What about it?"

"There was a story about some committee Mr. Tom is heading."

She looked puzzled. "Yes, and?"

"Herbert Waltham and Father O'Brien were both in the photograph that was with the piece."

"Oh. And who else?"

"I don't know. Eleven other men."

She flipped a hand. "I see those things all the time. A collection of stuffed shirts." She tilted her head. "Unless you think it somehow connects these murders?"

"I don't know." He moved on. "Tell me about Mr. Waltham."

"There's not much to tell," she said. "He showed up once every two weeks or so. He always asked for one of my younger girls. Sometimes, I had one available. If not, he'd go elsewhere."

"How young?"

She eyed him. "You know I make sure they're of age."

"Yes, I know."

"Of course, he came to spend time with my other guests, too."

Valentin understood. The high-class bordellos like Mahogany Hall also served as social clubs for men of means. They would dine and gamble to jazz music at Anderson's Café, then stroll to a Basin Street mansion to enjoy a night of refined entertainment, replete with fancy champagne and a professor at the parlor piano.

"In any case, he was always pleasant, quite jolly when he was in his cups, and he treated my girls well." Miss Lulu snickered. "Of course, at his age, they had to work extra hard to give him his pleasure."

"Anything about him that suggested trouble?" Valentin said.

The madam shook her head and the wig fluttered. "Not a thing. He was rather dull. Another wealthy fellow who cares only for money and a woman who is not his wife."

Valentin held out his cup and she poured more brandy. She waited until he sipped to say, "I told Mr. Tom about what happened to the Father."

He closed his eyes and sighed, trying to imagine what had compelled her to stir things up by calling Anderson. "How did he take it?" he asked.

"Completely shocked. Like it was the last thing he wanted to hear. He hung up on me without saying good-bye. Not like him. But he's—" The telephone on her desk had chirped.

Though he had never been much of a gambler, Valentin would have laid money that the call was from the same gentleman they were discussing.

Miss Lulu lifted the receiver and listened, her eyes shifting to her guest. She said, "If he comes by, I'll let him know," and placed the handset back in the cradle. "That was his maid. What's her name? Lily? Lucy? They sent for the doctor."

"The doctor? How bad is he?"

"He's not dying. He's just an old man." She settled back.

Valentin emptied his cup with a sigh of regret. "I'll pay him a visit. Right now, I'm expected at home."

Miss Lulu leaned over and picked up the newspaper, wearing her sweetest smile. "Maybe she'll love you, now that you're a star detective again."

Valentin stood to leave, thinking it was the last thing he expected her to do.

Rebecca had crept about the fringes of the crime scene, looking for friendly faces and hoping one of the officers would give her something for her next story. From a distance, she could make out the bloody patch where the body had lain. An old black man sat on one of the stone benches, staring at the stain as if he could not fathom it. She guessed that he was the one who had discovered the priest's body.

She had not failed to muse on the coincidence of two men who had appeared in a photograph that accompanied a story she had penned had turned up dead in as many days. The more she thought about it, though, the more she wondered if there was nothing ominous about it. Hadn't there been eleven other men in the picture? Still...

She returned to the street to find Lieutenant McKinney and the detective St. Cyr had escaped her once more. If only she could put bells around their necks. She laughed without humor, knowing that if she didn't figure a way to get what she wanted from them, she'd be back writing frills.

That thought propelled her along the banquette to the jitney the paper had hired for her. As she placed her foot on the running board, the sense of being watched assailed her once again. Perhaps it was just some copper leering at her rump as she climbed up? No, she knew that feeling and this was something else. Eyes were tracking her in a different way. She turned to scan the closest faces. Nothing; and just like that, the feeling went away.

*It's easy to get lost among the bodies, especially for someone dressed so plain. The reporter stayed after the policeman and the private detective left, walking from one officer to the next, asking a question, then moving on. It was clear they weren't helping her at all. That was not fair.*

*Well, one effort has already been made on her behalf. There will be more to come and more after that. Whatever it takes to keep the story alive.*

As rapidly as the word of Herbert Waltham's death had traveled, it was a slow stream compared to the gusher that followed the news of Father O'Brien's murder. Fevered noise rose from every corner of the city and from the top down. Mayor Behrman barely had time to digest the first tragedy when the second one landed on his desk. An important business magnate was bad enough. But a priest at one of the largest Catholic churches in the city? He raged, demanding action, including shutting down Storyville, though the District had nothing to do with the second killing—or at least as far as anyone knew.

It didn't signify. He ordered the Chief of Police into his office and those on the other side of the closed door heard him shout: "By God, John, I'll shut the whole goddamn city down! I'll fire you and every other copper on the force. *Do* something!" These same eavesdroppers swore that when the chief reappeared, the seat of his trousers was smoking. He looked neither left nor right, stalking out and snatching up the first telephone set he could find to summon Chief of Detectives Leroux.

Lieutenant McKinney listened as Leroux told him what had come down from no less than the mayor by way of the Chief of Police, demanding something—anything—that could stanch the angry barrages from the press and the public. By the time Leroux broke the connection with, "Finish the damned report and get over here," his ears were ringing.

He placed the handset back in the cradle. Why was he surprised? But he had learned from the Creole detective on the Rampart Street murder that rushing only made things worse. They had charged a hapless street rodent with the crime, losing precious time, and the guilty party almost got away clean. All because a noteworthy citizen was murdered and the city wanted results quickly rather than correctly.

The lieutenant decided he wasn't going to hurry, instead returning to his report on the murder at St. Rocco's. Normally, he would first make his way to the morgue and examine the body for yet another report, this one based on the coroner's comments. A detective worried about procedure would do just that, as the visit would be noted somewhere. He thought this a pointless waste of his time. What could the autopsy tell them that he didn't already know? He could match the severed finger that rested in his bottom desk drawer to the body later. There was no doubt in his mind where it belonged.

Anyway, Chief Leroux was expecting him. As he gathered his things, he remembered that he had told Rebecca Marcus she could call him at nine-thirty. He glanced at his watch; still twenty minutes to go, but she'd call sooner. So he made a quick stop at the front desk to have a word with the clerk, and was out the door and down the stairs.

The call came five minutes later. The clerk informed the reporter that Lieutenant McKinney had been summoned to headquarters at the last minute, just as that officer had instructed. Miss Marcus offered a clipped, "Thank you," and the line went dead.

Justine stood at the sink, washing the breakfast dishes, stopping every few moments to gaze out the window, her thoughts drifting back to the newspaper story that included her husband's name. He had brushed off not telling her about the reporter right away, as if it was just an absent-minded mistake. She wasn't so sure. Rebecca Marcus was no blushing violet. She would not have been sent out to cover a horrible murder if they thought she'd faint at the sight of blood. Or wouldn't take on the police and a certain Creole detective whom women still found interesting. Justine had seen the looks that were cast his way when they were out and about.

So now the lethal mix of a fine-looking woman who would meet the males she encountered head-on was part of the case. Justine had to admit she admired this, because she possessed the same kind of brass. And hadn't she in the past used both her looks and her wiles to get what she wanted? Now the same type of creature and perhaps some kind of rival had strayed into her husband's path.

Strayed? Hardly. Rebecca Marcus was not the sort to—

"We don't need another flood."

Justine turned, startled, to see Evangeline studying her in a quizzical way, half-smiling. The older woman gestured to the sink and Justine realized that she had been standing there, daydreaming, while the water had risen almost to the counter. She stuttered and in a swift motion, turned off the faucet and pulled the plug.

"Are you all right?" Evangeline said.

"I'm fine, yes," Justine said. She reached for a dish towel. "I think Valentin will be back soon."

She left the kitchen as Evangeline stared after her with concern in her eyes.

# TEN

After a half-hour walk that did not dispel the morning's bloody images or add any notion as to why a second murder had been committed, the lieutenant stepped through the doors of police headquarters on Royal Street and rode the elevator to the fourth floor. Chief Leroux's aide ushered him into the wood-paneled office.

The chief had been wearing out the carpet. He stopped when McKinney entered. "Goddamn it, Lieutenant," he said. "First the fellow who ran one of the largest companies in the city and now a man of the cloth?" He was all but moaning. "Is there any chance that it's not the same perpetrator?"

"We can't say for certain, but—"

"But you're pretty damn sure."

"Yes, sir," the lieutenant said. He waited to see if the chief had more to add before saying, "We did find something." He told Leroux about his interview with the deacon, what the nun had told Valentin, the visit to Father O'Brien's office, and the gory contents in the box on the desk.

"Jesus Christ." The chief moved to his desk and dropped into his leather chair as if a weight had settled on him. "Where is it now? The finger, I mean."

"In one of my desk drawers," the lieutenant told him. "I'll carry it to the morgue. I'm sure it will be a match."

"And Mr. Waltham's other parts? I suppose they'll be showing up, too?" It wasn't a question. "So we have a repeat murderer."

McKinney said, "It's the only explanation. Mr. Valentin agrees."

"Well, he would know." The chief pondered for a dark moment. "All right," he said. "At least we know what we're dealing with. What's next?"

"I'm going to work the physical angles. St. Cyr will get into the history."

"Because that's what he does."

"Yes, sir."

Leroux mused a bit more. "What have you told Warren?"

"Nothing."

"Good. Keep it that way. As little as possible."

"You don't want me to show him the finger?"

Leroux came up with a bleak laugh and waved a hand, dismissing him.

Just as the lieutenant was reaching the banquette, Valentin was turning onto Dumaine Street and pulling the Ford to the curb in front of number 4171. He shut off the rattling engine, climbed down from the machine and then stepped up the perron to the gallery.

She was slouched in one of the wicker chairs, her eyes closed, as a gentle breeze whispered in the trees. "You're back," she said without raising either lid.

"I am."

"Did you have breakfast?"

He stopped to realize that he hadn't eaten at all. The sight of the priest's slashed neck and the severed finger had quelled any appetite. Now he felt his stomach churn. When Justine made no move toward the kitchen, he sat down and heaved a relieved sigh. "Where's Evangeline?"

"Having her bath." She opened her eyes. "All right, tell me."

She didn't specify what she wanted to hear, so he described the murder scene, the victim's gaping wound, the pool of blood. The attack had been quick: one strike, a matter of seconds. Then he hold her about the interview with the deacon and his private talk with Sister Marie. He finished with the search of the priest's office and the package containing the severed finger.

She considered for a few quiet seconds, then said, "So you might have three more murders."

"Unless we stop him first."

"Him, again."

"Or her."

Another pause, then: "Speaking of *her*..."

He felt a chill. "Yes?"

"Rebecca Marcus. She used your name."

He said, "I didn't know she would do that."

"You didn't tell her not to?" Her tone was deliberate.

"I told her don't mention me as a source. I didn't say don't use it at all. I wasn't thinking."

"And why was that?" she said. When he didn't answer right away, she said, "What does she want, Valentin?"

"For me to help her."

"And what did you say to that?"

He produced a pronounced shrug. "*That's* what I said."

"Because telling her 'no' wouldn't stop her."

Why did he think she wouldn't understand that part of it? On the other hand, if she had suspicions about any of the reporter's other motives, she was keeping them to herself.

"She's after James. He's playing it safe, too. But we need to make sure she shares anything she knows that we don't. "

She let him stew for a few long moments before saying, "Anything else?"

He shook his head. "No, that's all of it."

She unfolded from the chair, stood up, stretched in a way that sent him a message, and said, "We have some eggs and ham."

Reynard beckoned to Rebecca from the door of Rolf Kassel's office and she paused, wondering if the editors had somehow gotten wind of the note she had hidden on the underside of a desk drawer, just the way she had read about in a dime novel. She prepared her best blank expression.

But when she joined the two men, the younger one said nothing about a missive from a murderer and Kassel looked his happy, half-drunken self. To her relief, Reynard asked only for a report on her visit to St. Rocco's.

"There was nothing to see. I mean aside from all the police milling about. They had it cordoned off. I tracked down McKinney and St. Cyr."

"And?"

"And they wouldn't say anything, except that the priest bled to death after being stabbed in the throat."

"Christ," Kassel said.

"It's something," Vernel said.

"I spoke to every copper on the scene. Asking for details. Or to be let in for a closer look."

"And they wouldn't help, either."

"I'm sure they're all under orders," Kassel said in his rumbling voice. "Two important men killed in two days? You'll have a time getting anything."

"The lieutenant said I could call him at nine-thirty," Rebecca said.

The senior editor produced a small smile. "So you called at?"

"Nine-fifteen. But he was already gone. Called away. 'Unexpectedly.'"

"Of course. Stay on him."

"Yes, sir, I will."

"How many men were in that photograph?"

She paused for a puzzled moment, then said, "Thirteen. Why?"

"I'm just curious," he said, "Have you seen the other papers?" She shook her head. "We're ahead of them. It needs to stay that way." The loose tone had cooled.

"I understand," Rebecca said. "I'll go ahead and write up my story and fill in blanks when I talk to him."

Vernel said, "You know he could hide all day. He and Mr. Valentin both."

Rebecca said, "Not from me, they can't." She offered a slight bow as she left the office.

Kassel looked at the younger editor. "Do you ever get the idea that she knows more than she's saying?"

"Always," Reynard said.

Valentin finished his breakfast and called Tom Anderson while he waited for Justine and Evangeline to gather their things for market.

The maid answered. "Good morning, Mr. Valentin."

"Lucy?"

"Yes, sir. Still here. George, too."

"Can Mr. Tom come to the phone?"

"Wait, please. I'll take it to him." She lowered her voice to a whisper. "He nearly done passed out when he heard what happened to that priest." Her tone returned to a false-sounding normal. "He's on the couch in the sitting room. I'm just going to carry it on in there."

Valentin heard some noises and then a voice that sounded even weaker than the day before. "Valentin. Thank you for calling." Anderson paused to draw a shaky breath. "My God. What is this?"

"We've seen it before."

"Not like this. I was acquainted with both of them. Dear Christ in heaven."

Valentin waited to see if Mr. Tom would mention the newspaper story. Instead, he coughed and the detective heard Lucy's soothing voice in the background, followed by the sounds of sipping. "They were both men of influence in this city. Who next? The mayor? The Chief of Police? Me?"

Valentin knew there was no point in listening to the old man while away in lament. "Can you think of a connection between them?" he said. "Other than the church, I mean. And these civic committees."

"No, I can't." Valentin came alert; the reply had been just a bit too quick. "I attended mass at St. Ignatius. I crossed paths with Waltham here and there, at city functions and what not. That's all."

"Both men had interests in the District, correct?" Valentin said.

Valentin read the silence that followed and understood. Mr. Waltham frequented the mansions. St. Rocco's still owned real estate in the District, like a half-dozen of the other churches did, and some of the properties were bordellos. He also understood that this did not on its own establish a thread between the victims.

Anderson broke into his thoughts, saying, "So are we just waiting for the next one to fall?"

"We want to prevent that." Even as he spoke the words, he felt a quiver of dread at what might happen once the sun went down.

"The police hired you?"

"Yes, they did. It was only for Mr. Waltham," Valentin said. "But then..."

"I understand. You're working with Lieutenant McKinney again."

"Yes, sir."

"He's a good man?"

"Yes, he is."

"Well, then, we'll hope for the best."

"Mr. Tom," Valentin spoke up before the old man could end the call. "If there's anything that comes to mind that ties the two victims together, I'd–"

"I told you, I don't know." Now he was sounding petulant.

"You might think of something. And you know where to find me."

"Yes, yes. I'm handing the phone back to Lucy now."

Valentin instructed the maid to get in touch if she was worried about the King of Storyville's health or state of mind. She promised to do that.

Valentin had just hung up the phone when the bell chirped again. This time it was McKinney letting him know that he was on his way to the morgue.

The detective was following Justine and Evangeline out to the Ford when it occurred to him that Mr. Tom hadn't said a further word about him paying a visit to the grand house on the corner of Coliseum and Fourth streets.

*By now, the package has been found. Had there been time to alert the post office to be looking out for more? Maybe so, but how could they hope to go through the thousands coming and going?*

*Anyway, this time it was different, a cigar box left behind somewhere, rigid and tidy, and no one would suspect until it was opened.*

*Did the tall policeman and the detective in the suit have any notion whatsoever? No, and they wouldn't; as long as care was taken, no one would know until the very end and then the truth would be revealed. That reporter, the pretty one, she can help. No. She will help.*

*But one step at a time. On this afternoon, it's the post office on Louisiana Avenue and it requires no more than ten seconds to drop the package, then fade back into the eddies of citizens moving about with no idea who walks among them.*

Valentin drove Justine and Evangeline to the French Market. After he helped the ladies out, his wife gave him instructions to be back in an hour.

"I could go in with you," he said.

"We'll be fine," she said. "And I thought you said you have an appointment at the morgue."

He nodded, looking doleful. She laid a hand on his arm and held his eyes. "The next time they ask, say no." She kissed his cheek. "I know, we need the money." She turned back and she and Evangeline walked through the wide archway into the market.

Dolores was putting away the last of the breakfast dishes, once again lost in thought over Mr. Waltham's terrible death, and was startled to see his son standing in the kitchen doorway.

"Oh," she said, when she caught a breath. "Mr. Herbert. Good morning."

"Good morning, Dolores."

She said, "Coffee, sir?"

"No, thank you," he said. "I'd like a few minutes of your time."

She was unnerved by the way he was watching her and by the fact that he had never had much to say to her. "Well, of course." She closed the cabinet door and waited.

He kept his voice low. "I've spoken to the rest of the staff about keeping our family's business private. If anyone needs to speak to the police or the newspapers, it will be me."

"Yes, sir."

"You understand that?"

"I do," Dolores said.

"Those two detectives who visited the day of my father's murder."

She kept her expression blank. "Yes, sir?"

"They asked if we knew of any reason he would be the victim of such a horrible attack. Of course, none of us did." He paused. "Do you?"

Now she was alarmed. "I'm sorry. Me? How would I know about–"

"Because maids see things, hear things. That's why." He waited.

"Anything come to mind?"

"Not a thing, no," she said.

He drew closer, almost hovering. "Dolores?" He tasted the name. "Have you always gone by that?"

She kept her eyes averted and mouth closed for a full ten seconds. Then she said, "There was this one thing, sir."

Valentin descended the stone steps to the cellar. He found James and Howard the attendant standing over the gurney upon which Herbert Waltham's corpse lay covered with a sheet. The lieutenant offered Valentin a faint nod, directing him to the opposite side. He laid the package atop the victim's thick middle, then drew the severed finger from his pocket and unraveled it from the cotton.

Howard muttered, "I'll be fucked. Where the hell'd you get that?"

McKinney ignored him as he raised the sheet a few inches and held the finger to the dead man's hand. "No," he said and reached across the corpse.

The right hand was a perfect fit. "So now we know what we already knew," he said. He turned to the attendant. "I need some gauze and a small tray with some ice in it. Please."

"Right away," Howard said and scurried to the supply closet that was attached to the examination room.

McKinney said, "Do you want to have a look at Father O'Brien?"

Valentin said, "There's no point, is there?"

"There is not," the officer said. "I'll report that we saw him, anyway."

The attendant returned with a metal tray holding the ice he had chopped in one hand and a roll of gauze in the other. McKinney wrapped the bloody digit and laid it back in the tray.

"Taking it home to Mae Rose?" Valentin inquired.

McKinney snickered, then said, "No, I'm going to trust it to our friend here." He treated Howard to a copper stare. "He's going to put it in their cold box and not let anyone else know it's even in the building." The stare hardened. "Correct?"

Howard said, "No problem with that, no, sir. None at all." He carried the tray out the door and his footsteps echoed down the corridor.

Valentin and the lieutenant left by taking the hallway in the other direction.

Once outside, McKinney produced his packet of Omars, gave one to Valentin, took a second for himself, and struck a lucifer for both. As they smoked, he related his visit to Chief Leroux's office and the Creole detective in turn told him about his phone call to Tom Anderson.

"The more I think about it, the more I'm convinced this is giving him a true fright."

"It wasn't just him hearing of another man he knew dying?" the lieutenant said.

"He says he wasn't that close with either victim," Valentin said. "And he's not involved in Storyville anymore. No, I think it was something else. I'll find out what." He puffed for a thoughtful moment, then said, "So how will you be spending your afternoon?"

"Checking on a couple other cases. And I promised Miss Marcus some information."

"What are you going to tell her?"

The lieutenant gestured toward the morgue doorway. "I'll tell her about the finger. No reason not to. Leroux is trusting me to handle her."

"What does Captain Warren say about that?"

"He's just glad to be out of it," McKinney said. "As long as I don't make him look bad."

Valentin said, "You think it's occurred to him that he was in the photograph, too?"

"I don't know what occurs to him." The lieutenant blew a languid plume of smoke. "What about your plans?"

Valentin admitted that he was expected back at the French Market. "I'll drop them at home. Then I'll drive out and talk to that maid at the Walthams'."

"Are we going to be one murder behind until all those pieces are gone?"

"I hope not," Valentin said. He dropped the cigarette into the gutter and produced a cool smile. "I'm not on the force. So if I don't get some results, I don't get paid."

McKinney laughed at the comment and sauntered off.

# ELEVEN

Their grocery baskets and sacks full, Justine and Evangeline found a table at one of the cafes and sat down for coffee and beignets. They talked over their purchases for a few minutes. Neither woman mentioned the chatter about the murders of the company president and the priest that they had overheard the entire time they had strolled the aisles.

Justine had long ago grown used to walking around such talk with the knowledge that the man she woke with every morning was one of the key players in the drama. She had seen from Evangeline's startled eyes that she was unnerved by it and that there would be questions coming.

The first one now arrived when the older woman stopped in mid-sentence and said, "The newspaper."

"What about it?"

"I saw the story by that woman. About the murder. Well, it's *murders* now, isn't it? What's her name again?"

After a moment, Justine said, "Rebecca Marcus."

"She mentioned Valentin."

"Yes, she did, I'm sorry to say."

"I'm sure that was a surprise."

Justine heard the odd note in her voice, as if she had felt something inside the house, like a voodoo woman without all the noise. Her husband put no stock in such beliefs, but she wasn't so sure. Some things couldn't be explained away, like the instincts of the woman sitting across the table from her, sipping her coffee as her eyes roamed the crowd of shoppers.

"He didn't tell me," she said. "Not at first, I mean."

Evangeline's steady gaze returned. "I wonder why. He's not that type."

"What type is that?"

The gray eyes were sly. "A sport. A rounder. The kind who's always slipping and sliding. Especially when it comes to women. That type."

"He was once."

"But not anymore."

"Well, he is a man."

Evangeline laughed, then stopped to study Justine more closely. "You don't like being on the outside."

Justine sighed and said, "No, ma'am, I don't. Not at all."

"Does he know that?"

Now it was Justine's turn to smile. "Oh, I'm sure he does," she said.

Back at his desk, Lieutenant McKinney called the newsroom and spent ten minutes with Rebecca Marcus. He began by confirming that the victim of the murder at St. Rocco's was Father O'Brien. The death was caused by a single neck wound that caused a massive loss of blood. "He would have been unconscious and then dead in less than thirty seconds," the lieutenant said.

"Do you have a suspect or motive at this time?"

He guessed that she already knew the answer. Still, he said, "No suspect. No motive."

"Do you believe it was the same person who murdered Herbert Waltham?"

"Yes, we do."

He sensed the surprise in her silence. She had been expecting *We have nothing to suggest...* or some other lame excuse.

"Why is that?"

"Because of the evidence."

"What evidence?"

He hesitated for a moment. "I'll tell you, but I want your promise that the information will not be in any story. For now. Will you agree to that?"

"Yes." She was breathless. "I agree."

"And, one more thing," he said. "You remember what I said yesterday about sharing any information that comes your way?"

There was a pause from the other end of the line, one that was a bit too long for his taste. She said, "Yes, I remember. And I will respect that."

"All right, then," he said. "One of the body parts removed from Mr. Waltham was found in the Father's office. It had been mailed on Tuesday."

"Which part?" she said.

"Not in the story."

"No, not in the story," she said.

"One of the middle fingers."

"Oh, my," she said. "Has anyone told the family?"

"No, and we'll keep it that way for now," he said.

"I understand. Is there anything else?"

"Nothing more I can share."

"Well, thank you," she said.

The line went dead. The lieutenant considered that he had been forthright with her, but he still couldn't be sure Miss Rebecca Marcus would return the good deed.

Valentin knew exactly where to find Each—if that character wasn't off on some hustle. He parked the Ford on the lot and walked to Fewclothes Cabaret, already open for business. His young friend was leaning an elbow on the bar, listening to some sot braying about *back in the days when...* It was a familiar refrain. Every saloon in the District contained at least one fat-mouthed fool who spent his waking hours cadging drinks and pontificating about Storyville when it was grand. Not like today.

Each saw the detective approaching and raised his hands in relief. He slapped the drunkard on the shoulder and moved away. The diatribe continued. "Back then, a man could walk in any door and he'd be..."

On this morning, Each had donned a suit of black-and-white checks that was not only years out of style, but ill-fitted to his odd frame, so that the coat was too long and the trousers too short. This was topped-off by the dusty black derby that he had been holding in his hand but now placed on his thatched head. "Buy you a drink?" he said with a smile of yellowish teeth.

"Not right now," Valentin said. "I need some help. And it pays."

Each's eyes brightened, then dimmed when the detective explained the assignment. "You're wanting me to guard some goddamn mailboxes?"

"Not guard them," Valentin said. "Watch them. To see if someone suspicious is dropping packages." He shifted his eyes and lowered his voice in a secretive way. "They contain certain body parts."

Now Each gaped. "You mean the..."

"Yes. One was mailed and turned up this morning. We're expecting the rest."

"All right, yes, sir," Each said. "I can do that."

"It's the twelve blocks around the Lafayette Square post office. There will be boxes at a half-dozen of the intersections. Find them and then keep circling. If you see something, get to the manager of the post office right away. Or use a call box and find a copper."

In his excitement, Each did not seem to understand or care what a long shot it would be to spot a killer dropping body parts in the mail. There was a chase on. He offered Valentin a solemn wink and when they reached the banquette shook the detective's hand in a serious way before hurrying off.

*The city is teeming—swirling, in fact—with all the thousands moving this way and that. Stop on any corner and within minutes, someone will say something.*

You read about these murders?

The head of that big company! A priest!

You can bet it's the same party, yes, sir. You got to wonder why... *and so on.*

*No, they would have no clue. That something that happens every day would drive such bloody mayhem. Because they don't know better and wouldn't care if they did.*

*What they also don't know is that among them walks a person holding a box wrapped in brown paper and inside the box is another part of the first one who died. Being carried along to the box. To be sent along just in time for the afternoon mail that will carry it across the city and into hands that cannot be expecting it.*

———

As Valentin approached St. Louis Street on his way back to the Ford, he heard strains of brass all low and mean. He turned the corner and came upon a lone trumpet player in a black suit, the brim of his hat pulled down so that his face was hidden from view. He stopped to listen.

The notes from the bell first growled, then started climbing the scale to swoop into a wail. Standing there, Valentin heard broken-hearted tears, a call to a blind God who was paying no mind, and the deepest shades of blue. Then came turns to the call of a bird sailing on the wind and a pealing like morning bells. And all the time, the player kept his eyes down and head moving just a bit from side to side. Valentin was wondering if the fellow even knew he was there (or perhaps *he* was blind) and he noticed that there was no bowl or cup on the sidewalk.

After listening for another few bars, he went fishing in his vest pocket for a Liberty half then stepped close and slid the coin into the player's vest pocket. The head dipped a slight inch and he felt eyes glide his way. He stepped back and moved off.

In his reasonable mind, he knew it couldn't be. Couldn't be that Buddy had somehow escaped the stone walls that confined him; couldn't be that he had found a way to return to the only streets that could have produced his wicked, mad, genius self; couldn't be that somewhere he had found a horn he could blow and call his children home. Couldn't be. And yet for a lingering few minutes, he pretended that it could.

Rebecca kept her pen and her typewriter busy when she was in the newsroom and then scampered out the door when her nerves got to her. She didn't know what she was doing and the illusion that she did wouldn't last. She was expected to deliver a story for the afternoon paper and another for the next morning edition, and they could not be the same piece with the words rearranged, the kind of work the two drunken beat writers Goings or Miller turned in.

She now walked the halls, pondering Mr. Valentin St. Cyr and a way to play him. She'd only been doing it since she was a young girl with any woman or man who could be of use to her and her skills were sharp.

She regretted that she didn't have any true connections to Storyville. As many times as she had daydreamed about transforming herself into one of those lovely Basin Street "doves," she had never summoned the courage to take that particular plunge.

Maybe someday. For the moment, she needed information on the Creole detective who had been a fixture of the District. The same part of the city that had been visited by thousands of society gentlemen... She stopped and turned back for the stairwell to the third floor, wondering why she hadn't thought of it before.

Beatrice Gillaume looked up from her desk, surprised at the sight of Rebecca coming her way. She ended her telephone call with a few quick words and sat back, smiling.

"Are you back?" she said. "Have you had enough of the blood and gore?"

"I have not," Rebecca said. She took the chair at the side of the desk and said, "I've come to ask you for some information. In confidence."

"Well, of course," Beatrice said. "About who?"

"Valentin St. Cyr." The editor smiled in a cunning way. "Well?" Rebecca said. "Come on, Beatrice."

Miss Gillaume lowered her head and her voice. "I know that name," she said. "He's pulled a couple dozen men of means out of scrapes. First it was in the red-light district. Lately, for some of the law firms on St. Charles. Cleaning up messes of one sort or another. Now he's on this case you're covering." Her smile widened. "Is that what this is about?"

"Does anything extra interesting come to mind?"

Beatrice Gillaume ruminated for a few moments before saying, "Yes, one very special little item." She went on to describe the murder of a wealthy businessman named John Benedict that had happened on Rampart Street some years before. "St. Cyr began digging up dirt," she said. "So of course everyone wanted him off the case. Everyone but the man's daughter." She paused for a delighted moment. "The young lady allowed that Creole to deflower her. There was a river of gossip over that." She studied her visitor. "Have you met him?"

"I have," Rebecca said.

"So what do you think? Is he wicked?"

"I'm not sure what he is," Rebecca said.

"But you want to find out."

"He might be the only one who can help me."

"And that's all?"

Rebecca stole a quick glance around then bent her head to whisper, "You know it's never all with women like us." She straightened, rose from her chair, thanked the editor with a smile, and walked away.

Valentin was waiting by the car at the north end of the market when the two women appeared from the shadows. He was held still for a dazzled moment by the picture of beauty coming his way. How could he be so fortunate?

He opened the trunk and transferred the sacks from their hands. Evangeline preferred the back seat and he helped her up first. Justine stopped with her foot on the step and treated him to a probing look, searching his face.

He said, "What is it?"

"That's what I want to know," she said.

"Oh," he said. "Something I saw. And heard. Someone, I mean."

"You'll tell me about it at home?"

"I will," he said. She climbed up and he stepped around to the driver's side.

And he did, once they got the groceries in the house and piled onto the table. "You didn't speak to him?" she said.

"No. I didn't want to interrupt."

"You mean break the spell."

"That, too."

"So, tomorrow night?" she said.

"Yes, tomorrow night."

"And now?"

"I'm driving back over to Esplanade to speak to the maid."

"What's her name again?"

"Dolores. She went by Dolly. Do you recall anyone by that name?"

"Maybe if I thought about it." She gave a slight shake of her head. "But I don't want to."

He raised her hand and kissed it. They stood together, looking out at the back garden with Valentin wishing he could stay in that place, and next to her, for a very long time. But he had the small matter of two murders to address and that meant a drive to Esplanade Ridge. He pressed his lips to her cheek this time and then moved away, leaving her to her thoughts.

He was almost to the door when the telephone rang again. Evangeline called from the kitchen. "Valentin?"

"Yes, I'll get it."

He wished that he hadn't. Sam Ross, the attorney at the firm of Mansell, Maines, and Velline who had kept him busy over the prior few years with dull but good-paying investigations on behalf of their rich clients, didn't bother with a greeting.

"Interesting story in the paper," he said, his tone half-mocking. "I saw your name."

"Sam, I was going to call."

"Too bad you didn't. We already knew about it. You weren't the only ears we had on the streets."

Valentin caught the *had* and guessed what it meant.

"You just never learn, do you?"

Valentin considered for a second before saying, "I guess I don't."

The attorney produced a laugh that contained no humor. "At least you're working for the police. And the victims are of the notable sort. That's something. But it doesn't keep you clean in these parts. You understand."

Valentin did. "I won't be expecting to hear from you any time soon." He was thinking *or anytime ever.*

"We'll see how this all turns out," Ross said. "If you find out who's doing these awful killings."

The detective got the message: if the guilty party got away, he'd be finished as far as high-toned law firms were concerned. And that even a capture might not be enough to salvage his career in those sober halls.

"I apologize for not handling it better," he said. "I know you've been fair with me."

"You probably have things to do," Sam Ross said. "Good luck, Mr. Valentin." The line went dead.

Valentin placed the handset in the cradle and called, "I'm leaving now."

Evangeline stepped into the kitchen doorway to say. "Please be careful."

Tom Anderson had recovered enough to return to the dining room table and the plate of bread, cheese, and fruit that Lucy laid out for him. In her thoughtful way, she also served him his coffee with a good drop of brandy. He sipped and closed his eyes.

"You all right, Mr. Tom?"

"Yes, I'm fine," he said. "I'll call if I need you."

She watched him for another concerned moment before leaving to attend to her duties in the kitchen.

Once she was gone, he heaved a troubled sigh. The call about the priest had brought a shock beyond the news of the brutal murder—the *second* brutal murder—of a man he knew in as many days. The start of fear that had knocked him to his knees had risen from a deeper place.

Something connected the two men that he only dimly recalled, and was lurking close by, which made it all the more disturbing. What veiled memory had caused him to totter and then fall like that? Something he didn't want to know? And was that the reason he hadn't pressed Valentin to pay a visit?

Lucy had poured a hefty shot into his cup and another sip of the laced coffee calmed him a bit more. He didn't remember murdering anyone and the only blood on his hands came by way of that same private detective and had been justified, the removal of miscreants of one sort or another within the bounds of his scarlet kingdom.

He stared into the swirling liquid. If there was some terrible something lost in his past, Valentin would unearth it. And if that was the case, he wondered if he would be the one asking for mercy.

Valentin couldn't remember if he had enjoyed the woman now calling herself Dolores during her days as a Basin Street sporting girl. It would not surprise him if he had. She had been a sharp-eyed, fair-brown dove with a wild air about her. Too wild; because she had landed in scrapes that then required his assistance with the police. She started her career as one of those who most often ended up wrecked or dead, taken down by the batterings of the life.

But one way out was the kind of escape she had managed, leaving the red-light district for a lovely mansion in a fine neighborhood where she spent her days quietly attending to the needs of wealthy employers.

He had called ahead and she was waiting on the corner of Rendon Street when he drove up, wearing a cloche hat with a sheer swath of fabric that was tied beneath her chin, hiding her features. She looked unsettled as she climbed in and he understood that she was worried about being seen.

"Mr. Valentin." She pulled the hat back and before he could speak a word, said, "Herbert, Jr. He took me aside me this morning. Told me not to talk to nobody. I only came out because it was you."

"Well, I appreciate that," he said. "Would you like me to drive?"

"Please," she said.

He put the Ford in gear and pulled out and started north. She didn't relax until he steered the machine into the shadows of the Delgado Museum and stopped, leaving the engine to idle. After a quick glance around, she settled back.

"So, Mr. Valentin," she said. "Look at you. Married and all. Justine Mancarre, is that right?"

"Did you know her?"

"Only from the women people talking. That she was the one to finally get the reins on you."

He offered a resigned sigh. "Yes, well..."

"But you didn't come up here to recollect them old days, did you?" she said.

"I did not," he said. "How's the family doing?"

"All right, I guess. It ain't a crazy house. Everyone's still..."

"In shock?"

"Yes, sir," she said with a slow shake of her head. "That was so awful what happened. And they're good people. For rich folks, I mean."

"How was it you came to be hired on here?"

"Oh, well. He was looking for a girl and a gentleman friend of mine told him I wanted to leave. He promised me he wouldn't ever say anything about where I came from. And he didn't."

"That was kind of him, wasn't it?"

He was eyeing her. She got the message and laughed. "Oh. You want to know... He never tried to fuck me, if that's what you're thinking. No. He only..." The former harlot began to blush.

"Only what?"

"He paid me to undress for him now and then." Her eyes wandered away and back to him and she dropped the fingers of her right hand to her lap. "And go to work on myself." She smiled a dim smile. "Five dollars extra every time. Once or twice, it was ten. To make sure I never spoke of it."

"And that's all?"

"That's all. The rest of the time, I was just the maid."

"What about the son?"

"He hardly ever said a word to me. Same with the daughter."

"And Mrs. Waltham?"

"She's a decent lady. Kind of dull. But decent."

"Is there anything else unusual you can think of? About Mr. Waltham, I mean."

She pondered for a few moments, her eyes shifting away. "Only thing was three or four times, he asked me about this one young girl back in the District."

"What girl?"

"He didn't know her name. He said she had been a trick baby in one of the houses on the line. I told him, you know, there's lots of them around."

"Did he mention the mother's name?"

"He said that it might have been Betty or Betsy."

"And he didn't tell you why he wanted to know?"

"He didn't say, no. He just kept asking. Like the next time I was going to tell him something different."

Valentin studied the rain. "Do you have any notion of why someone would want to harm him?"

She said, "I don't, no, sir. He wasn't nothing special. Another rich man."

"Does anything else come to mind?"

"No, sorry, Mr. Valentin. I mostly just keep my mouth shut and stay out of folks' way." He pondered the information, wondering how much she was keeping to herself.

"I better be getting back," she said.

"Of course." He sat up and dropped the shifter into gear.


Rebecca was twenty feet from her desk when she spied the envelope.

After the call from Lieutenant McKinney, she hurried to write her story for the afternoon paper. There were no copyboys in sight, so she carried the pages to Reynard Vernel and spent a few moments discussing the piece. On her way back to her corner desk, she caught a flash of white standing out against the black blotter, the gray typewriter, and the stacks of yellow copy paper. Her heart began to race.

Still, she affected a casual air as she read her name scribed in the same precise hand. One of the copyboys was passing and she waved the letter in the air and said. "Did you leave this for me?"

He peered at the envelope. "Oh, yes, ma'am. It was in the newsroom box with the other mail and I brought it up."

"All right, then," she said. He trotted off. With a languid glance to make sure no one was watching, she drew out the single sheet and unfolded it and read the words "Prepare for the next one. Soon."

She folded the paper and slipped it far in the back of her desk drawer and sat down to make notes for her story about the tragic murder of Father O'Brien. Anyone looking her way would have seen a smile creeping across her face.


*The light of the dying day turns the windows of the newspaper building into a pattern of deepening squares of red. Blood red, in fact, like what flowed out from the two men, in trickles and gushes. A sight to see.*

*A few streaks of cloud are drifting across the panes. The reporter, the woman who is telling the story, sits by one of them. By now, she has seen the second note. Which she got by keeping her silence about the first one. So she is an ally, a partner, someone to be trusted—for now.*

*Next is the one who stood by and let the crime go unpunished.*

# TWELVE

Valentin had spent the end of Thursday afternoon and the early evening puttering in aimless patterns about the house and back garden, wasting time with small matters and trying to push the two murders from his thoughts. It didn't quite work.

Yet another case had come along to prove how easy it was to manufacture carnage that could terrify a whole city. It required only the will of a mad mind, a way to commit the assault, and enough cunning to get away clean. In a place like New Orleans, blighted with dark corners, the last part was not so difficult.

It was the return of this nagging notion that, after a quiet dinner, quieter evening, and early arrival between the bedsheets, woke him an hour before dawn. Outside the window, a half-moon had risen over the trees and he whispered the words *mezza luna*. It was one of the first phrases in Italian his father had taught him and his sister and brother as they gazed up at the shape in the night, half in light and half in inky darkness. Soon he would begin to sing a few half-forgotten lines from an opera in his rough peasant voice.

The memory was something for him to embrace. Their stories had ended, his sister and brother taken by the yellow fever they called Bronze John and his father at the hands of a murdering mob. Did the simple weariness of a man reaching his middle years finding that the tragic too often prevailed have him clinging to fragments? And was a longing for crude justice driving him to pursue evil?

He turned to trace his wife's sleeping form, all curves and shadows. She had told him so many times that he could have different work and they another life, the three of them together. He would head in that direction, then circle back. For what? To right one of the ancient wrongs? So that every time he saved the city from another murder, a nail would be drawn out of a coffin? Or was it that chasing down the guilty was his way of holding back his fury over the wounds that those deaths had visited on him?

Justine stirred, bringing him off this murky path. It would be morning soon and he would start again. Back to chasing a killer driven by a rage that he could not yet fathom. Back to avoiding the web being spun by a woman who vexed him.

With a sigh at his foolishness, he pulled on his trousers and without waking his wife slipped out to the kitchen to start a pot of coffee. There he stood at the window studying the *mezza luna* for another minute, now wondering what would be crossing Evangeline's mind if she was watching it, too.

New Orleans awoke holding a collective breath in suspense over the possibility of another prominent citizen turning up dead.

It would be one of the late-night creepers or early risers, perhaps a maid or janitor or cook shuffling through the dawn streets who would happen upon the ghastly tableau and rush to report it to the nearest copper. From there the alarm would go out and the terror would flare anew. But five, then six, then seven o'clock came and went as a normal Crescent City morning.

And so a new day began under skittish clouds. Perhaps it had been two random killings that had nothing to do with each other. Yes, both victims had boasted notable names, but didn't things sometimes just happen? There had been only two deaths, after all, and at a time when men were being slaughtered by the thousands across the sea. So the minutes ticked by and the city began to unwind and settle back into its special rhythms.

After Thursday's flurry finally came to an end, Rebecca Marcus had found her way into the arms of a young woman in a house on Thalia Street. It was past midnight and they were both drowsy. The woman, a quadroon with hair dyed near-blonde, called herself Caroline, but who knew her real name? Her eyes were closed as she listened to Rebecca recount landing the assignment and chasing down leads, first for Herbert Waltham and then Father O'Brien.

Caroline laid a gentle hand on her cheek. "You having fun, ain't you?"

"Not fun exactly," Rebecca said. "The crimes are terrible. The work is exciting, though."

"That Waltham fellow?" Caroline said. "I remember him."

Rebecca came out of her drowse to prop herself on an elbow. "You do? From where?"

"He used to come 'round to Ruby Stein's when she had the house on Franklin Street," Caroline said. "Maybe once every two weeks."

"Did you...?"

"Entertain him?" Caroline's green eyes opened. "No, he'd just come for some drinks and one of the young girls. That was the kind he liked."

Now Rebecca sat up all the way. "Where is she now? The madam, I mean. Ruby Stein, did you say?"

"I got no idea," Caroline said. "Last time I saw her was down there and that was six, seven years ago. She might still be around. I don't know. She don't have the house anymore."

"Oh. That's too bad."

Caroline noticed the way Rebecca was staring at the wall. "Hey, are you working or what?" She began to reach for her.

Rebecca was already out from under the sheets and reaching for her underclothes. "I can't stay," she said. "I need to be at the paper in case another body turns up."

Caroline watched her slip into her skirt and shirtwaist. "When you coming back?" she said.

Rebecca finished dressing and bent to kiss her. "Soon," she said and was out the door.

————

A half-hour later, she arrived to find the newsroom quiet. Kassel's office was dark and Reynard Vernel was nowhere in sight. She crossed to the news ticker and found nothing on the local reports machine. She made her slow way back to her desk, slipped the two folded sheets from her bag and studied them again. The thirteen printed words convinced her that there would be more.

Sitting there, she knew that if there were, Rolf Kassel could decide that it was just too big a story for a lady reporter whose feet were barely wet and she'd be climbing the stairs to her old desk in the Society section.

James McKinney appeared in the section at eight-thirty and learned that the only body that had turned up overnight was that of a mattress whore found in the alley behind one of the dime-a-trick Robertson Street cribs. The trollop, who went by Sawed-Off Sal, last name unknown, had died with no outward signs of violence, which meant that a lifetime of being battered by whiskey and dope and a thousand cruel men had finally caught up with her. The lieutenant knew that there was little chance that her body would be claimed and her sad story would end in a pauper's grave out past Chalmette Battlefield. With that happy thought to buoy him, he reached for the telephone to call St. Cyr.

After they exchanged greetings, Valentin told the lieutenant about his conversation with Dolores.

"A young girl?" McKinney said. "You think maybe his daughter?"

"Maybe," Valentin said. "Though most times, a fellow like him would have the madam call up Dago Annie or one of the others to tend to the problem."

"That's if he knew about it soon enough. If he found out later..."

"That's possible, too," Valentin said. "I'll ask around. Maybe it's something else. But this has only happened about a thousand times." He went on to recount the tale of a particular man of wealth who had become infatuated with the daughter of one of the strumpets in Antonia Gonzales' mansion. "Made a complete fool of himself," he said. "Chasing after her like a schoolboy. She was only fourteen and her mother had kept her out of the life. He wouldn't give up and finally Anderson had me step in and end it."

"How did you do that?"

"I went to his office and asked him to join me at the window and told him that if he didn't stop, he'd be shamed in front of everyone on those streets down below. Every newspaper and rag in town would know. He'd be ruined."

"And?"

Valentin laughed, remembering. "I could see by his face that he was this close to saying 'I don't care. I love her.' So I told him I could make it easier and allow him to see her with me in the room. He agreed to it. And we did that. A couple years later, he dropped dead."

McKinney said, "Died happy, I guess. What happened to the girl?"

"She did well. He left her some money and she moved away."

The two detectives were quiet for a moment. The telling and the hearing of the story had been a pleasant way to begin the day. Now there was grim business at hand.

"The Father's service this afternoon," Valentin said.

"Pretty much everyone will be there," the lieutenant said.

"Everyone but Herbert Waltham," Valentin said. "On the other hand, maybe our killer will show up and surrender. Wouldn't that be helpful?"

*Not leaving another body to throw them. Patterns were how coppers and Pinkertons caught the ne'er-do-wells. So they would be watching. But they couldn't watch everywhere and there was the tongue and that other part still to go. And number three will require extra care. Though it will be done.*

*Time for the next package. This one is more grisly. People eat tongues. Not fingers, but tongues, yes. They served it in the restaurants.*

*There is this piece and then the other part, which is best kept out of mind until the time comes. And after that would be an announcement and then a disappearing act like in the magic shows at the Orpheum. The lady at the paper would be the one to receive the final word. After that there would be nothing left to say.*

*The piece of meat fits nicely in the same box that the bandages came in. On the outside, the same plain letters. So that the reporter will know that her special friend was back.*

*Funny that she and the coppers and Mr. St. Cyr will be at the church with their eyes wide open, looking for someone they won't see.*

Valentin finished his breakfast and sat dawdling over his coffee. The bed beckoned but he knew he wouldn't be able to sleep. Not with the city waiting for James McKinney and him to produce results in the form of a murderer in custody or dead.

Justine put the last of the dishes in the sink and joined him at the table to ask about his plans for the day.

"The service at St. Rocco's," he said. "It's at one o'clock."

She looked amused. "Oh?"

"No, I won't be going inside. James will be there." He sat back and sipped his coffee and treated her to a thoughtful gaze.

She said, "What?"

"You could come along."

"What for?"

"Another pair of eyes and ears," he said.

"One o'clock?"

"Yes. But before that, we'll need to go see Mr. Tom. Though I'm not sure he wants to see me."

Justine said, "Thank you for asking. I'd be delighted to join you." Her smile widened. "If I can drive."

He waited until just before they left to telephone the house and let Lucy know that they were on their way. "Tell him I'm bringing Justine. He hasn't seen her in a while."

"All right, Mr. Valentin," the maid said. "But maybe you better talk to him before you—"

"No, it's fine," he said. "We're leaving right now." He broke the connection and turned to find Justine waiting in a modest white shirtwaist and dark skirt, her curls pinned under a plain hat.

"You aren't concerned he'll go hide somewhere?" she said.

He opened the door for her. "Well, that would tell us something, wouldn't it?"

Rebecca was astonished to be put through to Lieutenant McKinney at Parish Precinct. She asked if there had been any developments in the two murder cases. The officer told her that there was nothing to add to what he had already shared with her, but that they were working every lead.

So she said, "Is it worth my time to keep calling?"

He didn't speak for a moment. "I'm doing what I can," he said. "And I can tell you what you get from me is going to be better than what you'll hear from Captain Warren. I just don't have anything to share right now. It's been quiet."

She changed her tack. "Isn't it true that the longer the investigation goes on, the less likely it is you'll catch the guilty party?"

"In most cases the answer is yes. This one's different."

"Because you're expecting more."

"There are still three pieces of Mr. Waltham out there." Before she could comment on that, he said, "What about you, ma'am? Have you come across anything of interest?"

Rebecca covered the half-second she was tempted to tell him about the letters in her desk with an absent shuffling of papers. She had no idea how much she could trust him or St. Cyr. What she was holding was precious. But what would happen if they found out anyway? She felt her heart begin to flutter.

"No, nothing more." After a pause, she said, "We're all chasing along behind, aren't we?"

"That seems to be the case," the lieutenant said and she thought she heard a note of dismay in his voice.

"Will you be at St. Rocco's this afternoon?"

"Possibly," he said.

"Well, we can speak again then."

"Anytime I can be of service," he said.

She wasn't sure if it was intended as a joke, so she thanked him and placed the handset back in the cradle. She now sat staring at her telephone, feeling a clutch in her gut. He had given her next to nothing and that wouldn't do.

The lack of a new murder was a reprieve, but how long would it last? She stared at the top of her desk as if her sheer will could penetrate the wood and read the two notes hidden there. Her newspaper career would end for sure if she continued to hold them without telling anyone. In the next moment, her fear that it was all a hoax returned. There was that, and the possibility that the writer would simply disappear and she would lose the only card she held.

She looked across the newsroom, lost in these thoughts. Reynard was at his desk, his head bent and his writing hand busy with a red pencil. A few moments passed and he looked up. Seeing her, he smiled his kind smile, then returned to his editing.

She pondered for another a half-minute before opening her drawer and reaching underneath. She stood, gathered her purse, and crossed the room. Reynard looked up again. "You off to the service already?"

"Not just yet," she said. "I need to talk to you. In private."

They climbed the stairs to the third floor and moved to the windows at the end of the hallway, one of the quieter spots in the building. Below, downtown New Orleans bustled as usual, but with the addition of a murderer walking among them.

"I want to keep this confidential," Rebecca said. "I mean, just take some time to think about it. Don't rush back downstairs."

Puzzled, he said, "I can agree to that. What do you have?"

She let the drama build before opening her purse and drawing out the first note. Reynard's eyes widened and he caught a sharp breath. "Is this...?" he began, then stopped to read the printed words again. As he was finishing the first one, she produced the second and pushed it into his hand.

"My God," he said, looking between the two. "Are these real?"

"I think so," she said. "I hope so." She waited while he went over them a third time.

"How long have you had these?"

"The first one came the day of Mr. Waltham's murder. And the second one yesterday."

"Why didn't you tell me right away?" His tone was faintly accusing.

"Because I thought they might be someone's idea of a joke." Her cheeks flushed a shade darker. "It's still possible they are. I know how some people feel about me." Reynard studied the notes some more. "What do you want to do?" she said.

"We have to tell Rolf," Reynard said. "And we can't keep them from McKinney and St. Cyr. Those two can be trusted." She wasn't so sure, but decided not to voice her doubts. "We do want to keep him writing."

"Or her," she said.

"Sorry?"

"It could be a woman. I can't tell from the handwriting. Can you?"

Reynard peered at the first note. "I can't, no. But a woman?"

"I think it's possible. And the police haven't ruled it out."

"Huh." He shook his head in wonder. "You know we've got something fantastic here."

"Does 'we' mean I'll be staying on the story?"

He said, "What? Yes, of course." He rattled the pages again. "These right here are your ticket." He handed the letters back and took her arm. "All right, let's go see our friend Mr. Kassel," he said.


Each felt his stomach growl as he stalked the banquette. It was a silly job and he wondered if Mr. Valentin had thrown it his way just to get him some extra pocket money. Walking along O'Keefe, he came upon the Jin Lee Laundry and stopped to study his reflection in the glass.

Did he look so ragged that the Creole detective felt pity? Whatever the case, he had not seen a single suspicious citizen at any of the mailboxes he'd been sent to check. Though of course such a soul could step up the second he turned away. He ambled on.

Another half-hour—until noon—and that would be all. He would tell Mr. Valentin he had other work. Which was true, in a way. He could always find a rounder who needed an extra hand or a citizen who needed a guide to the infamous red-light district. He had only been doing the same thing since he was a squirt.

He reached St. Joseph, debating what excuse would sound best. Yawning, he glanced across the intersection at the red mailbox in time to see someone wrapped in a coat that was too warm for the weather drop a parcel into the slot and scurry off on skittish legs. It took a second for him to come to his senses and realize that what he had witnessed was exactly what Mr. Valentin had described.

He dodged traffic to the other side, then walked at a fast clip along the banquette to the brick alley that cut through to Julia Street to see the figure skulking a hundred feet on. Whoever it was sensed him and shot a glance back. In the next moment, the shape evaporated.

Now he ran until he came to a sliding stop at the alley door of a hardware store and hurried inside, passing shelves and barrels of nails to the front counter, where an astonished clerk looked up at his red face.

"What's wrong?" the clerk said.

Each gasped out the words, pointing a shaking finger. "Did you see... did a... did someone just come through here?"

"When?"

"When?" Each was flustered. "Just *now*, that's when."

"Why, no. Who do you think—"

"What about back there?" He whirled around and peered into the dark recesses of the store.

The clerk said, "What the hell are you talking about? Are you drunk?"

"I'm going have a look," Each said and stalked from one rear corner to the other.

The clerk followed him, keeping his distance. "What's going on?" he said. "Do I need to call the coppers?"

"You don't need to call anyone," Each said. "Sorry." He walked out the door and onto Magazine Street.

Rolf Kassel had been wandering the building and Rebecca and Reynard waited in impatience for the quarter hour it took for him to come ambling back into the newsroom. His broad buttocks had barely dropped into his chair when the junior editor was in his doorway with Rebecca at his side. He took one look at Vernel's giddy grin and said, "What?"

Reynard ushered Rebecca inside and closed the door. Puzzled, Kassel didn't think to go into his drawer for his bottle. "So?" he said. "What's this about?"

Reynard turned to Rebecca and said, "Show him."

———

Ten minutes later, they exited the office, leaving the editor so astonished that he still hadn't reached for his Raleigh Rye. Reynard followed Rebecca to her corner, where they spoke in low voices.

"I don't understand why he wants us to talk to McKinney and St. Cyr first," she said.

"Because we cannot get on the wrong side of the police. Especially on something like this." She crossed her arms, sulking. "Rebecca. Look at what's happened in only a few days. You need to stay calm now."

She sighed. "I suppose you're right."

"Just carry on with your day."

"I'm going to St. Rocco's," she said. "I'll speak to the deacon. If St. Cyr and McKinney are there, I'll tell them then."

"*We* can tell them," Reynard said. "I'll meet you." Again, he sensed her displeasure. "We don't want them thinking…"

"What? That I wrote the notes myself?"

"You know they question everything."

"All right, all right," she said. "So I'll find you how?"

He said, "Don't worry. I'll find you."

# THIRTEEN

Justine frightened her husband only twice during the drive across town, once when she didn't give way to a bullying truck driver on Claiborne and the second time when she clipped the curb turning off St. Charles. She didn't blink in either instance and he had to admit she was becoming skilled behind the wheel, pulling up to the house and shutting off the chattering four cylinders with a flourish.

She removed her gloves and eyed him prettily. "Well?" she said. "Aren't you going to help me down?"

Lucy opened the door looking abashed and Valentin wondered if his wife's suspicion had been correct and Mr. Tom had found a way to avoid them.

"Is he here?" he said.

"He's here," the maid said. "But he ain't doing too well."

*Or pretending he isn't*, Valentin mused.

She led them through the foyer to the sitting room, where the King of Storyville was stretched out on a divan, his lap covered with an afghan. Even as he smiled at the sight of Justine, his appearance was to Valentin disquieting. He had lost some twenty pounds of his former girth. His usual florid cheeks were pallid and the eyes that had once glowed with both delight and icy anger were now a dull agate.

He was still sharp, though. He caught Valentin's look of concern and said, "Yes. I know. Time claims us all."

"Well, I think you look just fine," Justine said and stepped forward to kiss his forehead.

The old man's expression was wistful with another reminder that his days of philandering with the beauties of the world had ended. At that moment, the detective was doubly grateful that he had left all of it behind. Time, indeed.

Now Anderson was waving them to the armchairs at either end of the divan. Once they were seated, he treated Justine to a tired smile. "You're just as beautiful as ever," he said.

"And you're just as handsome."

The old man's eyes said he wished it was so. Though he had to know that it had been his power and wealth that had drawn most of the women to his bed over the years.

"Can I have Lucy get you something?" he said. "Coffee?"

Justine waved off the offer and Valentin shook his head. "We don't want to take a lot of your time," he said. "I want to ask if you've had any further thoughts on Mr. Waltham."

"That's why you came all this way?" Mr. Tom was perturbed. "What else can I tell you? He was a very successful businessman. He involved himself in civic affairs. Nothing unusual there." He took a sip of water from the table at his side. "He spent time in the District. He gambled a bit at the Café. Visited the mansions. Certainly not the type to make a scandal."

"I understand he had a hankering for younger girls."

"Well, he wouldn't be the only one," Anderson said.

"I heard something about one young girl in particular. Perhaps a trick baby. Perhaps his."

Was that surprise Valentin detected in the old eyes? Or something else? Whatever it was, Justine had noticed, too, her eyebrows peaking.

Anderson took another sip of water and cleared his throat. "Who was she?"

"I don't know," Valentin said. "But he was trying to find her before he died."

The King of Storyville weighed the comment, then said, "I'm sorry. I don't recall anything about that..." He made a vague gesture toward his head. "But you know my memory isn't what it was."

Valentin sat back, sure there was more and also sure there was no point in challenging him any further.

"Maybe Miss Lulu could help you with that," Mr. Tom said.

"What about Father O'Brien?"

"Oh, God. That poor, poor man." He did not meet Valentin's eyes. "You believe it was the same person who..."

"Yes," Valentin said. "The same person. Almost certainly." Valentin waited, then said, "Can you think of any connection between the Father and Mr. Waltham? Aside from Waltham being a parishioner, I mean."

Anderson said, "I can't, no. I wish that I could help. I just don't..."

Valentin and Justine waited, but the old man just let the statement hang in the air.

"Well, then." The detective and his wife exchanged a glance and he sat back, considering that there was a time when Tom Anderson could shift and dodge with the best of them. But those days were over. He now looked like a child trying to escape blame. For all that, he had for a decade held the title of the King of Storyville, still commanded respect, and Valentin knew better than to press him.

Justine studied their host with a kind smile, then turned to Valentin and murmured, "We should go."

"Yes," Valentin said and they rose from their chairs. "The Father's service."

"Ah, yes," Anderson said. "I wish I could be there. I'm just not feeling up to it." He spoke again without looking at the detective. "You'll keep me apprised of the news?"

"I will," Valentin said.

Anderson sat forward as if he had something more to say. But then he gave the slightest shake of his head and leaned back. "Thank you for visiting," he said.

As soon as they reached the gallery and Lucy had closed the door behind them, Valentin said, "So what do you think he's hiding?"

"What he knows about the two victims," she said. They descended the steps. "You think he'll tell you?"

Valentin opened the door and offered his hand. "He's not ready yet. I just wish I knew why."

She nodded, then stood with her arms crossed until he caught on, closed the door, and followed her around to the driver's side. Once she was seated, he stepped to the front of the machine and bent to turn the crank. The engine gurgled to life and he took his place on the passenger's side, wondering if he'd ever get to drive her again.

Lucy had returned from seeing the visitors out to find Mr. Tom slouched on the divan with one hand covering his eyes. She regarded him with concern. "You all right, sir?"

After a few seconds, he said, "No, Lucy, I'm not."

"Did Mr. Valentin say something to upset you?"

The hand came down. "It's not that." He managed a dim smile. "Could I have a small glass of brandy, please?"

The maid watched him for another moment before moving off to fetch the bottle.

The scene had been cleared, the barriers moved aside, and though the walkway had been scrubbed down, a faint trace of Father O'Brien's blood remained. Two patrolmen had been stationed at the corner. At least a dozen more would be arriving before the service.

Rebecca climbed from the jitney and made her way to the side door of the church. She found it open and walked along a corridor to a door with a gold placard engraved with **Fr. O'Brien**. She grasped the knob and turned.

"Help you?"

She gave a start. The man she had seen the previous morning sitting on the stone bench with the fractured look on his face was standing there in his work clothes, his hands in heavy gloves, one of them hoisting a toolbox. The thought that he could have been the priest's murderer came and went. The two detectives would have tended to that possibility. And he looked too ancient and too kind to commit such carnage.

"I'm a reporter for the *Times-Picayune*," she told him. "I'm writing the stories about Father O'Brien's murder." The man gave a perplexed nod. "And your name is...?"

"Henry, ma'am."

"Henry. Did you find his body?"

"Yes, ma'am. I sure did. Sorry to say."

"That's just terrible," Rebecca said. "Tell me, can you think of anyone who might have committed the crime?"

"The police ast me that, must have been ten times," Henry said. "The answer is no. Everyone liked him. They sure did." The caretaker was silent for a moment. "And they ast me why. Why would someone do such a thing? Answer is, I got no idea."

"Deacon Terrell."

Henry's eyes shifted. "What about him?"

"Is he here?"

"Believe so."

"I'd like to speak to him."

"He's over to the rectory. Gettin' things in order." He pointed. "This way," he said and led her down the hallway.

As they were moving up the walk, skirting the spot where the priest's body had fallen, they passed a nun walking along with her head down and hands folded before her. She waited until the pair had almost reached the house to turn and watch them.


Valentin had Justine drive them to Martín's for a late morning coffee and petit beurres. He asked to use the telephone and the proprietor waved him to the tiny kitchen.

McKinney came on the line and Valentin told him about the King of Storyville offering nothing except more questions.

"So you think he's holding back."

"I do," Valentin said. "Justine did, too."

"And she's the smart one," the lieutenant said.

Valentin allowed that that was true and meant it. "I think you and I need to pay Lulu White a visit."

"Whenever you want."

Valentin asked him what he had found.

"Well, I heard back from the chemist who works for us," he said. "It's what we figured."

"That's too bad." Every back-of-town bartender knew about chloral hydrate. A more exotic mixture would be possible to trace.

The lieutenant took the opportunity to wonder aloud about Rebecca Marcus, relating the moment of hesitation when he asked her if she had anything to share. Valentin knew that James had interviewed far too many suspects and was too clever a detective to miss the little hitches that meant a lie was lurking.

"You think maybe she's stumbled onto something?" Valentin said.

"I don't know. She's hard to read."

"But she's aware of what happens if she holds back?"

"She knows."

"What do we do about it?" Valentin asked.

"I'm thinking about putting someone on her."

"I'm married," Valentin said. "How about you?"

"You don't know Mary Rose," the lieutenant said. "I'd be the next victim."

It was a welcome moment of levity. McKinney said, "If you can occupy yourselves for a little while, I'll pick you up in a police vehicle. Drive out to St. Rocco's."

"We're at Martín's," Valentin said.

"I'll see you in an hour," the lieutenant said before clicking off.

It required exactly three minutes for Rebecca to realize that Deacon Terrell was likely to spend whatever time she had with him in a state of agitation.

To begin, once he got over his surprise that the woman on his door-step was a reporter for the newspaper and after he offered her a seat on the heavy white couch, he remained standing or pacing the carpet as if he was ready to either open the door and shoo her out or bolt for it himself.

"Do we have to do this now?" he began. "We have the service to prepare for. The Archbishop is coming. And a—"

"I'll only take a few minutes," Rebecca said.

"On today of all days?" he said. "I don't have a few minutes."

"Please, sir."

"Well, all right..." he said, though it clearly wasn't.

"I want to begin by asking–"

"You know the police already spoke to me," the deacon said in a pinched tone. "I told them everything I knew. Which was nothing that could help."

Rebecca sensed that he had turned back and she was in danger of losing him again. "I understand," she said. Then: "Of course, you want the church represented in the possible light. After such a terrible event right on the grounds."

Terrell stopped, detecting something, and meeting her eyes for the first time. "Well, yes, of course we do," he said.

"And I'll make sure it comes out that way. But, sir..." Here she paused to compose her face with sincerity. "I'm wondering if there's anything that you didn't tell the police that you can share with me?" The deacon's eyes flicked and she said, "Nothing I would quote directly, you understand."

Terrell stood very still for a long moment before lying. "If I think of something, I will of course let you know."

The lieutenant spent part of the walk to headquarters mulling Mr. Valentin's comment and entertaining several lewd thoughts about the reporter in various stages of undress. Not one of them dissuaded him of his suspicions about her. He put all of it aside when he entered the building.

Chief Leroux was waiting in his office. "You're going to the service?"

"Yes, sir," McKinney said. "St. Cyr and I both. Watching the crowd." He chose not to mention that the Creole detective's wife would also be there.

"All right, what else do you have?"

The lieutenant told him what little St. Cyr had learned from the Walthams' maid and Tom Anderson. The chief was mollified to hear that something—anything—had surfaced that might lead somewhere. "So all you need to do now is locate a trick baby in the District. How hard could that be?"

McKinney came up with a dry laugh. Some strumpet was going into labor every other day.

"What do you know about this girl?" Leroux said.

McKinney said, "She could be anywhere from fifteen to twenty, as near as we can figure."

"And any idea what house she came out of?"

"We know he spent time at Mahogany Hall," the junior officer said. "So maybe there. St. Cyr said we'll do well to go talk to Miss Lulu and see if she has anything to tell us."

"Well, she does have her nose in everyone's business." The chief came up with a smile that contained actual amusement for once. "Do you know her?"

"I've met her, is all. She and St. Cyr go back. So the three of us will sit down and talk."

"You'll enjoy that," Chief Leroux said before waving him out the door.

# FOURTEEN

By one o'clock, the streets surrounding the church were thick with automobiles and the banquettes teeming with bodies, most of them clad in somber blacks and grays. Mourners had begun filing into the chapel an hour before the start of service and the pews became a small sea of fluttering fans.

Women wept openly as men stood shaking their heads in woe. A murmur ran like a wave through the crowd when a Packard limousine pulled up and the Archbishop's mitre floated to the doors, a bobbing flower of bright red. Father O'Brien had been a much-loved shepherd to the flock and the crowd seemed a single creature animated by grief.

Those who chose to wait in the relative cool outside gathered in clusters at the front and sides of the church. Lieutenant McKinney had commandeered a police sedan and driver and collected Valentin and Justine from Martin's. They rode to the southwest, then turned onto Carrollton. The closer they drew, the more traffic they encountered, and the driver crept the sedan through the crowd until they reached the corner and climbed out. The lieutenant went off to speak to Chief Leroux, who was standing by the front door with a group of a dozen other senior officers.

Valentin and Justine crossed the street and in their best casual poses turned to survey the crowd. After a few minutes, he said, "So?"

"Impossible," she said. "Could be anyone."

"I'm wondering if this particular person would recognize me," he said. "I mean now that my name has been in the paper for the whole city to see."

She snickered. He was still miffed. But whose fault was it? She said, "No one is going to come out in the open."

"Well, we do have a lunatic on our hands."

She squeezed his arm. "Maybe you could just identify yourself to the crowd."

"Or hang a sign around my neck."

He was turning around to locate the lieutenant again when he heard a familiar voice call out, "Mr. Valentin!"

*There he is again and with that same preying animal pose as the silly-looking fellow in a suit that doesn't fit right steps up to shake his hand. The one who gave chase. Good time to stay back. Now he's bowing his head over yelling out like that, but the detective looks cool. Maybe because of the lovely woman beside him, the quadroon. His wife? Funny how he turns this way and that and every time he does, his face changes. First he's a dago, then a Negro, then a Cherokee, then something else entirely. But ain't lots of men and women that same way? It's what happens in a place where all kinds of people are laying with each other. Mr. St. Cyr presents himself as a decent fellow. Like others who are not.*

Valentin pinned Each with a sharp look and the younger man, realizing his gaffe, slapped a hand to his mouth, and whispered, "Sorry I did that. Sorry." He swallowed, then turned his pink face to Justine. "And you... you are looking pretty as ever."

"And you're more grown every time I see you."

"That's 'cause it ain't very often," Each said, now sounding crestfallen. Valentin and Justine were the only folks who qualified as family in his world.

Valentin said, "Do you have something to report to me?"

Each snapped out of his haze. "Christ, yes," he hissed. He recounted seeing the person dropping a package then scurrying off. "I chased after, but I lost him."

"So it was a man," Valentin said, keeping his voice low. "You saw that."

"What?" Each blinked his large eyes. "Well... I thought it was... I guess it could have been a woman. Small person. I guess I ain't sure."

Valentin felt Justine pinch his arm in punctuation. "And this was on what street corner?"

"Julia at Church," Each said. "I was just..." The full extent of losing the suspect was dawning on him and his face fell. "I just lost him. Her."

"It's all right." The detective tilted his head in the direction of the church doors. "You see Lieutenant McKinney up there? Go tell him I need a minute of his time right away. We'll be around the south side. Tell him to bring one of his street coppers along with him."

Relieved at having an errand to run, Each ducked into the crowd and scurried off. Valentin took Justine's arm and steered her around to the walkway that led to the back of the church, a match for the one on the other side where the priest had fallen. They found a spot beneath a spreading maple tree and a few minutes later, McKinney appeared with Each and a uniformed officer in tow.

The lieutenant said, "What do we have?"

"There's a mailbox at the corner of..." He turned to Each, who said, "Julia and Church."

Valentin said, "All right. We need to get to the Lafayette post office and have them hold the contents of the box. If it's already been picked up, we want them to find and hold it."

Valentin had Each repeat what had happened earlier, complete with the upsetting conclusion. When he finished, the lieutenant said, "I think it's a damn wonder you even happened to spot him."

"We're not sure about the 'him' part," Valentin said. "It was a small person and covered up. So he didn't see any features."

McKinney mulled this, then spoke over his shoulder to the patrolman. "You got that?" The officer nodded. "Get someone to drive you or take a car. On my orders."

"Each needs to go with him," Valentin said.

McKinney waved a hand and the cop hurried off with Each following along behind him. "You really think it could–" A heavy bell tolled once, again, then a third time. "I'll see you after," he said and moved off.

Rebecca slipped around the edge of the crowd, a veil in place lest she be recognized as the *Times-Picayune* reporter, a Jewess on Christian grounds, or both. She came upon Henry standing at the back of the church, smoking a hand-rolled cigarette, and staring at nothing, his eyes as sad as ever.

She spoke to him for a quiet half-minute, pushed a coin into his palm, and followed him to the side door. She just missed Lieutenant McKinney stepping up to the church office and was able to make a quiet entrance into the chapel. A gentleman shifted in the pew to allow her a place to sit. She opened her fan and waved it before her face as she watched the newest arrivals and wondered if one of them was a murderer.

The lieutenant used the priest's telephone to call the First Precinct. As he explained to the commanding officer about the mailbox, he studied the spot on Father O'Brien's desk where Valentin had found the bloody parcel. From what Each had said, the appearance of the next package was only a matter of time, a day or two at most. And then there would be two more after that and unless they could do something, three more bodies to match.

The sedan rounded the corner onto Church Street and Each pointed and said, "That's it right there." The corporal steered to the curb. As Each climbed out, a harried man in a blue uniform stepped from a delivery truck with U.S. Mail emblazoned on the side.

He introduced himself as Mr. Rollins, the station manager, and shook Each's hand. Then he delivered the news. "The mail in this box was picked up almost two hours ago. It's already been dropped."

"And that means what?"

Mr. Rollins said, "That means someone's going to have to go through some bags."

"How many?"

"Maybe twelve," Mr. Roberts said. "But that's only if they haven't already been sorted and sent on."

————

The service had ended. Valentin spotted her descending the steps and his first instinct was to turn tail and run. Even if he tried something so childish, his escape routes were blocked by the bodies on every side. As she was boring in on them, he heard Justine say, "Is that..." He dared not look her way.

It didn't matter. When he finally did glance at her, he saw that she was regarding the reporter with eyes so cool that Rebecca came to a stop while still a half-dozen paces away.

She said, "Mr. Valentin."

"This is my wife," Valentin said "Justine. This is–"

"Rebecca Marcus," Justine said. "From the newspaper. I've seen your photograph. And read your stories."

Rebecca smiled more broadly, pleased to be recognized, though Justine hadn't specified which stories. When she addressed the detective a moment later, her expression grew serious. "It's important that I speak to you and the lieutenant," she said. "I have information about your case."

Rebecca turned her most charming face back to Justine. "You don't mind if I steal him, do you?" She let a few beats go by and then said, "Just for an hour?"

Justine offered the barest shake of her head. Valentin took a moment to consider if they were being tricked into something. There was only one way to find out. "I'll find the lieutenant. We'll meet you in thirty minutes."

"Where?"

"We left our machine at Martín's on Magazine Street," Justine said before he could reply. She fixed the reporter with a steady stare. "Do you know it?"

Rebecca returned the stare, though with a softer edge. "Of course," she murmured. "A lovely place."

Now Valentin sensed his wife drawing back and he knew that whatever he said was going to land him in some kind of trouble, so he nodded agreement—to something.

"I'll see you there." Rebecca cocked her head in a pert way and said, "Mrs. Justine," before hurrying away.

Valentin said, "I need to..."

"Find James," Justine said, her voice dusted with ice. "Yes. Let's go do that." She went ahead and he followed.

The lieutenant summoned the police sedan, opened the door for Justine and Valentin to climb in back, and took the front passenger seat. Because of the driver, they discussed only minor matters during the ride along St. Charles and then over to Magazine. Justine barely spoke at all.

When they pulled up in front of Martin's, McKinney turned in the seat and ask if she would be joining them.

Justine said, "I think the lady would prefer I not be present." She glanced at her husband. "So I'll drive myself home."

"Yes, yes," Valentin said and slid out to hurry around the back of the sedan and open the door for her. McKinney climbed down from the front seat and the driver pulled the sedan down the curb.

Justine could tell by Valentin's posture as he cranked the engine that he was not pleased with her navigating the city streets alone, but was in no position to protest. For her part, she was both excited and anxious. But it was too late for him to make amends or for her to change her mind; the four-cylinders were clattering out their metallic beat.

Valentin and the lieutenant stood watching the sedan disappear into the afternoon traffic. "I guess marriage is a complicated business," McKinney said.

"Sometimes," Valentin said and made for the front door of the café.

They had been seated for ten minutes when Rebecca appeared, this time in a hesitant way instead of her usual breathless rush. Before she sat, she said, "I want to let you know that Reynard Vernel will be joining us."

Valentin glanced at the lieutenant, who shrugged. He stood to hold her chair and ask what she would like for a refreshment. He and the lieutenant had already ordered coffee.

"They have a nice jasmine tea," she said. He stepped away to place the order.

When he returned, she had settled into her chair. "While we're waiting, is there anything you can share with me?"

"Nothing more than what we discussed on the telephone," McKinney said.

"That's what I expected," she said. She turned to Valentin and warmed her tone. "Justine," she said. "She's very pretty."

"She'll appreciate the compliment," Valentin said.

"Have long have you been married?"

He had to think. "Three years, now. It felt odd talking about it with her and he could sense a next question being readied.

It never landed. Looking over her shoulder, he saw Reynard Vernel stepping through the door. He waved a hand and the editor approached the table.

Reynard and McKinney had crossed paths a dozen times, mostly during Valentin's cases, and they exchanged quick greetings. Rebecca's tea had arrived. The editor waved off the offer of a beverage and took the remaining chair.

"So," the lieutenant said. "What do you want to discuss with us?"

Rebecca treated Reynard to a hesitant glance before opening her purse and drawing out the two sheets of cream-colored paper. She handed the first one to the lieutenant, who spent a few seconds reading. When he passed it to Valentin, she handed him the second one.

Once both detectives had read the letters twice, Valentin placed them in the middle of the table. "So you believe they're from the person who committed the two murders."

"Who else?" Rebecca said.

"Someone looking for attention or playing a hoax," McKinney said, though he didn't sound too sure about it. "What do you plan to with them?"

"We haven't decided," Reynard said. "I was thinking we'd wait for one more contact. Whatever it might be."

Valentin noticed the flicker of disappointment on Rebecca's face, followed by her eyes darkening. He understood; she wasn't the type to wait. So he knew he'd make her more unhappy when he said, "I think that's a good idea."

Vernel said, "Lieutenant? What would be the police department's stand on this?"

"In general, we prefer nothing be shared with the public. It only encourages others. So I do think waiting would be wise." He sat back. "But of course we can't stop you." ,

Now Rebecca was staring into her cup, her lips pursed. Valentin looked at the editor and tilted his head her way. Vernel said, "It's your story, Rebecca. Everyone will know you got these. But it will be better to wait." She raised her head and nodded, barely mollified. He pushed away from the table. "I need to get back to the newsroom."

"Wait, I'll join you." The men stood up with her. "There's something else," she said. "I have a feeling that I'm being followed. Watched."

Reynard said, "You didn't tell me that part."

"Because I'm not sure," she said.

She felt the Creole detective's eyes on her. "I wouldn't ignore it," he said.

Surprised, she said, "No?" She had been expecting something like mockery for a silly woman's fancies.

"No," he said. "Be careful."

She mulled this, said, "Gentlemen," and turned away. Vernel waved and followed her to the door.

The two detectives sat down again. "What do you think?" McKinney said.

"I'm not sure," Valentin said.

"I'm not either," the lieutenant pondered for a few moments. "What if she wrote them herself?"

"That crossed my mind."

"What about Vernel? Would he be in on something with her?"

"No," Valentin said. "I don't see that at all."

"What if she's putting something over on him?"

"I doubt it," Valentin said with a bemused smile.

"And why's that?"

"Because I was watching him. And he doesn't trust her, either."

The lieutenant offered to have the driver carry him to Bayou St. John, but Valentin demurred and they walked instead to the streetcar stop on the next corner. "What's waiting for you at home?"

"I have no idea," Valentin said.

"About Miss Marcus. I hope those letters are real. But I'm sure there are a lot of people don't like the idea of a woman reporter covering crimes."

Valentin said, "She couldn't do any worse than some of the sots they have now."

The Canal Line car came clattering to a halt. The doors opened, but Valentin made no move to climb on and the car rolled away. The lieutenant told him that he had police business to attend to, laid a hand on his shoulder, said, "Good luck," and ambled off. When he reached Commerce Street, he turned to see Valentin had begun walking east.

Though Tom Anderson had felt too poorly to attend Father O'Brien's service, he was recovering by the end of the afternoon, thanks to a nap and two more glasses of brandy. After Lucy was satisfied that he was fine on his own, she left him to tend to her chores.

He returned to the dining room and tried to distract himself with some papers, but it was no use. The two murders circled his head like dark birds. At least now the panic that had caused him to be untruthful with Valentin and Justine had passed and he could think with more clarity about what had happened – or what he could do about it.

He pulled a chair close to the window so that he could sit and watch a street in the light of a spring afternoon. He wanted calm. He needed to think.

He had never been one to pay much mind to the voodoo that so engaged the women of Storyville, many of whom were either pious Catholics or rowdy Baptists. Wasn't the most trusted follower of Jesus a harlot? Earlier in his career, he had given nods to both beliefs as they served his ambitions. Now, as the years dragged on him, he found great solace in the Church and had left all the silly superstitions behind.

But as he sat watching rain clouds rising to the west, he wondered if there was a curse lurking. One that had touched first Herbert Waltham and then Father O'Brien. He thought about who else might fall and wondered if he could be among their number. Wasn't he at the center of the photograph?

It was this thought that pushed him out of his chair and into his office, where he closed the door and picked up the telephone. He knew the number by heart.

Miss Lulu was interviewing a young lady whose background, like so many others who came to her, was vague. She was a pretty one, though, fair-skinned, freckled, and blonde.

"Where did you work before you came here?" the madam inquired. The woman—who said her name was Sally Anne—named a house in St. Louis that Miss Lulu had never heard of, and she knew the class bordellos in a thousand-mile radius. She guessed that Sally Anne was on the run from someone or something. She paid this no mind. If the young lady was willing and passed her little test and the doctor's examination, she'd be a money-maker.

She was explaining her expectations when her telephone rang. Genevieve, the mulatto house girl, had been waiting outside the door and appeared in an instant to answer it. She listened for a few seconds then gave the madam one of their signs, this one meaning the call was important. Miss Lulu responded with her own silent gesture and said, "I'm sorry, dear. I have to take this." Genevieve ushered Sally Anne out into the foyer, pausing to mouth the name, "Tom Anderson" before closing the door behind her.

The madam was not surprised. She had been expecting the call. She removed the heavy earring, pushed up the curls of her wig, and placed the handset to her ear. "Mr. Tom," she said in an easy voice.

"I had to speak to you." The voice on the other end of the line carried about half the timbre it had boasted not six months before. And there was something shaky about it. A man in fear, she surmised.

"About the murders?" Miss Lulu said.

"About the reason for them."

"I'm sorry, Mr. Tom? The rea—"

"I never did anything." Now the voice was plaintive. "I still asked God to forgive. Forgive all my sins."

*Good lord,* the madam mused. *What is he talking about? Is he going to confess to me?* Before he could go any farther, she said, "Isn't it more likely a coincidence?"

"No," Anderson said. "I mean I don't know. But I can feel it."

Miss Lulu said, "Feel what?"

"Something drawing closer." He let out a loud breath. "And I'm wondering if Waltham and the Father felt the same way only a few days ago."

The madam felt she had listened enough to the foolishness. He was not going to be soothed. "What can I do?"

"Be my ears on Basin Street for the next few days," he said. "I can't come there anymore. My health..." As if to punctuate the point, he coughed.

She rolled her eyes. "Isn't this something you can ask Mr. Valentin to do?"

After a pause, Anderson said, "He's with the police now."

"Well, I still think you can trust him," Miss Lulu said.

"Maybe so. Maybe so." He sounded weary. "For now, please, if there's anything you hear..."

"All right, Mr. Tom." The madam dropped the handset in the cradle and sat still for a brooding moment. Rousing herself, she called out, "Genevieve? Please bring Sally Anne back in."

When Valentin arrived home, he was relieved to find the Ford intact and his wife in a quiet mood. If she had any thoughts about what had transpired with Rebecca Marcus, she didn't voice them.

They were on the front gallery, she tending to the plants in the boxes that sat upon the railings and he sitting on the perron, watching the afternoon traffic and pleased to be there rather than any place he could name. The smells of Evangeline's dinner wafted from the kitchen. He wondered how much better it could be—except for the small matter of two murders and possibly more to come.

He described the notes that had landed on the reporter's desk, a minimum of words in a hand so precise that it defied identification.

"And that's all?" Justine said.

"That's all." His eyes followed the Chevrolet truck that was rolling past. "Well she did say she felt like she was being followed. Watched. But that could just be her imagination."

"Yes, I suppose." The comment was delivered in an even tone and she did not wonder aloud that it could be another ploy for her husband's attention. He knew that at times like this, his wife tended to keep her opinions tucked away. Since the subject was Rebecca Marcus, he was fine with that.

"So McKinney asked that they wait to see if there's another one," he said. "And if that happens, they can publish them then."

"I'm sure any reporter would hate that," Justine said. The shears went still. "What's the possibility that she–"

"Wrote them?" Valentin said. "We talked about that. I don't think the time fits. And I'm not sure she's that clever."

"Or that stupid. It's just asking to be caught."

He stood and stretched. "I agree." He waited to see if she had anything to add. When she went back to her plants, he said, "I'll go fetch us something to drink."

"I'm ready," she said. "And remember..."

"I know. Tonight. Mangetta's." He stepped close to kiss her cheek before disappearing into the house.

# FIFTEEN

Justine began having second thoughts as she dressed for their evening out. She had not set foot onto Storyville's scarlet banquettes for over a year and that time for bare minutes. This night would put her back there for hours, though it was true that they'd spend most of the time hidden in Frank Mangetta's night-time saloon. Still, it bothered her that she could not shake a last inkling of that twenty-block square's bizarre magic.

Standing at the mirror, she lost herself in memories of her life as a scarlet princess, with men pampering her as she serviced them, living the privileged life of a courtesan, all this after she had come from nowhere with nothing. She recalled in a moment of relish the dance halls, gambling parlors, cafes, bordellos grand and mean, the drink, the hop, and the music that had been her world. And all the women. The reason that the plot of Uptown real estate had existed as a red-light district for close to a hundred years: the women.

With a sigh, she released the images and returned to her preparations, applying more mascara and lipstick than her day-to-day faint touches. When she opened the closet door, she passed by her wifely dresses for one with a hem that reached only to her ankle—just a few inches above, in fact. Let them look. The skirt and the bodice were thin cotton and lace in a medium purple and supple enough to show off her figure. She chose a hat that was more a wide band about her head with a plume on one side, then spent some time before the mirror getting everything right.

When she stepped into the front room, Evangeline saw her first, stopped mid-sentence, and smiled with delight. When Valentin turned around, she wished she could hold the dazzled look on his face forever.

They gaped at her in various states of pleasure until her latte cheeks blushed deep red. Valentin only came out of his daze when she said, "Is it time to go?"

Rolf Kassel often worked late, but he liked to linger on Friday nights in particular to make sure the weekend editors picked up the batons for their issues and because he had nowhere else to go, his wife having left him for another man twelve years before over his hours and his drinking.

On this Friday night, after standing at the windows to watch the purple night cast a veil over the city, he passed Reynard Vernel's desk and was surprised to find the junior editor still at work, his head bent to a stack of copy pages. "You after my job?" he inquired.

Startled, Reynard jumped, then laughed. "I have these to finish. And I feel like if I leave, something will happen."

"I know what you mean." Kassel motioned for the younger man to join him.

In his office, he dropped into a chair that had sagged from punishment from his girth and instead of reaching for his Raleigh Rye, dug into a different drawer for a pint of McIver's Malt, his weekend drink of choice. Reynard was happy to accept the offer of three fingers.

They sipped for a silent few moments and then Kassel said, "About our Miss Marcus."

Vernel said, "Yes, sir? What about her?" Though he had some idea of what might be coming.

"She's traveled very far very fast, hasn't she? And now these letters. I'm still wondering if she's up to the task. I'd be concerned if it was a long-timer." Reynard waited while he took another ruminative sip of his whiskey and then lifted a stack of sheets of white, cream, and yellow paper.

"On the other hand, we've already had dozens of letters about her. And more dozens of telephone calls. Some are on the negative side. 'Why is that woman writing about such gore?' Or 'Why is a woman doing a man's job?' That sort of thing. And some very crude ones." He waved the sheaf in the air. "But a lot more of them say they love the idea. Most are from women, of course. Do you know why that matters?"

Vernel did, and very well. He also knew to let the editor answer the question himself.

"Because the women are the ones who do most of the buying of our advertisers' goods, that's why." He dropped the pile. "This is where we find ourselves."

The junior editor waited again, this time for Kassel to take a slower sip of his drink, before saying, "So what's the verdict?"

"She stays," the editor said with a sigh. "And partly because I'm not sure what she'd do if I pulled her off. She's got some kind of temper. But we're going to have to watch that her notoriety doesn't get out of hand. We keep her on as long as she delivers on her stories and it benefits the newspaper." He raised his glass in a bleary toast. "And she keeps receiving letters from murderers."

"And if it doesn't?"

"Then we'll make a decision about Miss Rebecca Marcus."

She let him drive this time and he parked at his usual lot on St. Louis. He helped her down to the banquette and they strolled the narrow streets of the Vieux Carré, taking in the sights. At the corner of Dauphine Street, he came to a halt and looked back over his shoulder.

"What is it?"

He surveyed the intersection, looking for some special shard of motion, but saw nothing. He turned back to see her studying him. "Valentin?"

"It's all right," he said. They continued on.

*How can this not be a true cause? On the way to the next one and there he is, not forty paces away, walking with the lovely quadroon's hand linked in his arm. Once again, he moves like an animal on the prowl, though now more at ease. How close before he senses something?*

*Fifteen feet and now he stops and his head begins to turn and there's just enough time to slip from view behind two women wearing wide hats.*

*He and his quadroon walk on in the direction of the District. There's no time to follow. And no good to try. Too much risk in trying to dodge those sharp eyes. There's another place to be and an appointment to keep.*

Before they left the French Quarter, he asked if she preferred to take a roundabout way to Mangetta's. He knew how she felt about Storyville.

"It's all right to cross here," she said. "I'd like to see how Basin Street looks these days."

As she took his arm again, he spent a moment wondering if it was rather that she wanted to let Basin Street see how *she* looked. Which was fine by him; he was happy to show her off.

When they reached the other side of the tracks, she stopped to give the famed boulevard a long inspection. Though it was still a mighty sight, she thought the lights dimmer, the milling crowd of men thinner than when she had seen it the previous year, and the facades of the mansions showing more of their age.

The stares she received as they moved up the block humored her. It had been like that back when she paraded with the other sporting girls in their finery. Before Valentin had come into her life. Had it really been almost nine years?

By the time they arrived at the corner of Conti, she'd had enough. She said, "All right, let's go see Frank," then took a last lingering look. "It won't last much longer, will it?"

"No," he said. "I don't think it will."

When they stepped inside, the saloonkeeper was standing at the end of the bar, talking to one of his regulars. He looked up, spotted Justine, and let out a little cry.

He rushed to embrace her, then squired them to the booth in the back corner, where he took her hands in his and kissed them. "You're so beautiful. *Bella. Bella.*" He tilted his head at Valentin. "So what are you doing with this *cafone?*"

"He's rich," she said, her eyes dancing. "That's what he told me." Then: "What? He isn't? He's been lying all this time?"

Frank shook his head in mock woe. "Just another poor *paisano*." The play was over and he clapped his hands. "I'll be back."

Valentin caught his arm. "What about Mr. Cecil?"

"We'll see." The saloonkeeper gave a Sicilian shrug.

He returned with two bottles of wine and three glasses. The room was beginning to fill up and the five members of the Silver Moon Band ambled in and began unpacking their instruments. Valentin did not expect to be entertained. Over the past year, more dozens of the best players had vacated the city for St. Louis, New York, and Chicago, and those who stayed had neither the skills nor the spirit, faint echoes of the crazy revolt that Bolden had started and a score more had carried forward. Jass had taken twenty years to explode, invade proper New Orleans, and then travel off to more lucrative shores.

As if he had conjured the man with these thoughts, a smallish, nervous-looking fellow in a dusty derby and with the pale features of someone who didn't get out much launched himself into the room and started glancing around. Mr. Cecil.

Frank, who had returned to the bar to order food for the table, spotted him at the same time and gave a wave. Valentin leaned over to whisper to Justine, then stood up. Frank took the fellow's elbow and steered him to the booth.

"Mr. Cecil," he announced. "This is Valentin St. Cyr. He grew up with Bolden. Stayed friends until..."

"Until he went away," Valentin said. He reached out to shake the clammy hand, nodded toward Justine. "My wife."

"Ma'am," the visitor said, touching a finger to the brim of his hat.

"Would you like to have a seat?"

"Sure enough," Mr. Cecil said and slid onto the bench with a jerky motion.

Frank said, "Something to drink, sir?"

"A whiskey would do just fine," Mr. Cecil said.

Frank moved off. Valentin regarded the man across the table. "So you made the recording of Bolden and his band."

"Called himself Kid Bolden back then," Mr. Cecil stated.

"What can you tell me about that night?"

"It was in the daytime. Late in the afternoon. At Preservation Hall. Before they played their show." He shot a glance toward the bar. "Wasn't much to it. I came in, set up my machine, and they played three tunes. That was the arrangement." When he continued his voice held a note of pride. "I had a nice Edison model. There wasn't but a half-dozen in the whole city." He frowned. "I had me a good business. Then the record disks come in and that was that. I had to—"

Whatever tale of woe was to follow was interrupted by Frank arriving with a glass of whiskey. Mr. Cecil quaffed half the liquor in a single long slug, then let out a long breath. "What I remember most is how loud it was. Damn. About blew me over."

"That was Bolden, all right," Valentin said. "Do you recall the songs?"

"'Careless Love' was one," Mr. Cecil said. "There was a gutbucket kind of thing. And a rag. I don't remember the titles to them two." He helped himself to another sip and the rest of the whiskey disappeared.

Frank treated Valentin to a sly glance. The Creole detective shook his head. *Not yet...* He had been holding back the question. Now he said, "What happened to the cylinder? Do you know where it is?"

"Oh, yeah," Mr. Cecil said. "I got it right here." He dug into one of his coat pockets and produced a white box that was six inches long and two wide and high and worn at the edges. Valentin stared at it and said, "You'll have another whiskey?"

Mr. Cecil said, "Yes, sir, thank you." Frank waved a hand to his barkeep.

Justine stole a peek at her husband, then said, "Mr. Cecil? What are you planning to do with it?"

"What am I..." The bloodshot eyes wandered to the bar, came back. "I'm wanting to sell it. If the price is right, I mean."

Valentin said, "What price would that be?"

The barkeep approached the booth and placed a glass before Mr. Cecil, who snatched it up. "What price?" He studied the amber liquor. "Mr. Bolden, he got to be quite the thing, didn't he? And as far as I know, he never made no other recordings." He looked up at Valentin. "That's right, ain't it?"

"I don't know," Valentin said. "But suppose it is?" He had to work to keep his eyes off the box.

"Then I'd say it's worth quite a bit." He took another sip of his drink. "I'd say a hundred dollars." His eyes did a cunning shift as he tried to gauge the detective's reaction. "I ain't talked to no one else about it. But I plan to do that. Tomorrow."

Valentin had been practicing a poker face all his life. Now he displayed it for Mr. Cecil's benefit, even as he considered the price. A hundred dollars was what he had paid for the Ford that was parked on St. Louis Street. It amounted to a working man's wages for a month. They didn't have that kind of money just lying about.

"You have a deal," he said. "After I listen to it."

One of Mr. Cecil's brows hiked at the same time Justine's and Frank's heads turned. They had only heard the number. They didn't grasp that the cylinder in the box was a treasure and that he had read Mr. Cecil as a man who could not be trusted with it. He had already considered what a wonder it was that it had survived almost twenty years, not only in the heat and humidity of the Crescent City, but three hurricanes and multiple floods.

Mr. Cecil recovered from his surprise at how easy the sale had gone. "Say, maybe I should make it one-fifty or two—" He froze in the heat of Valentin's stare, drained his glass and said, "A hundred will be all right. Yes, sir. Just fine."

"You can leave it with Mr. Mangetta," Valentin said. "He's got a safe on the premises. As soon as I hear all three songs are in good shape, the money's yours. Fair enough?"

Even through the whiskey swirling in his brain, Mr. Cecil sensed it was best to go along and not cross the Creole with the hard eyes. He didn't care about the damn thing, anyway. "That's fair enough, sure." In the next moment, he realized that it was time to make an exit. "So I'll come 'round tomorrow."

"That will be fine," Valentin said.

Mr. Cecil performed a clumsy wave of farewell and headed for the door. Valentin sat gazing at the box. Then he heard Justine say, "Excuse me? Where are we going to get a hundred dollars?"

Before he could respond, Frank sighed and said, *Da me*. *From me*.

Bartlett Barry made the call to the Pinkerton office before turning his attention back to his notes on the case coming Monday. After a few seconds, he stopped, his thoughts so scattered he could barely remember what he had just written down.

When he settled again, his eyes came to rest on the afternoon edition of the *Times-Picayune* that was laying on his desk with another article about the two murders. Written by a woman, of all things.

The moment he heard about the priest, he felt a jolt of fear from a dark well of memory. Then he told himself that what he imagined could not be possible, not after so much time. When the next morning arrived with no reports of any new horror, he held back an urge to make phone calls to certain parties. So far, it had been two murders. A pup fresh out of law school would know better than to set off alarms.

But with night coming on, the fingers of dread returned and he decided it would not hurt to have protection and called for the security man who was even now on his way.

He rose from his desk, opened the French doors and stepped onto the balcony. The Vieux Carré's Friday nightlife was just beginning as the late shoppers were moving out of the stores and the diners and drinkers were gathering at their preferred establishments. As always, a throng was milling on and off the banquettes. He could pick from among them the gentlemen who had spent their early evenings in Storyville bordellos and were now hurrying to meet their wives for dinner.

His eye, honed on eleven years in the justice system, also spotted the usual miscreants: hustlers, pickpockets, second-story men, and their like, along with a few strolling strumpets. On the fringes, random drunkards and hopheads were making their staggering ways down the banquettes to the next bottle or pipe.

He stood enjoying the spectacle and thinking about his night ahead, beginning with a few hours of gambling to the music at Anderson's Café and later more intimate pleasures with a Basin Street octoroon named Grace. He could afford to keep her for the night and wake in her arms come morning. The Pinkerton would be close by just in case.

His musings on the last time he had seen her were interrupted by the rapping of a knuckle on his office door. He pulled out his watch: pressing on eight o'clock. His man had arrived sooner than expected; all the better to get a start on lifting the grim cloud. He left the doors open to the night and went to receive the visitor.

The face he greeted was not that of any Pinkerton and he gasped and took a half-step back, "You..."

"Yes, me."

He was reaching to slam the door when a hand shot out and planted a syringe into his solar plexus. "What... what did you do?" he said. In the next seconds, his breath was coming short.

The response was a harsh laugh and the words, "What did *you* do?"

He felt his legs go weak as if they contained no bones. A few seconds more and he pitched to one side and into arms that held him upright. In a blur, they passed through the office and onto the balcony, where the lights of the Quarter were multicolored stars in the night sky. As his hands grasped the railing, he felt something going around his neck and in a murky corner of his mind, realized what was happening. The thought lasted until he pitched forward and down.

As promised, Valentin let his *zio* take the little box to his safe. He explained to Justine that he'd get the money to Frank as soon as he could. She shook her head over his foolishness, but let it go. The wine that kept pouring had gotten to her, too.

They listened to the music for an hour or so and when the band took a break, said their good-nights and stepped out onto Marais Street. Justine led the way down Bienville to Basin Street. She stopped when they reached the corner and now instead of hurrying to cross over into the Quarter, paused, looking pensive.

"So, do you miss it?" she said.

Did he? Valentin paused to weigh the question. Did he miss not knowing what would come next, because no two nights were ever the same? And did he miss being royalty in this little empire, with almost no one to tell him what to do? He considered all this before saying, "Only now and then."

"But you're still here."

"Just for now." He looked back the way they had come. "Anyway, I told you. It can't last."

Justine sensed that there was something more. "And?"

"And I'm tired of it," he admitted.

"Then maybe when this is over..."

He took her hand and smiled at her lovely face and said, "Yes."

"That would suit me," she said and drew him along the banquette in the direction of St. Louis Street. They strolled the edge of the Vieux Carré, passing the corner where the trumpeter had played, and leaving all the lights and noise and bustle. They reached the little lot in the shadow of the cemetery wall.

Valentin helped her into the seat and had just closed the door when they heard the racket of an engine and were splashed with the light of headlamps of a vehicle sliding to a stop. Justine shielded her eyes as James McKinney emerged from the cloud of dust. She said, "Oh, my lord."

The citizens strolling St. Philip Street were startled then horrified to see a body tumble over a balcony railing and come to a sudden, jolting halt at the end of a rope. The form shuddered and the legs kicked a half-dozen times and then went still. The pedestrians stood with mouths agape at the gruesome sight until a fellow who worked for the railroad came alert and rushed into the saloon he had just visited to yell to the barkeep to call the coppers. Then he stepped back outside to stare at the hanged man some more.

The first words out of the lieutenant's mouth were apologetic. "Valentin... Justine... I'm sorry."

Valentin had helped his wife back down to the banquette. "Where was this one?" he said.

The lieutenant paused for a breath and jerked a thumb. "Right back there. St. Philip."

"Has the victim been identified?"

"Do you know Bartlett Barry?"

Valentin said, "He used to be a city attorney. But he left for a private practice."

"He was in that photograph," Justine said.

Valentin looked at her, then at McKinney again. "How did he die?"

"Hanged. From the balcony outside his office."

"*Hanged?*" Justine said. "So how do you know it wasn't a suicide?"

"Because he got stuck with a syringe," the lieutenant said.

"Just like Waltham," Valentin said.

McKinney placed his middle finger on a spot just below his sternum. "Right there."

"When did it happen?" Valentin said.

"About two hours ago."

"I'll be damned," Valentin said. Then: "How the hell did you find us?"

"I called your house. Miss Evangeline said you had gone to hear some music. I figured it was Mangetta's and called over there. You had just left. And I know you park here." The lieutenant now dipped his head and said, "Miss Justine. I'm so sorry..."

"But you need him," she said.

Valentin turned to her and said, "Why don't you come along."

She thought about it for a few seconds, then reached out a hand.

They crossed back over on North Rampart and turned down St. Philip.

At the corner of Dauphine, they found a police barricade. McKinney flashed his badge and spoke to the officers. Valentin noticed their eyes flicking at his wife when they passed through.

Bartlett Barry had been brought down on a stretcher that now laid in the narrow walkway between his building and the next one over. The lieutenant asked for a lamp and he and Valentin bent to study the body. The Creole detective saw that the rope burns around the victim's neck were raw and his face bloated, an added insult for a man who clearly tended to his appearance. His hair was trimmed and oiled. The suit he wore was tailored and of fine mohair and his shoes were of the best black leather. Not that any of it would help him now.

The two men stood up and made their way back to the street to collect Justine from amidst the gaggle of police. The three of them stood gazing up at the balcony while the coppers watched them and traded whispers.

"You had them leave the rope?" Valentin inquired.

"I did," the lieutenant said.

Valentin eyed the distance from the railing to the banquette. "Somebody got a hell of a surprise," he commented.

"All right," McKinney said, "Let's have a look upstairs."

He opened the door for Justine and Valentin. Inside, the stairwell was dark and glass crunched on the steps. "The bulbs were broken," McKinney said from behind them. "Figure the perpetrator did that." When they reached the second floor, he guided them across the short hallway to an office with an open glass door bearing the inscription "Bartlett Barry —Attorney-at-Law."

The office was tidy. The lawyer's large and ornate desk occupied the right wall. Smaller desks were placed in the two opposite corners. Cases filled with legal tomes were arranged from floor to ceiling. Valentin poked about the shelves. Justine crossed to the desk.

"I already had a look," the lieutenant said.

Justine said. "Did you see this?" She held up a cigar box and waited for her husband to produce an odd, short laugh.

"What is it?" A few seconds went by while the lieutenant studied the desk. "No ashtray."

"Leave it for now," Valentin said. Justine was happy to replace it.

Valentin surveyed the room before stepping to the door. "So someone knocks and he, what? Gets up to open it. Then..." He made the motion of a syringe being thrust. "A few seconds pass and he starts to go out. The visitor gets him across the floor..." He now turned to the open French doors and stepped out onto the balcony. The lieutenant and Justine followed to find him standing at the spot where the rope was still attached to the railing. "Square knot," he said. "Simple." He stood back. "So the visitor has him out here. Props him up long enough to get the noose on and tie the knot to the railing. And then..." Now he mimed a two-handed shove. "Over and down."

McKinney came up with a doubtful frown. "I don't see it," he said.

"All right, I'll show you." Valentin turned to Justine. "Help me with this." He untied the rope from the railing, handed it to her, and led her back to the office door, where he said, "We'll do it just like I described." He laid the rope over her shoulder and then sagged against her. "The drug would have begun to work right away. I'm getting weak but I can still walk. Or at least stumble."

He motioned to Justine and she wrapped an arm around him. "So the assailant walks me outside and to the railing." He now slouched more of his weight on her. "She can still hold me upright." Justine pinned him to the railing. "Now the noose..." At this, she hesitated. "Go ahead," he said. "I'll take it right off." She looped the rope over his head with her free hand. "Now pull the knot tight." She did as she was told. "All right, push me," he said.

She said, "Valentin..."

"No, it's all right," he said. "Quick!"

She slammed her palms against his chest so hard that McKinney had to reach out and catch him before he did topple over the wrought iron. She treated him to a look that was first startled, then angry, and she barely softened when he kissed her cheek and said. "I'm sorry. We had to do it." He turned to the lieutenant. "So?"

"So let's have a look at that box," he said.

They left the office and started down the dark stairwell. Halfway along, Justine stopped and said, "I can't believe someone..." She caught a breath. "So two parts left. The tongue and his... Oh, good God." They continued downward, feeling their way.

McKinney said, "I'd sure like to know who is going to all this trouble."

"And why," Valentin said.

In the hour after Bartlett Barry had been murdered, calls went out to both Lulu White and Tom Anderson from their friends at City Hall. The madam took the news in grim-faced, tight-lipped silence. When Lucy answered the telephone at Anderson's house, she heard something in the caller's voice that told her more bad news had arrived and made an excuse about Mr. Tom having gone to bed. This was partly true, but he was not asleep; rather, he had taken to the downstairs guestroom with a book and the day's last glass of brandy. Whatever had happened could wait until morning.

Rebecca could not be reached at all. Frazzled by the day's events, she found her way to the mechanic who kept an apartment over his shop just off Broad Street. They had met when he was repairing a gentleman friend's sedan and she made a return visit on her own. He liked to take her riding in the machines in his shop, which was how she had once ended up hunkered down in a Marmon Raceabout and another time on the back of a Brougham motorcycle.

On this night, they drove past the lake in a beautiful Grant two-seater that he at one point pushed to seventy miles per hour, whipping her curls in the night wind and drawing tears from her eyes. When they arrived back at his messy flat at the bottom of Dufossat Street, he stretched her out on the bed, afterward leaving her in a sagging, sopping heap, dead to the world. So she failed to call and did not learn that another of the thirteen men in the photograph that accompanied her Society page piece had died a horrible death.

# Sixteen

Miss Eloise, the landlady of the house on the corner of Dauphine and Elysian Fields where Rebecca Marcus roomed, was a good Christian woman and did not care for goings-on of any kind. She expected her young ladies to retire and rise early, be on time for the meals she served, and go to the house of worship of their choosing on Sunday.

In another city, she might have been able to enforce these rules, but in New Orleans it was a losing battle. There were too many distractions— and more every day. Young ladies were no longer dedicating their lives to the joys of courting and marriage, but smoking, wearing scandalous clothes, chasing careers, and arguing for the right to vote.

And wasn't one of these truant females right under her nose in Room 12? She had been stunned when the name Rebecca Marcus appeared in a news story about a terrible crime, even though that young lady was a wild one who did what she pleased and sometimes didn't come home at all. Like the previous evening.

Miss Eloise knew because she encountered Rebecca reaching the door just as she stepped out to collect the milk bottles and the morning paper. She watched what looked like a racing machine roar away before eyeing her boarder up and down, noting that she looked ragged in a way that did not come from toiling at a typewriter. Shameful—whatever she had been doing, though it didn't take much to guess.

Rebecca was not in the least abashed. "Miss Eloise," she said, sounding only a bit dizzy. "Good morning."

The landlady's response was a curt, "Morning." Rebecca didn't notice the discourtesy as she passed by to open the door. Miss Eloise waited until it had almost closed to say, "There was a message for you."

Rebecca stopped and stepped back onto the gallery. "Message?"

"Some boy from the newspaper come by last night." The landlady scanned the street in an idle fashion, a bit of torture.

"Well?" Rebecca said. "What did he say?"

"For you to get to your newsroom right away."

Rebecca closed her eyes, said, "Oh, no," then rushed inside to change clothes.

Since Valentin had begun working as an investigator for St. Charles Avenue law firms, he got to enjoy early Friday nights and languid Saturday mornings with his wife. Unless the weather was bad, Evangeline would make her own way to one of the street markets in the neighborhood, leaving them alone in the house for a delicious two hours.

He did not expect there to be any such idyll this Saturday. He had been awake before dawn, staring up at the ceiling, picturing the scene on St. Philip and wondering why he just hadn't said no to James McKinney in the first place. Sam Ross and the others might never call back and then where would they be? Working for high-toned attorneys and their spoiled-rich clients had given him little satisfaction. What they had given them was steady money and he knew that Justine had been thinking about that, too.

Though not at the moment. He felt her hand on his back and turned around. She was treating him to a pretty, sleepy smile that tugged various parts of his body. She sighed and her chest heaved. "You can't stay, can you?"

In response, he stood up, dropped his sleeping drawers to the floor, reached out with both hands, and drew her from under the sheets. Her eyes took on a shine as he turned her so that her back was against the wall. He pulled the sash and her night dress fell open. With an arm wrapped around her back, he edged his thighs between hers.

She let out a gasp and a little moan as he lifted her from the floor, a bit of music he had heard time and again but never tired of. Now she closed her eyes and with her arms circling his shoulders and the fingers of one hand locked into his curls, drew him to her naked self.

He pushed with a hard thrust and she bit down on the cry that rose from her throat and wrapped her legs around his waist as he did it again and then a third time. Her sighs were lost in the wind through the trees outside the window.

Justine felt like he was going to drive her up the cool plaster all the way to the ceiling. There was wet between them, Mississippi wet, and he was tightening his throat to still his own moans. She began to whisper in his ears, words from a strange language that tumbled from her lips with every breath. An electric tingle began somewhere near the base of her spine, a current that rose and spread, whirling through the middle of her body and just as she imagined him driving her right through the wall and into the next room, the shocks became a small explosion that threatened to tear her into pieces. She bit his shoulder and for ten long seconds was blind and deaf.

Ever so slowly, she came out of her trance in time to hear him give a last, long groan as he pinned her against the plaster. She held him tight until he lifted her again, turned her around, and laid her back on the bed.

She laughed a quiet laugh and he said, "What?"

"Now I remember why I married you."

She saw him to the front door, where she kissed him and said, "Are you going to need my help?"

"Yes," he said. "I'll call you in a while."

He stepped off the gallery and reached the Ford in time to see Evangeline approaching along the banquette with a basket under her arm. He said, "Good morning. Can I take that?"

"No, it's fine," she said. She looked closer and frowned. "Did something happen?"

"Yes, ma'am. Another man was killed."

"By the same person?"

"Yes. The same one."

She shook her head. "I do wish you had kept to your more peaceful work," she said.

"Sometimes I wish I had, too."

"But not today." Her eyes were knowing. "Today you're on the chase." With that, she turned and climbed the steps to the gallery.

Valentin set the ignition and choke and went to the front of the machine to crank the engine and ponder the wise woman's words.

Lucy took the early morning call and when she heard the words "New Orleans Police," explained that Mr. Tom was still not available, which was in fact true, because he had been in the downstairs bathroom for the better part of a half hour.

She had been following the newspaper articles written by the woman about the two murders, the first the wealthy businessman in the red-light district and the second the priest at St. Rocco's Church. By keeping her mouth closed and her eyes perked, she learned that her employer had known both victims, had been photographed with them, and that their deaths were putting a fright in him.

She didn't know why, but understood that she now had to be more careful around the subject. So when he appeared in the dining room, she let him get settled at the table before saying, "You had a telephone call a few minutes ago."

He had been lifting his cup for the morning's first sip. Now he placed it back in the saucer. Keeping his eyes on the plate, he said, "Who was it?"

"Your friend at the police," Lucy said. "Didn't tell me nothing. Just that you're to call him back."

When he picked up his cup again, it rattled against the saucer, spilling some of the coffee onto the tablecloth. He murmured. "Well, I'm a mess this morning."

"I'll get that," the maid said, keeping her voice low. She crossed to the oak sideboard and retrieved a fresh napkin.

As she was dabbing at the stain, Mr. Tom reached out and grasped her wrist. "Where's George, Lucy?" he said.

She was taken aback, wondering what in God's name the old man was up to. She had seen the way he eyed her curving parts, even now. "Went to collect some sacks of soil for the flower bed," she said. "Why do you ask?"

"Sit down, please."

Lucy hesitated. He had never asked her to join him at the table. She pulled out a chair and sat. "What is it, sir?"

"I want to tell you something," he said. "But before I do, I want you to make me a promise."

"Sir?"

"That you won't tell anyone else. Not even George." He waited, watching her face. "If you don't feel you can, I'll—"

"No, you can trust me," Lucy said. "I won't say a word to anyone. I swear."

"But if something was to happen to me... then..." He took a sip of his coffee, his hands now steadier. "Then you can tell Mr. Valentin. Right away. Understood?"

"Yes, sir. I understand."

He bent his head and whispered, "This was I think seven years ago..."

*So here it is another morning and still no police pounding on the door. Still not a hint that they know. Passing within a few feet of the detective St. Cyr three times without being spotted. But every time, it was crowded and noisy. What about on a silent street?*

*The lawyer was easy, starting with the prick of the needle. That such a small, plain thing can do such damage. Just the way some people can. Oh, the way the fear came up on his face as the poor fool began to sense what was happening to him. On the balcony and up against the railing he was like just another sloppy drunk, so the rope part was easy. He grabbed the railing and there was the one second when his eyes cleared and he understood. Remembered. What, who, and why. Then he went over. Number three, gone. Only two more to go. And then it will end.*

Lulu White cursed her foolish notion that Friday coming and going without another murder had been a good sign. A killer so clever as to evade the detectives of the New Orleans Police Department *and* Valentin St. Cyr would have sly tricks to play, like throwing pursuers by creating two days of carnage followed by one of calm. And then strike again while everyone was taking a breath.

There was something especially horrid about the murder of the one-time city attorney Bartlett Barry. Victims died at the end of knife blades all the time, from gunshots and strangulations and poisonings. But to be hanged from a French Quarter balcony on a busy Friday night? It was spectacular in a hideous way. Now she'd see if there would be an outcry, as there always was whenever Storyville was the scene of the crime. See if there were now demands that the Vieux Carré be burned to the ground.

She calmed herself. At least she wasn't Tom Anderson. What that old man must be thinking! He had known Barry as the city hall official responsible for the red-light district. Just as he had known Herbert Waltham and Father O'Brien from their places in the scarlet web. And yet he was still hiding whatever truth he knew from Valentin St. Cyr, the one person who might be able to help him.

During his years as a street detective, Valentin had been a regular at the newspaper morgue, combining the research for his cases with visits with Joe Kimball, who had lurked among the dusty piles of newsprint with his bottles and his cigars. But Joe was dead, murdered in fact, because he had discovered something that pointed to the guilty party in one of those cases. He had managed to leave a message in his dying seconds and Valentin never got over his admiration for the heroics or his guilt over his part in the poor, sweet man's death.

He knew the regular supervisor slightly, but that fellow didn't work weekends and so he walked into the musty basement to find a young man half-asleep at the desk that had once been Joe's. The clerk showed no interest in him and didn't offer to help, preferring to ignore him while he chortled over the morning comics.

Valentin crossed to the cabinet that held the file cards, wondering if Rebecca Marcus had been there ahead of him or had yet to figure out such an essential habit. He detected no woman's scent as he pulled the sheet of paper from his pocket and began with the first of the nine names who, as far as he knew, were still alive—and who were not Tom Anderson.

Rebecca walked into the newsroom four floors up to see Reynard Vernel beckoning her from Rolf Kassel's office doorway.

"You're a hard person to find sometimes," the senior editor said in a tone of voice she'd never heard from him before. Reynard kept his arms crossed and his eyes on the floor.

"Have you heard anything more from your friend?" Kassel said.

"I haven't, why?" She sensed something in the hard silence and turned to Vernel. "Was there another one?"

Reynard said, "Yes. This victim was in the photograph, too."

"And we had nobody on it." Kassel bit off the words, stinging her. "Nobody! How many reporters do you think the *Sun* and the other papers have out there right now?"

Rebecca felt a faint wave of nausea come over her and wished to disappear in a puff of smoke. She pushed past that. This was no time to quail. She forced herself to move, to dig into her bag for her pen and pad, then get out the words, "What happened?"

In a few terse sentences, Vernel explained the details of the demise of Bartlett Barry. Rebecca was stunned. A man hanged from a balcony in the French Quarter? How could it be? She had to choke back a crazed laugh at the sheer horrible absurdity of it.

"On a Friday night," Kassel said, as if to punctuate her thoughts. He roused himself, rising to his feet and carrying a section of newsprint to the corkboard behind his desk and punching two thumb tacks into it so hard that the frame shook. Rebecca recognized the photograph.

The editor produced his red pen and drew lines through three of the faces. "Oh, look," he said, his voice dripping as he snapped his eyes over his thick shoulder. "Only ten more to go."

Rebecca waited for Kassel to sit again before turning to Vernel. "What about the victim?"

"He used to be a city attorney," Reynard said. "He handled criminal cases of different kinds. For maybe ten years."

"In the French Quarter and Storyville," Kassel added.

"Yes. Then he went into private practice. Set up shop on St. Philip Street. I don't recall much about his family. I think he was a bachelor." He glanced at the senior editor, who frowned, still piqued.

Rebecca dropped the pen and pad back into her bag. "I'll talk to McKinney and see what I can find out. If I'm still on the story, I mean."

She looked between them, surmising that they couldn't let her go after she had come up with the killer's missives—and in spite of their obvious suspicions that she had planted them herself. Still, for a terrible few seconds, neither man spoke.

Then Kassel hunched forward and barked, "Go!"

Vernel jerked his head. She went.

# SEVENTEEN

Valentin caught up with James McKinney at Parish Precinct. They met in a lobby that was buzzing for a Saturday morning. The lieutenant approached him, holding the cigar box in one hand, and muttered, "With me," and headed for the elevator. A dozen pairs of eyes followed them.

On the way up, Valentin recounted the hour he had spent in the newspaper morgue, sifting through cards that mentioned the men in the photograph. He skipped Anderson out of hand and there wasn't time for a detailed search, but he found no obvious connections to Storyville. If time allowed, he'd carry the names to Lulu White and Mr. Tom and see what they could tell him.

The elevator doors opened. "So nothing there," McKinney said. "All right. It had to be done. And better you than me."

Just before they stepped into Chief Leroux's office, Valentin glanced down the hallway and saw Captain Warren standing in his doorway and watching them with an expression he couldn't read.

Chief Leroux was behind his desk, tie-less, wearing cotton trousers, an everyday shirt, and a thin spring jacket.

"I don't want to be here," he said by way of greeting. "But there's a murderer out there taking down one victim after another, one *important* victim after another, and it appears that my detectives can't do a thing about it. Four days. Three bodies. Christ."

He noticed what McKinney was holding. "You bring me a gift?" he said. When the lieutenant described the contents, he made a sound of disgust and said, "What are you going to do with it?"

"Get it to the morgue."

Leroux turned his attention from the box. "You know who woke me up in the middle of the night? Not the Chief. The mayor. His goddamn Honor the *mayor*." He slammed his fist down, then began stalking back and forth, steam all but shooting from his ears. After a moment, he stopped and caught a breath.

"But, oh yes, I did hear from Chief Reynolds," he said. "And you know what he wants? To begin, he wants ten more detectives assigned."

"Oh, no," the lieutenant said.

"That's not all." He jabbed a finger at his visitors. "He wants you and you sent down."

The lieutenant said, "Chief," he said. "We're doing—"

"Stop," Leroux said, holding up a hand. "I know it's not the two of you. It's happening too fast. I understand. And that's what I told him." He dropped into his chair and planted his palms on either side of his desk blotter. "He started to argue. Make threats. I told him if he was going to fire people, he could start with me. And turn the case over to Warren."

"And?" the lieutenant said.

"And there was no further discussion of that point." Now becalmed, he said, "But I will put more officers on just to make him happy." He caught McKinney's frown and said, "They won't be in your way. They'll be assigned to the other men in that fucking photograph."

McKinney and St. Cyr exchanged a glance that the senior office noticed. "I know. It can't hurt, can it?"

Valentin said, "Could we make it nine, Chief? I'll get someone on Mr. Tom."

Leroux shrugged, then said, "I'd like to hear your thoughts on this whole mess, sir."

Valentin said, "It's been rushed. There's going to be a mistake. We can set a trap for him. Or her."

Leroux stopped to stare. "What do you mean 'her'?"

"A woman could have done the killings." He didn't see any point in adding that his wife and Rebecca Marcus had both voiced the same notion.

The chief said, "Do you agree, Lieutenant?"

"I'm still seeing a man. But, yes, it could be either."

"Oh, wonderful. More possible suspects." Leroux swiveled to stare out the window. "What kind of trap?" When neither detective answered, he said, "That's what I thought." He turned his chair back around. "All right. Do you still have my home telephone number, Lieutenant?"

"I do, yes, sir," McKinney said.

"I want a report at the end of the day. Even if there's nothing. Talk to me. Understood?"

"Yes, sir," McKinney said.

The Chief of Detectives waved a doleful hand, shooing them out.

Things didn't get any easier when they reached the lobby. Rebecca Marcus was waiting by the front desk and when they stepped off the elevator, she lunged and blurted, "Another murder and I'm about to lose my job."

"You aren't the only one," the lieutenant said.

She stopped, confused. "What?"

"Never mind," McKinney said. "I'll tell you what we know, all right? But outside." He ushered her across the marble floor and Valentin opened the door for her.

They descended the stone steps and the lieutenant moved her off to the side.

"Any more letters?" Valentin said.

"No. But of course I'll inform you when the next one arrives."

They waited while she gathered her writing materials, and then McKinney told her about the discovery of the attorney's body, their inspection of the office, and the staging of the murder on the balcony. "You staged the murder? Like in a play?" She came up with a quizzical smile. "That's a good story right there."

"Please, not now," McKinney said. "Maybe later. We just wanted to see if it was possible. We do that at times."

"And it was," Valentin said.

Now she turned her dark eyes his way. "How did the two of you manage that?"

"We had another party's assistance," he said.

Her gaze settled. "Would that have been Miss Justine?" She hiked an eyebrow. "Wait. Was it to establish if a woman could have committed the murder?"

McKinney spoke up. "We're keeping our minds open."

Rebecca pondered, then poised her pen again. "Do you have anything more that connects the three victims?" she said, looking between them.

"Nothing we could describe as solid," the lieutenant admitted. "But it's a line we're pursuing. I will keep you informed."

She closed her notebook and said, "Cooperation is pleasant, isn't it?" If her smile wasn't sincere, she made a good show of it. "Thank you both," she said. "I expect we'll speak again soon." She walked off.

The lieutenant watched her go. "I hope we're not fucking this deal," he said. "Or getting kicked off the force would be the least of my troubles."

Valentin caught something moving on the edge of his vision and turned to see Captain Warren again, now standing just outside the street doors and peering in their direction. He nudged the lieutenant, who turned in kind.

"Now what?" McKinney murmured.

"I saw him upstairs when we got to Leroux's office," Valentin told him.

McKinney said, "Wait here a minute."

Valentin watched as the two policemen moved a few paces down the banquette and then stopped. The lieutenant crossed his arms and bent his head to listen as Warren spoke with a jerky animation that was peculiar for such a straight-backed fellow. The exchange took less than a minute and the captain climbed the steps to the door and disappeared inside. McKinney motioned and he and Valentin walked off in the direction of Toulouse Street.

"What was that about?"

"I was asked not to tell you. Or anybody."

"So?"

"So I'll tell you."

As they strolled on, he explained that Captain Warren had said that it was important—no, *urgent*—that he be kept up on the progress of the case. In fact, he asked that every new detail be shared with him as soon as it was gathered.

Valentin said, "I thought he didn't want to know anything."

"So did I." They stopped at the corner and McKinney turned to glance back at the precinct. "He's quite bothered."

"About being kept out of it?"

"About something else," the lieutenant said. "Just what I need. Him in our business, too." He closed his eyes, already weary. "I told him I'm going to have an officer assigned to him. As a precaution. He put on a stiff spine, but I could tell he liked that." He opened the left eye and fixed it on Valentin. "It's not too early for a shot of whiskey, is it?"

"Not in New Orleans. Anyway, there's someone I need to talk to."

*The precinct has a place for the police and a place for the jail. He is among those coppers who walk in and out every day and so is easy to trail. He's just there. Like he was that morning when he appeared out of nowhere. Started the whole thing. Him. He knows all about that fat business fellow. The priest. Now the one on St. Philip Street. He was supposed to be on the right side. He is the law. So there must be a special punishment for him.*

As soon as they stepped into the grocery, the buzz of voices, some calling out orders, more going on about a third murder in four days faded and then ceased. Enough of the customers recognized Valentin St. Cyr and others knew Lieutenant McKinney from some place or other. In the muttering silence, Frank raised his head from behind the counter. Valentin pointed to the saloon. The made their way out and the chatter resumed.

Valentin sent McKinney to a table, then stepped behind the bar to select a bottle of rye and three short glasses, pouring two of them half full. They sat sipping and gazing through the gaps in the front curtains at a sleepy Marais Street.

"What the hell are we going to do?" the lieutenant after some long minutes had passed.

"I don't know." Valentin let the liquor clear his thoughts. "We can try a lay-out."

"I'm for that," McKinney said. It was a technique they'd both used before to clarify the pieces of an investigation.

Valentin settled back. "Three victims killed by the same party. They all knew each other. At least from their civic activities."

"And they all had business in Storyville."

Valentin said, "That's right." He took another sip. "The other serial cases I know of, the killer takes one victim, then waits a while, then the next, and like that. But three in four days? That doesn't happen." He sipped his whiskey. "And there's something else. Each murder was committed in a different way. The others find something that works and repeat it. Until they get caught."

"Or stop. Or take their crimes elsewhere."

"Yes," Valentin said. He knew neither of them wanted to think about these prospects. "Only Waltham had body parts removed."

The images from Eclipse Alley returned. Had it really been only five days? He drained his glass. When the lieutenant did the same, he refilled them.

"So it begins with that victim and with a sexual angle," McKinney said.

"And in Storyville, of all places," Valentin said. McKinney snickered over the comment. "That's why I think it all goes back to him. He's the key. We just don't know why."

"Yet."

"Yes. Yet."

Valentin went on. "Unless it's a trick, our killer is contacting the newspaper. One newspaper. The one with the female reporter."

"Does that point to a woman?"

"It doesn't point away. And I think our someone was a victim. Or feels that way."

"And most victims are females."

They stopped there, watching the street and musing on the case until Frank appeared from the grocery. "So busy this morning. And everybody talking..." He glanced at the policeman, then at his godson, and delivered a cool smile. "*State nascondendo?*" he said.

Valentin spent a few seconds working through the vocabulary, then laughed. "Are we hiding? *Non lo so. I don't know.* James? Are we?"

"We are, indeed." McKinney raised his glass. "I'd stay here all day, if we could."

Frank poured a glass for himself and took the third chair. "Valentino," he said. "That cylinder? I found a machine. Customer of mine, Signore Pizzelli, he still owns one. To listen to his old opera rolls. He says it works fine."

Valentin explained the Bolden recording to McKinney. "That's some story," he said.

"It is, isn't it?" Valentin said. "And it—" He fell silent, gazing into space.

"It, what?" Frank said.

Valentin said, "You know I don't believe much in coincidence."

"You've mentioned it a few times, yes." The lieutenant was smiling; it had been more like dozens. "What coincidence are you talking about?"

"I haven't heard anything about Bolden for years, now," Valentin said. "There's been no news. Nothing. And then just as this case is beginning, out of nowhere, someone shows up with the only recording he ever made."

McKinney shrugged. "So?"

"I don't know," Valentin said. He pondered a few seconds, then asked Frank what would happen next.

"I'll go collect the machine once things slow down. This afternoon. You can come by later and play it." He produced a grim smile. "If you're not busy with your *pazzo* killer, I mean."

"If I'm not coming, I'll let you know," Valentin said.

"You two ate breakfast today?" Frank said and stood up.

Valentin knew there was no point in answering. The saloonkeeper was already moving toward the kitchen. Valentin pushed his glass aside. "So now we eat something," he told the lieutenant. "*Then* we go catch this *pazzo* killer."

On hearing the news of the lawyer's murder, Rebecca Marcus made an instant decision to swear off pleasures of the flesh until the story ended. There was too much coming too fast and she could not afford to be distracted by carnal games.

It was in this chastened mood that she marched back into the newsroom and crossed directly to Reynard Vernel's desk. He noticed her heading his way and sat back in his chair. "What do we have?"

"I talked to McKinney and St. Cyr and there's nothing new. So they say."

"What else?"

"I went to St. Philip Street," she said, explaining that Barry's neighbors said that he was a professional who did not bother anyone and had no obvious vices. None of his clients would raise eyebrows. He did not engage in criminal law, devoting his attention to contracts and other business matters.

"Was Herbert Waltham one of his clients?"

"I called the house and spoke to the son," she said. "He was not."

"Then so far that yellow fever committee is the only thing they have in common."

"So far."

"There has to be something else," the editor said.

Rebecca said, "I'm working on it."

Reynard nodded. "Are you going to the funeral?"

"I am," she said, doing her best to hide the fact that she expected to hate every somber minute. But she had to attend, just in case she stumbled on something. That, and the likelihood that she'd encounter Mr. St. Cyr, with or without his pretty wife.

"We still don't know much, do we?" Reynard said.

"No, we don't." She placed her bag on his desk. "Will you join me for a cup of something?" she said.

She led him to the lobby and down the staircase one floor, and to the small employee lunchroom. A Negro woman named Bee, who had been behind the counter since the Hayes presidency, was serving coffee, tea, and pastries. Reynard ordered two coffees with cream and sugar and carried them to the table where Rebecca was waiting.

He took a sip from his cup. "I checked on your desk and down at the lobby and in the mailroom. No new letter." He hiked an eyebrow. "Unless you're hiding it."

"I'm not." She was brooding. "Is that the only reason I'm still on the story, Reynard?"

He didn't answer her question directly, instead saying, "Rolf has not changed his mind. But if there's not a third note in the next twenty-four hours, you'll have to come up with a new piece of the story."

She sat back, fuming. "I could if I had some help. Those bastards Goings and Miller won't lift a finger. They treat me like dirt. And I know Rolf is watching everything I do." She tapped her fingernails on the table. "Tell me something, Reynard. Are McKinney and St. Cyr just using me?"

He cocked his head and treated her to an unsure smile. "Are they... I don't know. Do you think they are?"

"At least some."

"I don't know McKinney all that well," he said, "I can tell you that Mr. Valentin will help you if he thinks you can help the case."

She nodded in a pensive way, as if it was the answer she had expected, and said, "Then I'll just have to do that, won't I?"

Lulu White had been prepared for another visit from Valentin. This time, he brought James McKinney, the police detective who was in charge of the investigation. They arrived on her doorstep at ten o'clock, both appearing quite relaxed for the early hour.

She ushered them into the sitting room and onto the plush divan and disappeared for a few moments. In the kitchen, she instructed the maid to fetch fresh coffee. She also told her that while it was brewing she was to go upstairs and inform any gentlemen who were lingering that there was a police officer and a private detective on the premises and that they could avail themselves of the back staircase.

She returned to her visitors. "So," she said, settling into her armchair with a pronounced sigh. "Mr. Barry," she said. "That's what you're here about?"

Valentin said, "Him and the other two."

"What a horrible way to die. And in sight of all those people."

Valentin guessed that she was as appalled by the indignity as she was the gruesome violence of the attorney's death. What could be worse for a woman who imagined that one day hers would be the most dramatic passing and grandest funeral in New Orleans?

"How well did you know him?" he said.

"Oh, I met him a number of times," the madam said. "He prosecuted cases in here for years. I remember he was not a difficult man. He would come by to talk to me about matters that concerned the District." Valentin could hear the pride in her voice when she added, "There were things that he chose to bring to me instead of Mr. Tom."

The coffee arrived. As the maid served them, Valentin heard the creak of the back stairs. Once the girl left the room, Miss Lulu said, "Of course, he had to pay heed to the interests of the property owners. He understood how things work. He did not cause problems for anyone. Except for the miscreants, of course. He spent time at the Café, rubbing elbows with that crowd."

"A requirement of the job," Valentin said.

"Correct," she said.

McKinney spoke up for the first time. "Do you know anything personal about him, ma'am?"

Miss Lulu said, "I recall that he was a regular guest at Ruby Stein's mansion," Miss Lulu said. "You remember, Valentin? It was back on Franklin."

"I do, yes." Valentin said. When the madam didn't continue, he said, "Regarding Herbert Waltham. Before he died, he had been trying to find a girl who had been a trick baby."

"Oh?" She looked at him. "Was he the father?"

"We don't know."

"Well we have too many of those to count."

Valentin recognized the way her gaze skittered away. He saw that the lieutenant had caught it, too, and said, "Was there something else?"

The madam shifted her chair. "I seem to recall that he spent time at Miss Ruby's as well."

Both detectives sat back. After a moment, the lieutenant said, "Where is she now?"

"Ruby?" Miss Lulu said. "She's been gone for five years, at least."

"Gone where?"

"She left the city. That's all I know."

"Who took over the house?"

"It was closed up for about a year. I believe Kate Markley got it. I believe she's still there."

Valentin said, "Do you know who owned the property?" Now the madam tensed, something he had rarely seen in her. "Miss Lulu? Was it by chance St. Rocco's?"

In the next moment, she surrendered. "It was. And still is." She reached for her cup. "And that's all I know about it."

Valentin doubted this, but did not wish to press her. "So two of the victims spent time in the house that was owned by the church that the third victim pastored. Is that right?"

She peered at him over the rim of her cup with a look that told him she did not like his tone. "I told you everything I know of the matter. And I certainly can't solve these crimes for you."

It was all she had to say and Valentin knew that forcing the issue would only drive her to deeper cover.

The tense moment passed. "Have you spoken to Mr. Tom?" she said.

"Yesterday," he said. "We went by the house. Why?"

"Because you'll want to speak to him today."

"Does he know something you don't?"

She smiled a tight smile. "Doesn't he always? Isn't that what he's famous for?"

Valentin said, "Once. Not anymore."

"Well, he's not dead yet," Miss Lulu said.

Neither Valentin nor the lieutenant knew what to make of the comment. But the madam had at least given them a push in a certain direction. They spent a few more uncomfortable minutes talking about nothing before making their escape.

Once outside. McKinney said, "She's a tough one."

"She is," Valentin said. "Always has been."

"Why didn't she just tell us whatever the hell is going on with Tom Anderson?"

"Because she's not ready to yet."

"What are they protecting?"

Valentin didn't have to think about it. "Each other," he said.

————

Lucy had left Mr. Tom at the table and wandered the house in an aimless way, trying to think through what the old man had told her. It was so disturbing that she had been tempted to run to George, no matter what she had promised. But then she realized that he wouldn't know anymore what to do with the information than she did. He'd just tell to keep her mouth shut about it.

She reached the second floor, slipped into the bedroom, crossed to the window, and looked down on Coliseum Street, wondering why people who had everything still did such terrible things.

If only he had found someone else to tell. It wasn't her business and she had no wish to hear about it. But he had told her and she couldn't remove his words from her ears. She sighed, idly watching the figure that appeared on the opposite banquette and moved closer to the house, huddled in a coat that was too warm for the weather. Now the figure stopped and turned. Even from that distance and the shadows, she felt the gaze rise to the window. A shiver ran up her spine. Her heart thumping, she drew back.

She let a few seconds pass before leaning to the glass again. The figure was nowhere in sight and she wondered if it had only been her mixed-up brain. She turned to leave the room, now thinking how much she would like to tell the detective. He would know what to do. But she had promised Mr. Tom. She had promised.

# EIGHTEEN

Miss Tracy had stepped away from her lobby desk to get more change for the customers who appeared in a steady stream to buy papers. An envelope was there when she returned, marked **REBECCA MARCUS** in a precise hand. She studied it for a long ten seconds, then snatched up her telephone and asked the operator for the newsroom. The copyboy must have flown down the steps because he arrived to collect it two moments after she hung up.

Reynard Vernel called to Rebecca and she rose from her desk and crossed to Kassel's office. The senior editor was holding the envelope. He handed it to Reynard, who handed it to the reporter.

"So?" Kassel rumbled. "Let's hear it."

She drew out the page. "'I have seen you but you have not seen me. I see everyone but no one sees me. Until it's too late. No one has even come close. I have not been touched.'" Rebecca paused to glance between the two editors. Then: "'You are my friend. So I will tell you to watch for the next one. Maybe today. Maybe tomorrow. Thank you.'"

"Next what?" Kassel said. "Letter or murder?"

"It doesn't say."

The editor folded his hands before him and hunched his shoulders. Rebecca looked at Reynard with a question stitching her forehead. Was the editor now going to back away from his promise to let her go to press with the notes? The pause went on for so long that she was about to open her mouth when Kassel straightened, unclasped his fingers, and laid his palms flat on his desk.

"All right, Miss Rebecca," he said. "Write your story. We'll run the complete text from all three notes in a separate column." Rebecca stifled a smile as she turned for the door. "Have it in Reynard's hands in an hour," he called after her.

The two editors spoke for a few minutes more after Miss Marcus had scurried back to her desk.

Kassel poured three fingers of rye into his glass and one into a glass that was somewhat less dirty, this without asking. He handed the second to Reynard and sat back in his squeaking chair. She was close enough that they could hear the machine gun staccato of her fingers on the keys of her Underwood.

"What's our move here?" The senior editor tilted his head in the general direction of the racket. "This could get out of hand. We'll need to keep her in line."

"Have you shown her any of those letters yet? Or told her about the telephone calls?"

"I haven't. We don't need a prima donna."

"I know," Vernel said.

"And we're still not sure that any of this is real, correct?"

"That's right. And we might not, until it's all over, one way or another."

"We're going to look worse than fools if it's someone's game. Hers or anyone else's."

Reynard said, "St. Cyr and Lieutenant McKinney were convinced by the first two."

Kassel picked up the third note and held it out. "Can you show them this one?"

"If I can track them down."

"Do that. Because if they see anything amiss, I'm going to hold her story."

"I'll call Mr. Valentin right now." Reynard took the note and folded it carefully. "What if I can't find him?"

"Then I'll take the gamble and run with it. I did promise the young lady." The editor sat back, helped himself to a doleful sip of his whiskey, and said, "Even though that means our heads might end up on the chopping block."

———

Evangeline had been up early, awakened by a telephone call, someone from the newspaper looking for Valentin. When she told the caller that he was sleeping, the fellow said not to bother him and that he'd call back.

After an hour working at the counter, she took her coffee out to the back gallery and settled in one of the wicker chairs. She saw dark clouds in the distance and felt the first wisps of wind that would be bringing a spring storm. The breeze was gentle and she closed her eyes. After some moments, she heard a child's voice from one of the houses down the block and an image rose in the back of her mind, in hazy color and slow motion.

Since the morning she had roused Valentin to answer the call about the first killing, she had been worrying that he was heading for danger. She had sensed it all the more in the way Justine watched him, even as she drifted to anger at him getting involved in the mess. The young woman who crossed his path had added another dose. Though Justine's ire had evaporated the moment she was asked to join the hunt.

Evangeline understood all this from watching the little dramas around the house. And because deep in her mind were lodged distant memories of having a man who was not always wise and children who engaged in small battles. They had been her life once.

Where had they gone? Her husband had died by violence. Her children had faded away, their young lives taken by raging fevers. She had lost them all, there was nothing she could do, and now they were hidden in the shadows of time and injury. She had been a year living under Valentin and Justine's roof and wandering their back garden, draped in their kindnesses and feeling little by little that she had a home as the dark places gave way to light.

But that light was also shining on her fears that they would be in peril, that their marriage would crack as they sometimes did, or that both would come to pass. More immediately, she sensed the threat from the woman who wrote the newspaper stories. Perhaps Justine had good reason for her suspicions.

She was nursing this thought when she heard that young lady in the kitchen. Soon she would be going about her chores, though announcing with every word and movement that she wanted to be with her husband.

Evangeline closed her eyes again, willing both of them safe.

———

Valentin was on his way to the bathroom when the telephone clattered.

James McKinney was on the line. "Waltham's funeral," he said.

"Yes," Valentin said. "What time?"

"One o'clock."

"Who will be there?"

"Every–damn–body," the lieutenant said, "The Mayor. The Chief of Police. A half-dozen commanders. City councilmen. Other business owners. And some–" He caught himself. "Oh, yes. There's word that Tom Anderson is coming."

Valentin was surprised. "When we were there, he could barely make it from one room to the next."

"I guess he's feeling better." He sensed something in the Creole detective's silence and said, "What is it?"

"Nothing, I guess," Valentin said. "And what about Father O'Brien?"

"I spoke to that deacon. He'll be buried on Tuesday. They need the time to make preparations."

"And Mr. Barry?"

"He's at the morgue."

Justine passed the archway and offered him her husband a wan smile. "Do you need me there?" he said.

"I don't," the lieutenant said. "And I don't know if I'll bother with it. Probably not. I can just talk to the coroner. We know what happened." A soft voice drifted in from somewhere behind him. "What about the funeral?"

"We can talk again in a while," Valentin said.


Valentin found the women sitting at the table and he got a sense from the silence that Justine had been recounting their Friday night. Evangeline told him that a fellow from the newspaper had called, but didn't leave a message.

"Reynard Vernel," he said as he crossed to the stove to pour his coffee.

"When is this going to end?" Evangeline asked him

"When?" he said, turning to lean against the counter. "Soon, that's when."

"How can you be sure?"

"Because there are likely only two victims left," Justine said. She looked at her husband. "Isn't that right, Mr. Detective?"

Valentin let out a sigh that was weary for so early in the day. "And that's if we're lucky," he said.

He spent an hour reading the newspaper, making a point to avoid the front page. He saw that the United States Navy had laid siege to the Dominican Republic in order to, as one official put it, "restore order to the chaotic situation on the island."

He shook his head in disgust. If he was still gambling, he'd wager that the invasion would result in an occupation that would be as deep with muck as a Louisiana swamp. Three or four years down the road, it would all collapse, leaving some other official to bemoan the folly that cost lives and millions of dollars to no worthwhile end. The country would meanwhile be ravaged. He was not an old man, but he had seen it before. They never learned.

At the bottom of the story was an announcement of construction beginning on a new Navy base just downriver from New Orleans, with thousands of sailors to be stationed there. So Storyville might have reason to rejoice. But only after a particular felon was brought to ground.

He was glad to be drawn from the news by Justine coming into the kitchen from her bath and smelling so fresh that her scent filled the kitchen. Valentin treated her to what must have been a foolish smile, because she gazed back at him, bemused. He couldn't think of any words to say, so he turned to Evangeline and said, "I do want to keep her from harm."

The older woman studied him for a few seconds before saying, "I think she can take care of herself, don't you?"

Justine laughed and Valentin said, "I do, yes ma'am."

After pouring her coffee, Justine joined them at the table. "So, the funeral."

Valentin didn't respond directly. They had never talked about the details of a case in front of Evangeline. He saw from his wife's eyes that she was thinking the same thing. She gave a minute shrug.

"Yes, this afternoon," he said, and proceeded to share what McKinney had told him about those expected to attend. When he got to Tom Anderson, she was as surprised as he had been. "And what about you?" she said. "And me?"

"I've been thinking about that."

He expected her to be miffed when he explained his plan. But when he finished, she produced a faint smile and said, "'The Sign of Four.'"

He looked across the table. Evangeline was regarding him as she might any man off on a foolish caper.


Three hours later, Lieutenant McKinney parked his Dodge in a restricted space near the corner of City Park and Canal and affixed his police card inside the windshield. Each had been riding in the passenger seat and they both climbed out.

On the ride over, the lieutenant recounted the Creole detective ending their conversation that morning swearing he was going nowhere near Greenwood Cemetery. "What he said was, 'I spend too much time around dead people as it is.'"

"Ain't like him to miss something like this," Each said.

"Well, maybe he changed his mind." McKinney tugged at his collar. "All right," he said. "Let's go."

They joined the swelling stream of mourners moving along the avenue. When they drew close to the grounds, the lieutenant instructed Each to peel off, skirt the crowd, and keep an eye out for anyone suspicious—especially anyone who resembled the person he had chased just the day before. Once again puffed with importance, Each strode away.

The lieutenant had just reached the cement pathway leading to the gravesite when a rough-looking fellow appeared from behind a tree and began wavering his way, one of the sots who loitered at the cemeteries, doing small services for and cadging dimes from visitors. People visiting their late loved ones often felt charitable. He was dressed in a stained shirt and ragged and torn trousers and wore awful-looking shoes of cracked leather. He wore a black Stetson that looked like it had been run over in the street.

Such characters could sense the presence of a policeman in or out of uniform and McKinney was surprised that this one didn't balk, but stepped up to grunt, "Empty your pockets, you bastard!"

The lieutenant glared, then peered closer. "Well, I'll be damned. Look at you."

"Justine helped me," Valentin told him, careful to sway like a drunkard. "We dragged all of it out of the rag bin. What do you think? I might go around like this from now on." He didn't mention that he had gotten the idea for the hat from the mysterious horn player and the rest from the world's best-known fictional detective, as Justine had noted.

McKinney waved a hand in front of his nose. "As long as you're not expecting to make any new friends," he said.

"It's a good way to be ignored," Valentin said.

"Well, I hope you happen on something worth the trouble," the officer said. "And the smell."

"We can't do a lot worse," Valentin muttered before skulking away.

He was at the edge of the moving mass of bodies when he heard a murmur rippling and turned to see a familiar maroon Packard 12 pull to the City Park curb. Tom Anderson's Negro driver Edward jumped down and hurried around to open the passenger side door and reach out a steady hand to the old man. Valentin watched as Mr. Tom made a gradual trek across the low grass with the help of a cane. Other eyes followed their progress and then the person that emerged from the crowd to approach them.

*So of course they're all here. All but the Creole detective. Unless he's lurking somewhere with those hawk eyes. That's probably so. How many times will it take to get close enough to touch one of them? They have to know that the person who made three men dead, the one they're after, is walking among them, as invisible as a ghost.*

———

Rebecca knew about Tom Anderson from the newspapers, from seeing him across the ballroom at a charity event, and the times some society someone had mentioned his name. He had been one of the city's larger personalities for the better part of twenty years. She now beheld a crabbed gentlemen showing his age as he moved along the path aided by a tall Negro, his creeping pace noted by heads turning and whispers.

She knew if she didn't make a move, she'd have to wait half the afternoon, so she weaved her way through the bodies and directly into his path. "Mr. Anderson?" she said. "My name is Rebecca Marcus."

Valentin saw her approach Mr. Tom, who stopped and took a half-step back, so sudden a move that Edward had to grasp his elbow. The reporter spoke for less than a minute, too little time for Valentin to amble close enough to hear. Before he could curse his luck, he saw Each appear behind the King of Storyville, as casual as could be. The kid turned his back to study a copy of the program for the service and Valentin wanted to kiss him.

Their conversation ended, Rebecca offered a slight bow, turned around, and walked away. Anderson watched her go, his face darkening as his hands clutched the head of his cane. Each slipped off before he was spotted and melted into the crowd. Valentin did the same.

It was not what he had been hoping to achieve by showing up in a rough disguise but it was something, and he now made a wide circle to intercept Each back among the white marble biers.

The kid studied the tramp who was heading his way, his lips tight with disgust. Valentin drew closer and the lips twisted into a smile. "God damn," he said. "Mr. Valentin. Ha!"

Valentin wasted no time. "What did you hear?"

"Not much," Each said, "When I came close she was asking him how well he knew that Mr. Waltham. And Mr. Tom, he draws back like she accused him of something. Then she said 'Well, you were friends, correct?' And Mr. Tom said that was true, but not close. And then the lady says, 'Was that from Storyville or someplace else?' And Anderson just stares at her and then he says, 'I knew him, that's all.' He was getting angry. Looked worried. Maybe a little scared."

Valentin mulled all this as he peered through the low branches. A few mourners were drifting away from the main crowd. The service was about to end. "We don't have much time," he said. "Here's what I need you to do."

The sun was getting warmer and he wished he had brought some other clothes. Though he didn't expect to be there long.

He was not. Within a few minutes, he saw Each leading Dolores his way, a gawky, off-kilter figure next to a quiet ballet of curves. As they drew closer, he could tell from Each's dazed smile that he was already smitten. Valentin didn't blame him. She had always been a comely woman.

Now she stopped and stared. "Mr. Valentin?"

"Don't mind this," he said. "A stupid idea."

"They didn't notice me going," she said. "The confusion and all. But they'll be missing me soon." He could see the tension in her eyes. "What is it, sir?"

Valentin said, "Who is she, Dolores?"

The maid hedged for a long moment. "I don't know," she said. "I never did find her."

"But he sent you out looking."

"He did. She was long gone from the house where she had been."

"Ruby Stein's on Franklin?" Valentin said.

"Yes, sir."

"Did anyone remember the child? Or the mother?"

"No one I talked to," Dolores said. "But the house had been closed up for a while. Some other landlady had it."

"What about Miss Ruby?"

"They said she left New Orleans." She glanced over her shoulder, fidgeting. "And that was all I could find out."

"And you told this to Mr. Waltham."

"Yes, sir. He said I should try some more. 'I've got to find out where she is.' That's what he said. But I didn't do any more. I was done with it."

"Those words?"

"Yes, sir, just like that."

Valentin could see by the way she stiffened that she was about done with him, too. She had shared all she knew, in any case. "Thank you for your help," he said. "My associate will see you back. He looked at Each. "If you don't mind."

"Oh, no, sir, not a bit," Each blurted and took Dolores' arm.

Valentin made his shuffling way out of the cemetery, feeling more of a fool with every step. What had he been thinking? The truth was, he hadn't been thinking straight at all. In his frustration at being beaten at every turn, he had dreamed up a silly scheme. In the end, it was Each who had done the real work, eavesdropping on Rebecca Marcus and then fetching Dolores.

In any case, it was too late to do anything more and he walked along, careful to keep his eyes cast downward as mourners moved in a slow parade to his right, heading for the iron gates. It was mostly quiet, laden with the sad drama of a man being laid to rest.

There would have been no such glum scene at an Uptown funeral. Instead, the brass band that had followed the procession in with a mournful dirge would be waiting to do their part in the second line, blasting the departed on his or her happy way into the clouds. There would be much drunkenness and random lechery and by the time the line arrived back in town, it would be a full-blown revel.

When he reached the Ford, he decided that was exactly what he needed—or at least a taste of it—and would drive to the saloon on Marais Street, dirty clothes and all, to hear King Bolden's horn for the first time in ten years. The case could spare him for an hour.

After her strange encounter with Tom Anderson, Rebecca got a few moments with Clarice Waltham, offering condolences. Now it was her turn to be taken aback, because the entire family was on guard against her. The greetings were polite but icy and they all but formed a phalanx around the widow as she left the bier. Rebecca would be getting nothing more from any of them.

As she walked to the gates, she noticed a man moving on slow legs a hundred feet ahead, a tramp who struck her as oddly familiar. But how could that be? She watched as he exited the cemetery and turned left, disappearing. Her thoughts retreated to Anderson and the gambit she had played with him.

It had come from nowhere, a sudden urge that told her to step up and say something and see how he would react. The King of Storyville just might know something.

So she walked into his path, introduced herself, and saw his blue eyes go wide. He stuttered something she didn't catch. She asked some questions that he barely answered. Before he could duck away, she said, "I know more about this than I've reported." It was a pointless statement and she did not expect what happened next. The old man glared at her and in that instant saw that she, in fact knew nothing at all. Even at his age, he was that quick.

She saw a sudden blade of fear in his eyes. He stared at her, unblinking, until she backed away, then turned and walked off. When she got some distance and glanced over her shoulder, she saw a thin young man with an odd face and dressed in a suit that didn't fit standing close enough to have heard most of what was said. With a start, she recognized him as the fellow who had called out Mr. Valentin's name at St. Rocco's, and she turned to watch Anderson and the driver move off.

She had reached City Park Avenue where her jitney was waiting. On the ride back into the city, she thought of nothing but the revelation that Tom Anderson, once the King of Storyville himself, was part of her story.

Valentin used the upstairs bathroom to wash. He dropped the jacket and hat in the trash. When he returned to the saloon, Frank was waiting by a table where the wax cylinder player Frank had borrowed sat under a cloth. A bottle of wine and two glasses were waiting as well. The saloonkeeper allowed a dramatic pause before drawing away the shroud to reveal an Edison machine of polished wood and gleaming brass and steel.

After he attached the copper bell, he poured two glasses full, lifted his for a sip, and said, "You want to go ahead?"

"Let's wait a bit," Valentin said. "I don't want to hear complaints from that fool if it doesn't play." He drank a bit of wine. "I appreciate what you're doing, *zio*."

Frank brushed this aside and asked Valentin about any news on the murders that had the whole city on edge. The detective began explaining, but only out of respect for his godfather. He was saved from repeating more of the vexing details when Mr. Cecil flapped into the saloon, a jittery bird.

"So, did you listen?" he said. "Can I get my money?"

"Not yet," Valentin said. "We wanted you to be here."

"All right, that's fine," Mr. Cecil said and, as before, Valentin was struck by how edgy he sounded. Like he was guilty of something. Frank noticed as well and hiked a puzzled eyebrow. The little man sniffed over the machine. "Just like the one I used to have," he said. He drew the cylinder from the box and placed it on the spindle, then lowered the arm that held the needle and turned the crank.

The first few seconds were rough noise. A voice whispered, "One, two..." and Valentin was just catching a breath when the music began.

That it was far from perfect didn't matter. It was Bolden. Even with the scratches and the wavering speed, there was no mistaking that silver cornet. Valentin looked at Frank, shaking his head in wonder. Had it truly been that raw and wild in the Rampart Street dance halls where he had made his name?

For most of the next nine minutes, Valentin kept his head bent and eyes closed. When it was over and Mr. Cecil stopped cranking and lifted the armature, he looked up and said, "We agreed on a hundred dollars."

Mr. Cecil nodded like a pecking sparrow and showed his yellow teeth. Frank produced five twenty-dollar gold pieces and placed them on the table. Mr. Cecil began to reach for them when Valentin said, "Wait." The little man's hand stopped in midair.

"Why did you come here?"

Mr. Cecil said, "'Cause you said you wanted—"

"I don't mean today," Valentin said. "Why did you come last Saturday night to tell who told you to come here and tell Mr. Frank about the cylinder?"

Mr. Cecil's smile dimmed and his eyes flicked. "Don't know what you mean..."

"Yes, you do. Did someone send you?"

The little man stood frozen in place as his eyes shot from the detective to the saloonkeeper.

He surprised them with his speed. In a sudden instant, he took a step back, whirled around, and bolted into the hallway, through the grocery, and onto the banquette. After a startled second, Valentin and Frank gave chase, but the street was Saturday-afternoon busy, and Mr. Cecil had vanished.

"*Gesu!*" Frank said. "*Cos'è successo?*"

Valentin made a last survey of the street. "I wish I knew," he said.

He was finally able to shed the filthy shirt and trousers when he got home. "I say we build a fire," Justine said and carried the clothes out the back door. She returned to the stove where she had been starting on dinner and he sat at the table with Evangeline and recounted his afternoon, from the collision between Rebecca Marcus and Mr. Tom, Each's spying, his brief questioning of Dolores, and then the weird interlude at Mangetta's.

When he finished, Justine stood quietly for a while. Evangeline hadn't said a word, holding her gaze steady.

"You think he was sent?" Justine said. "But why?"

"I have no idea," he said. He turned to look out at the afternoon sky.

"Things often connect, don't they?" Evangeline said as she returned to her knitting.

After a moment, Justine said, "Feels like a long day already."

"It does," Valentin said, "I'll call James and tell him about all this. And then, just for tonight, we can put it aside."

"Unless...," Justine said.

"Yes," Valentin said. "Unless."

# Nineteen

It was Captain A.G. Warren's habit to eat his supper at the Baronne Diner—named for its location—every Saturday evening. In fact, he dined there every day of the week save on the Lord's Day and ordered one of two selections from the menu—a pork chop or chicken breast with mashed potatoes, and a steamed vegetable—except on Friday when, like all good Catholics, he had fish.

The captain also always sat at the same table in the booth farthest from the front door and at the last of the windows that looked out onto the banquette, held for him as a special courtesy to a regular customer.

On this Saturday, his routine had been changed by the street copper who was one of those assigned to accompany him day and night until further notice. This, because his face had been one of thirteen in a newspaper photograph. Though he made a show of protesting the order, he was hugely relieved. He had in fact been in a state of fright since the body of Father O'Brien had been found. His jangled nerves and a shred of memory told him he had reason to be.

The officer, a burly old-timer named Wilson, one of those patrolmen who stopped at two stripes with no desire to go further, took the first stool to the right of the cash register so that he could intercept any citizen who appeared to be homicidal. Whatever that meant. As he waited for his pie and coffee, the corporal considered that he couldn't do much about it if someone decided to blast the captain through the window. He thought the duty a waste of time and other officers around the precinct agreed that it was unlikely that a nobody like Warren would rate any killer's list.

The captain had taken his place and the waitress, whose name was Maggie but whom he had never called anything but "Miss," greeted him with his cup of Lipton tea. The cook had spotted him and began preparing his meal. There was no need for a page from the server's pad, as the captain was not expected to and had never offered to pay. Though he always left a single nickel by his plate for his server.

A copy of the *Times-Picayune* had been left by an earlier diner and he gave the front page only a cursory glance. He had already seen the story about the ghastly murder of the former city attorney and didn't need his appetite ruined any further. Instead, he turned his attention to the plate that Maggie slid before him. As he ate, he glanced out the window at the darkening street, barely noticing when a hunched figure moved past and dropped something in the trash can.

Ten seconds later, a fearful racket and a burst of multicolored blades of light erupted from the can. The diners at the counter and in the other booths turned to the windows and some stood up. Corporal Wilson hoisted himself off his stool but observed nothing but the aftermath of some foolishness. The noise and sparks went wild for another half-minute and then fizzled into sudden silence. The customers returned to their seats, chattering and laughing.

Presently, Maggie made her way along the booths, refilling coffee cups. When she arrived at the last one, she saw the captain wearing an odd expression, his eyes wide open and mouth partially-so, with what appeared to be a dribble of gravy at the corner of his mouth.

"Captain?" she said and waited. "Captain Warren?" Another few seconds went by and she said, "Oh, no."

Valentin, Justine, and Evangeline were in the living room, sipping glasses of brandy. They were taking turns with stories and Justine was relating one about her and her two brothers and two sisters chasing a boar through the bayou thickets while their drunken father staggered far behind.

"We didn't think about whether it was male or female," she said. "We just wanted the meat. So we ran it into this tangle and then we found it. It was a sow, with little ones, and she came charging back at us with these piglets right after her. She was grunting like..." She made a guttural *ruh-ruh-ruh* sound. "...and the little ones were squealing and running all over the place." She stopped to laugh, her eyes merry. "We all went up into trees like we were monkeys. And stayed there until they went away." She shook her head at the memory. She left out the part where their father raged at them and beat her oldest brother over losing a winter's worth of food.

In the silence that followed, Evangeline raised her eyes to find the husband and wife watching her in expectation.

"Well, let me see now." She lowered her needlework to her lap. "This keeps coming back to me."

Closing her eyes, she recalled a morning in May and sunlight that broke through the leaves of the trees and between the buildings and cast swaths of gold on the dirt path that would soon be a banquette of wooden slats. At that time it was hard sand but could have been strewn with rocks or been a field of wheat, because she had no thought, save that her child walked happily ahead of her, straining at her reach, and she knew it wouldn't be long before she couldn't hold him back anymore. He was his father's son.

A bird—a bluebird, she recalled—lit on a branch a few feet ahead of them and he laughed at the sweet music and pointed, his face aglow with wonder as the moment stopped for mother and child.

"That's all," she said, opening her eyes once more. Valentine and Justine waited to see if she would go on, but instead she kept her eyes on him. She was still waiting for him to say something when the telephone clattered.

He broke her gaze, said, "I'll get that," and made a quick move to the foyer.

Ten seconds later, the women heard him say, "What? My God," and then "All right. On the way."

He stepped back into the room and hesitated only a second before addressing Justine. "You'll need a wrap," he said.

They emerged from the curious crowd to find the lieutenant standing outside the diner. He treated them to a death's head smile when they emerged from the curious crowd. Though his mouth was tight, his eyes were almost merry. "This one sure has some crazy skills," he said and tilted his head for them to follow him inside. "And some fucking gall, too."

Except for a dozen policemen in uniform and plainclothes, the restaurant was empty. The officers moved aside to allow the lieutenant and the Creole detective and his wife pass by. In the last booth, they found Captain Warren sitting up very straight and very dead.

McKinney lowered his voice. "So listen to this. He sits down to eat. The copper they assigned to guard him is parked down there." He waved a hand in the direction of Corporal Wilson, who stood dazed, like he still didn't understand what had happened. "Outside, someone throws a string of firecrackers into the trash can and a couple those..." He configured a small canister with the fingers of one hand. "Uh..."

"Sixteens?" Valentin said.

"Yes. A couple of those in there. You know they're loud as hell. So they all go off and make this huge racket. The customers and the folks who work here all go to the windows. The corporal got up, but it just looked like some kind of prank. Street rats. Anyway, it's thirty seconds of light and noise until the firecrackers burn out. Captain sits back down to enjoy his dinner. Within another minute, he's dead. Only thing I can figure is poison."

"How can you be sure it wasn't a heart attack?" Justine said.

"Usually, that would be my first guess, yes," the lieutenant said. "But the girl who brought his dinner said he looked perfectly fine when she left his plate."

Valentin leaned closer. "No blood. So that means he wasn't stabbed or shot. Wasn't time for someone to get close and strangle him." He stepped back. "So while it's all noisy and the lights are flashing and the customers are scrambling for a look, our friend slips inside, gets through the crowd, passes by the booth, and drops something in the..." He looked over the plate. "...the potatoes. And then out the door while everyone is going back to their seats." He shook his head in wonder and said, "Brilliant."

Justine stared at the dead man's graying face. "What kind of poison?"

"Strychnine or cyanide, most likely," Valentin said. "Anyone can buy it. It works fast." He shrugged and said, "So there's all that..."

"And he's in the photograph," the lieutenant said.

The diners who had been shooed outside had been joined by more onlookers, swelling the crowd, and he reached over the table to pull down the window shade. Valentin heard him say, "Oh, Jesus," and turned to see Chief Leroux coming through the door and heading their way, shooting a warning from his eyes.

Chief of Police Reynolds was right behind him with two majors following along. The coppers gathered inside ceased their chattering. A few came to attention. The two senior officers passed by and stopped to stare at the body in the booth.

"Christ in heaven," Reynolds said.

"He was poisoned, Chief," McKinney said.

Reynolds turned his way. "What?" It came out more like a bark. "How the hell did that happen? Is the food that bad here?"

It wasn't intended as a joke, but Valentin, Justine, and McKinney were at the edge of their nerves and stifled laughs while the chief glared. Valentin bit his lip and nudged the lieutenant, who went ahead and repeated his scenario of the murder.

Reynolds listened, blinking hard. When the junior officer finished, he said, "What about his escort? Where was he?"

"Wilson, sir. It would have been pure luck for him to spot someone in all the confusion."

Reynolds said, "So is it the same one?"

"Probably," the lieutenant said. "Yes, sir."

The chief uttered another curse, then turned to Leroux. "What about him?" He waved a vague hand toward the dead man. "Anything that would make him a murder victim? I mean other than being in that damned photograph with those others? Money problems? Women? Some felon getting revenge?"

"Not him," Leroux said, "No, sir. He was mostly—"

"A bookkeeper," the chief cut in.

"More or less."

Reynolds seemed to notice Valentin for the first time. His attention shifted to Justine. "And who is this?" Though the question was polite, his eyes were sharp.

"My wife," Valentin said. "Justine."

"I see," Reynolds said. Then, "Ma'am."

Valentin sensed that he was waiting for something more and said, "She assists me on some of my cases."

"I remember," the chief said. "That fellow last year. Went by..."

"Gregory," Valentin said.

Reynolds treated Justine to a last blank glance before turning back to his officers. "Do you need to assign more detectives?" he asked Leroux, who turned to McKinney.

"Lieutenant?"

"I don't see where that would do any good, Chief."

"Oh, no?" the chief said, his face going red and his tone brittle. "What would do good, then? Because this is the fourth innocent citizen murdered in five days. And by the same person. I guarantee there's a package on his desk back at the precinct. People around the city are panicking, gentlemen. We're getting beaten on this one."

None of the officers dared break the silence that followed, so Valentin spoke up. "But we're not going to lose," he said.

Reynolds stared at the Creole detective. Leroux and McKinney both had to sense to stay quiet. "How so?"

A second passed and Valentin said, "There's going to be another attempt in the next forty-eight hours. The last one. And when it happens, we'll be waiting."

He was aware of the heads of the lieutenant and the Chief of Detectives swinging around and Justine's eyes going wide.

"I'm going to count on that, sir," Chief Reynolds said. He glared at the body in the booth for another moment, then turned around and stalked away.

Valentin faced his wife and the two police officers and said, "I have no idea."

McKinney returned from escorting the brass outside to find Justine and Valentin seated on stools. He had collected a tablecloth along the way and draped it over Captain Warren in an unceremonious manner.

He turned to regard Valentin with a befuddled expression. "We're going to be waiting, are we?" he said. "So I guess we need to do something."

Valentin was regarding the draped body with his head resting on the palm that rested on the counter. "What did he do?" he asked at last.

"What did he *do*?" McKinney said. "He spent a career showing up and used his time finding ways not to do anything."

"But he knew something."

"We know he was worried," the lieutenant said.

Valentin explained to Justine about seeing the captain that very morning inside Parish Precinct and then again outside, where he showed a sudden interest in every detail of their investigation.

Justine said, "And this from someone who didn't want to know."

"Correct," McKinney said.

Valentin said, "So, for you?"

The lieutenant said, "I'll go back to the precinct and secure the package from his desk."

"That would be number three," Justine said. "So there's one left."

The two detectives winced at the reminder of which part would be the last.

After a pensive few moments, Justine said, "Men."

The detectives paused at the curious comment. "You always say the little things matter," she went on. "Things that might not appear to at first."

The lieutenant came up with a crooked smile. "He does say that. I've heard it myself."

"Well, I think it matters that the first victim had the parts he could use on a woman removed."

"Yes, we talked about that," Valentin said.

"And so...?"

"They're here for the body," the lieutenant announced.

Valentin and Justine stood up and moved out of the way. She said, "What? Did I speak out of turn?"

"No, not at all. I'm thinking about what you said. And I'm wondering why I didn't fix on it more."

She said, "You know it makes it even more likely that it's a woman."

"Yes, it does," he said.

McKinney returned. "They're carrying him to the morgue."

Valentin said, "I can meet you there tomorrow. Or we can."

"There's no need for that," the lieutenant said.

Justine looked relieved. "Then what do we do?" she said

Valentin stood up and offered a hand to his wife. "We go home, so we can start again in the morning."

*That was some performance, all right. It could not have gone better. It's easy to get lost when there's so much excitement. No one sees anything. Like the magician. Look at my left hand while the right one is doing the trick. And now it's not just some coppers and the red-haired police detective and Mr. St. Cyr and his pretty wife. This time it's the police chief himself marching in and marching back out.*

*One more to go. And the grandest prize of them all.*

# TWENTY

Murders or no murders—and mostly because of them—Justine was not about to miss mass, and if there had been any hesitation on her part, Evangeline cured it by rapping on their bedroom door. Outside, a gray morning was beginning and from the look of the clouds, they'd be carrying umbrellas.

Valentin felt guilty lying about when she had stayed up with him the night before, so he rolled out of bed and shuffled to the kitchen to start the coffee. He knew the women wouldn't eat anything but communion wafers until they got back. As he ground the beans, releasing their special perfume, he thought about the two of them bending their knees as the incense wafted and the voices chanted, the one part of the service that might bring him some peace at the breaking of this day.

But there would be no such respite. Even if he wanted to go, the case was calling him, crowding him, in fact. If there was still a case at all. Indeed, their murderer might have decided to trick them again and finish the work. The last assault could already be done, the body yet to be found, and the perpetrator of now five gruesome killings on a train smoking out of Union Station. If this happened, he and James McKinney would both be finished in New Orleans, blamed and shamed and compelled to find livelihoods elsewhere. Because he had promised the Chief of Police that they would end it in forty-eight hours. As early as it was, the thought sent him into the cabinet for the brandy bottle.

After he poured the coffee and liquor and drank off half his cup, he stepped out on the gallery to collect the Sunday *Times-Picayune*. Rebecca

Marcus's story was planted prominently in the first column on the left above the fold.

### THIS TIMES-PICAYUNE REPORTER
### RECEIVES MISSIVES
### FROM PURPORTED MURDERER
by
### REBECCA MARCUS

Over the past four days, this reporter has received three messages from a person claiming to be the murderer of Herbert Waltham, Father John O'Brien, and former city attorney Bartlett Barry.

The Time-Picayune's editors believe that the notes, which were left at the front desk of the newspaper's offices on Tulane Avenue, are genuine.

The three notes are printed in their entirety on this morning's front page.

He looked at the last column on the page and the three missives that appeared so ordinary to the point of making it hard to believe that the killer of at least four men had penned them.

Ten minutes later, he stepped back into the kitchen and found the ladies dressed for church and with steaming cups in hand. Justine gestured with hers as he dropped the newspaper on the table. "Miss Marcus must be losing her mind," she said.

Valentin allowed that this was true. For the second—or was it the third time?—a murder had occurred too late for the next edition. The reporter could join Justine, James, and him in trailing behind.

"What are the chances they'll put out some kind of special edition for the captain?" Justine said as she studied the front page.

Valentin said. "Good. Because if they don't, someone else will."

He was correct. Rolf Kassel arrived in the newsroom and woke Reynard Vernel, who had been asleep with his head on his desk. The junior editor groaned, opened one heavy eye, and managed to get to his feet and stumble off to the canteen.

Rebecca was standing at her closet, deciding what to wear for the long Sunday ahead, when Miss Eloise yelled up the stairwell that there was a call for her. She ran down the steps and grabbed the telephone. It was Kassel. She raced back upstairs, threw the first shirtwaist and skirt she could lay hands on, and hurried out to find a jitney to carry her to Tulane Avenue.

In the meantime, Reynard had made his shaky way to the print shop in the building in back to ready the staff for the single sheet with a new front page that would wrap the few thousand copies of the Sunday edition that had yet to hit the streets. It would not be pretty, but they'd be first and Kassel and the publisher had decided that getting the jump was worth the trouble. The worst they could do was lose a few dollars. The back page advertisers would be happy with the free extra placement.

Rebecca swept into the newsroom and crossed to Reynard's desk. He appeared ragged and she wondered if he was slowly turning into his boss.

She said, "Did you sleep here last night?"

"Not here," he said. "But I didn't make it home, either."

He left it at that and she went off to pound away on her Underwood. He took his red pen to the copy she handed him, and a half-hour later, it was carried to the fastest typesetter in that section, who placed the copy and reworked the front page to fit it. The copies of the new edition were carried out the doors just before noon and were gone within two hours, snatched up by later-rising readers who devoured the story.

### NEW ORLEANS POLICE CAPTAIN
### IS LATEST MURDER VICTIM
#### by
#### REBECCA MARCUS

New Orleans Police Captain A. G. Warren was murdered at the Baronne Diner, located in the 700 block of the street of that same name, last night at approximately 8 o'clock.

Police are reporting that the captain was

the victim of poisoning by some substance that
was placed in his dinner. No one on the staff is
a suspect at this time. No further details are
available as the investigation is ongoing.

The police would neither confirm nor deny
that the crime is the work of the same individual who has claimed three other lives in
the past five days.

Lucy had been jumping every time the telephone rang and the
evening before had been no exception. She had been in the front room,
paging through one of the magazines the last Mrs. Tom Anderson had
left behind. That gentleman and her husband had gone off to bed and she
was trying to keep her mind on the photographs of the handsome men
from the moving pictures when the telephone in the foyer clattered.

She dropped the magazine and fairly leaped from the couch, whispering, "Oh, my Lord," before she knew what the call concerned.

Or maybe she did, because she could have recited the first words
spoken by the voice on the other end of the line from memory. "Tell
Mr. Tom there's been another murder," the caller said. "A police officer
this time. Captain Warren from Parish Precinct. He was poisoned at
the Baronne Diner." She heard a click before she could say a word in
response. She replaced the handset.

It had been only five days since the madness had begun and she was
tired and frightened. Tired from worrying over the old man in her keep
and frightened because of what he had told her at the table. Even if his
was a made-up fear, she had been infected. And on top of all this, the
image of the odd, skulking figure she had glimpsed from the upstairs
window kept returning. It was nothing, she told herself, just some
random someone moving along the banquette. When she described it
to George, he frowned as if she was talking nonsense. But he hadn't seen
what she had.

She gave a start, realizing that she had been standing there for minutes,
lost in her thoughts, and decided she needed some air. She stepped out
onto the front gallery to let the night breeze wash over her. Faint stars
were twinkling through the branches and it was quiet, save for the sound

of an automobile rolling away on the Coliseum Street cobblestones. The tail lights glowing a merry red in the darkness marked it as a newer model. The accessory had been added to machines only in the past two years.

Her nerves calmed by this trivial detail, she was just turning to go back inside when she caught sight of a dark shape on the opposite corner. She peered again. Had it moved? She felt a chill prickle her arms and scalp. She was about to call out to George, then realized he'd never hear. Her hand found the brass knob and she pushed her way inside.

After she closed the door, she pulled back the curtain and watched the street. All was still and whatever she had seen—if she had seen anything at all—was no longer visible. She went for the whiskey bottle, but this time it wasn't for Mr. Tom.

She stood in the pantry, letting the whisky work its magic. Maybe he would be angry at her for not waking him. But it would mean that they'd both lose even more sleep. It was all getting to be too much for her and she thought about talking to George about finding another situation.

Though she knew what he'd say. What could be better than working for the King of Storyville?

Unlike Tom Anderson, Lulu White had learned about Captain Warren on Saturday night, before the officer's body was even cold. Her friend inside the police department didn't have any details to share and so she telephoned the house on Bayou St. John to find out what she didn't know.

"You've heard." Valentin said. He took the box containing the Bolden cylinder from the shelf and turned it over in his hand.

"Well, of course," she said. "So what about it?"

"It's the same one," he said and went on to describe how the fatal poisoning was carried out.

"My God," the madam said. "What's going to happen the next time? Someone getting thrown in front of a train?"

Valentin was about to tell her how there wouldn't be a "next time" when she said, "I remember him."

That caught his attention. "Captain Warren?"

"From years ago," she told him. "He was assigned to a detail here. It was back just before you started working for Mr. Tom. But I never met the man. He was only around about nine months, as I recall. I'd just hear someone mention his name in one place or another. I think he was avoiding me. And just about everyone else down the line."

"Well, that makes sense," Valentin said. "From what I know of him, I mean."

"What had he been doing since?"

"Sitting at a desk."

"Then I don't understand," Miss Lulu said. "The other three had some standing around the city. The kind of men who might make enemies. And he wasn't. So why do you think it's the same person?"

"It happened right on top of the others," Valentin said. "The way he was killed. And now you're telling me he had a connection to Storyville."

She was quiet for a moment; too quiet, in fact, and he came alert. "Miss Lulu?"

After another beat, she said, "What about the way he was killed?"

She had dodged him again and again he knew she'd get slippery if he tried to snag her, so he said, "The spectacle. They've all been like that." He didn't want to confess that he was beginning to harbor a grudging admiration for the crafty way the four homicides had been pulled off, each one unique and bizarre. He could only hope that the victims were evil in some—

The madam was going on about what Mr. Tom must be thinking when he said, "Pardon me, Miss Lulu. Something's come up. I need to go. I'm sorry."

"Wait," she said. "At least tell me what's going to happen now."

The detective said, "What's going to happen now is our last chance." He hung up the phone and stood turning the box in his hand, over and over again.

He was in the kitchen refilling his coffee when heard the front door open. A moment later, Justine appeared. He was about to start in about the case when he realized that she was alone. "Where's Evangeline?" he said.

"She was invited to breakfast by a lady from church." Justine was smiling. "I think some gentlemen were asked along, too." She saw the sudden concern on his face and said, "It's all right. I know them. She'll be fine. They'll drive her home after."

Valentin was confused at the news and unsure of his feelings about it. Except for her trips to market, she had been with one or both of them or at home since they had first brought her under their roof. But he knew Justine was protective, too, and pushed it aside to tell her about taking the call from Miss Lulu and her news that Captain Warren had once been assigned to the District. "So it keeps pointing one way."

"Now what?" Justine said.

"We need to get together with James and Each. I have an idea."

"When?"

"Now," he said. "Today. We can make breakfast."

"Not here," she said. "If she comes home and finds I cooked for company without her, she'll have a fit."

"Then we'll find someplace in town."

"Mangetta's?"

He shook his head. "I've been spending too much time there. And I'm not going to drag him in on Sunday morning."

"Where then?"

Valentin thought about it before coming up with an odd smile.

Rebecca hadn't eaten all morning and was famished. She was also curious to know if the Baronne Diner would be doing business as usual, so she grabbed her bag, left the building and started south on Loyola to find out and perhaps have breakfast. She had gone only a few paces along the banquette when the feeling of someone watching came over her again. This time, she didn't jerk around and start scanning nearby pedestrians, but walked to the kiosk on the corner and stood with the others, as if waiting for the streetcar. Only then did she cast a casual eye about.

It was hopeless. A person clever enough to get away with now four murders while fooling the police and a certain private detective at every turn was not going to walk up holding a sign or make an announcement, *Hello, it's me!*

With a last glance around, she continued to Poydras to Baronne Street and crossed over. Halfway down the block, she stopped and stared.

Valentin St. Cyr was helping his wife down from the driver's seat of a Model T Ford in front of the diner. Rebecca moved out of sight in the entranceway of a furniture store and watched until a Dodge pulled to the curb and Lieutenant McKinney slid out from behind the wheel. The silly-looking young fellow she had seen at the cemetery climbed out the passenger side. The lieutenant stepped up to rap a knuckle on the glass. The door opened, the four passed inside, and the door was pulled shut behind them.

So the diner had indeed been shuttered in the aftermath of the murder. Now she was dying to know what the two detectives working the case and the two others were doing back there the day after.

*So they're all together again. It hasn't failed yet. The reporter leads to them, even if it's by accident. Like they all decided beforehand to be in the one place.*

*Who knows what they're doing there? Looking for clues that don't exist? Or for a trail from there to here, to this very spot and the person who stands on it? Or are they making a final plan before it ends?*

*She can't wait all day and walks off. It wasn't in the plan to deliver the next one here, but who could pass up the chance?*

Rebecca's stomach was growling. She knew Selby's Restaurant near Lafayette Square would be open and started in that direction. As she waited to cross at Girod Street, two women dressed for church stepped up.

"Miss Marcus?" the older of the two—possibly the mother—called out.

They were both smiling. "We read your stories about these awful murders. And they're grand. Not the murders, of course. They're horrible. But your stories are grand."

Rebecca didn't know what to say. Her pieces were so simple that a cub reporter could have written them in his sleep.

"We sent letters to your editor," the younger one said. "To tell them how pleased we are to see a woman getting a chance to show what she could do."

Rebecca stared between the beaming faces for a moment before recovering. "Oh, yes," she said. "The letters. Very kind."

"I'm sure ours weren't the only ones," the older of the pair said.

"They weren't," Rebecca said. "But still appreciated." She thanked them and they went on their way. She stood thinking about how she was looking forward to seeing Kassel and Vernel back in the newsroom and the talk they'd be having. Unless, of course, another body had been discovered.

As she turned and started off, her bag brushed a passing pedestrian. "Oh, excuse me," she said, and clutched the strap. Whoever she had bumped had moved on and she whispered a scolding word to herself. She really did need to get her thoughts straight. She walked a half-dozen paces before slowing to a gradual halt, whispering to herself in a different way.

It was right there, peeking out the top in the same cream color. She crossed to the park and found the nearest bench, where she sat down, drew out the envelope, and opened it.

"'So now we share something. This is good. I can say to you that it will soon be over, perhaps tonight. And when it is, you'll know who and why, and you can put that in the newspaper, too. You are fair and I am grateful.'"

Rebecca folded it back. After sitting still for a half-minute not daring to look up, she rose to her feet. She wasn't hungry anymore.

Captain Warren wasn't the only policeman who took meals at the Baronne Diner. It was a regular stop for officers from the Parish and First precincts and so a simple matter for Lieutenant McKinney to arrange for Maggie the waitress and the night cook to be on hand.

After the two detectives spent a few minutes questioning both to confirm that no details had been overlooked, the lieutenant told them they were ready for breakfast. Relieved, Maggie jotted their orders on her pad and went to fetch coffee while the cook fired his stove.

They moved to the booth at the far end of the room from where the captain had taken his last bite and sat down to eggs, boudin, biscuits, and coffee, speaking of everyday matters for the next half-hour. The case wouldn't be going anywhere. The lieutenant had called the precinct to tell the desk sergeant where he'd be if there was news.

Throughout, however, Justine could feel her husband's edgy impatience and see it in the way he stared into the distance. She knew the look, knew it meant that one part of his brain was hard at work.

Maggie appeared to take their plates and fill their cups. Valentin, finally able to move, crossed to the counter for a toothpick, but instead of sticking it in his mouth, used it as a tiny pointer. He turned first to McKinney. "Well?"

"It was on his desk, wrapped in butcher's paper."

"What was?" Each asked. Then said, "Oh..."

The lieutenant's tone turned ruminative. "You know, a human tongue is not very large," he said.

"Good lord," Justine said. Each looked as if he might swallow his own.

"So here's what we have," Valentin said. "Four dead. About to be five. I don't have any doubt about that. And we've been chasing behind all this time." He produced a slight smile. "Yes. *All this time.* We haven't gotten close. Though I believe our perpetrator has gotten close to us. And to Miss Marcus." He kept his eyes off Justine. "She told us she had a feeling."

"And there's the letters," McKinney said.

"Yes," he said. "The letters."

Valentin turned to his wife. "Friday night, when we were in the Vieux Carré? I thought someone was watching me." She nodded. "Someone was."

He took a sip of his coffee. "Something came to me when I was on the telephone with Miss Lulu this morning. I was telling her what an amazing trick this individual has pulled off. It's been almost..."

"Artistic?" Justine said.

"Exactly." He jabbed with the toothpick. "And something to be admired. As horrible as it's been."

James nodded as if he had been thinking the same thing. Each, on the other hand, was frowning, puzzled at the direction the detective was going.

Valentin said, "And I had this thought that if all this had to happen, I really hope the victims were evil."

"I think that whenever someone is murdered," the lieutenant said. "But it's not the case very often."

"I know," Valentin said. "But what if this time, it was?"

Watching them, he saw Justine catching up, James close behind, and even Each coming alert to say, "So the victims, they were all evil people, is that it?"

"Not quite," the lieutenant said.

"Each one committed an evil act," Justine said, then after a few seconds, "Or took part in the same evil act."

Valentin sat down on a stool, planted the toothpick between two teeth, and stared at the floor, arranging his thoughts. "Storyville was always the most important factor," he said. "We found Waltham in Eclipse Alley. I was thrown off by the priest's murder, but we can trace him to the District through the church. The church where Waltham was a parishioner."

"The nun," McKinney said.

"She told me she heard them arguing about something." He stood up, tossed the toothpick, and began to pace a few steps this way and that. "Next is what Dolly told me about Waltham and a trick baby."

"Dolores," Justine said.

"Dolores. Yes. And how he was desperate to find her. So this child, who is now twenty or so, is somehow in the middle of it. Maybe she's his daughter. Maybe she's not, but knows something about her. Or maybe something happened to her because of it."

"Or maybe she's the murderer," Justine said.

"Yes," Valentin said. "Maybe she is." He mused on that point before moving on. "We know that Barry and Warren also had business in Storyville.

But it's not just the place that they have in common. It's the place at a particular time."

"Six or seven years ago," the lieutenant said.

"Correct. And something happened."

He stopped his pacing and paused to consider where they had all been. He was gone, because Justine had taken up with a rich man. McKinney was a street copper on his way up the ranks. And Each had still been Beansoup, though he was old enough to sprout whiskers.

He put the memories aside and continued. "Whatever it was has drawn the four dead men and the girl together. And how did that happen?"

"The photograph," Justine said. "She saw the photograph."

"I'll be damned," McKinney said. "And two days later, Waltham is dead in Eclipse Alley."

"The rest come one after another," Valentin said, snapping his fingers. "Father O'Brien. Bartlett Barry. Captain Warren."

"There were thirteen men in that picture," the lieutenant said.

"Yes. But as far as I could tell from reading those old papers, none of the others had any dealings in Storyville."

At this, Justine raised an eyebrow and McKinney and Each snickered. Valentin offered a dim smile. "I mean the kind of –"

"We know what you mean," Justine said. "Only the four who've been murdered."

"And one more."

"Tom Anderson," she said.

Maggie appeared with a coffee pot, refilled their cups, and disappeared in back.

The lieutenant said, "So where does this leave us?"

"Back where it started. With Herbert Waltham."

"Except he ain't around," Each quipped.

Valentin said, "He's not, but Dolores is. And I have a feeling she knows more than she's been telling me."

"But what if she doesn't?" Justine said.

"Then I have no idea. But I'll be going to Esplanade Ridge to find out."

"When?"

"In just a little while."

The lieutenant said, "And what do you want us to do in the meantime?"

"I want you and Justine to go into Storyville. Visit as many houses between Basin and Liberty that you can. It will be quiet and most of the madams will be in."

"Visit for what?" Justine said.

"To ask for any piece of information about a trick baby who was born about twenty years ago. About a madam named Ruby Stein. Or anything else you can shake loose."

"What about me?" Each said.

"You're going to Tom Anderson's," Valentin said.

"What for?"

"To guard his person."

Each's face fell and Valentin guessed he had already been thinking about spreading his charm from one sporting house to the next. Now he'd be spending his day as nursemaid for an old man.

Valentin said, "This is important. A murderer could be coming that way. I need you out there."

As he expected, Each's scrawny chest puffed with the duty that was his, complete with a chance to be a hero. To sweeten the pot, Valentin said, "I'm sending you to Lucy, his maid. She's a fine woman." Each produced a rounder's smile, then put it away in the silence that followed.

Valentin offered him a few instructions and he stood up and made for the door, his expression solemn with the gravity of his mission.

Once the door closed behind him, Valentin addressed his wife and the lieutenant. "It will take you maybe two hours. I'll be done by then. And we can meet up at Fewclothes." He caught Justine's pained expression and said, "All right, not there. The Café. At one o'clock."

He noticed them exchanging a glance and said, "What is it?"

The lieutenant said, "I don't know, it seems like a long shot."

"It is," Valentin said. "It's what we have. And we've done long shots before. More than once."

The policeman stood up and stretched. "All right, then. I'll see you at the Café." He sauntered to the door.

Justine watched him go, looking distracted. Some seconds passed and they heard the Dodge rattle to life. Valentin took the moment to step behind the counter to use the telephone.

Lucy answered. "Oh, Mr. Valentin, he's in the—"

"I don't want to talk to him."

She said, "Oh."

"I'm sending a man out there."

"A man?" she said.

"One of my people. His name is Each. Mr. Tom knows him. He's going to be on the premises all day. Maybe longer."

"All right, then. But I'll need to explain this."

"That's fine. Tell him that it's either Each or a copper he doesn't know. Tell him I said it's necessary. And to trust me."

"All right, sir." She was silent for a few moments. Then she said, "Mr. Valentin..."

Her voice sounded strained, quavering. "What is it, Lucy?"

Another pause. "Never mind. It's nothing. All this has me in a state."

Valentin shook his head, hearing more in what the maid didn't say than what she did. Just like Dolores and Lulu White. He had known Anderson long enough to recognize his hand in the background, however feeble. And what would those three women have to say if the King of Storyville was the next—and the last—to turn up dead?

"Mr. Valentin?"

"He's on his way," he said and hung up. His next call was to the Waltham house. A man answered and he put a soft country burr on his tone to ask for Dolores.

She was not pleased. "What is it, now?" she said in a voice so low he could barely hear.

"I'm coming to see you," he told her.

"When?"

"In a half-hour."

"What for?"

He didn't reply, letting the silence linger until at last she sighed and said, "All right, then. All right. I'll be where I was before." The line went dead.

He sat down across from his wife. She lifted her cup for a sip of coffee, found it cold and put it down again. "I'm not looking forward to this, Valentin. Not one bit."

"I know," he said. "And I'm sorry. We have to do it." He thought to tell her that she could change her mind, but he knew what her answer would be. "Some of the women will be glad to see you. Miss Antonia. Miss..."

She treated him to a droll smile as she slid out of the booth.

They ducked the raindrops and climbed into the Ford. Valentin drove to Canal Street, then turned north. When they reached Union Station, they sat studying a Basin Street that was Sunday-quiet under the gray clouds.

"I'll be watching for Mr. Cecil, too," she said.

"Mr. Cecil." Valentin said. "Yes. I doubt we'll see his face again, but who knows? Nothing else has made much sense."

She opened the door. He climbed out and walked around to help her down. She opened the umbrella and they stood gazing across the way.

"Do you actually think this will do any good?" she said.

"I don't know." He hesitated. "But, listen. The person we're after. She's shown that she's willing to—"

"I know," she said. "I understand. I'll be careful." She turned his way. "How come you didn't tell James and Each the same thing?"

"Because I'm not planning on waking up tomorrow morning with either one of them, that's why."

She smiled, kissed his cheek, and walked away. He waited until she had crossed the tracks before climbing back into the Ford.

# TWENTY-ONE

Tom Anderson woke later than usual and it was almost eleven o'clock when Lucy heard the mattress creak and his heavy footsteps from behind the door. She began preparing his coffee and breakfast, which would be no more than some fruit and a biscuit with butter.

She returned from the kitchen as he was stepping out of the bedroom. After doing maid work for twenty years, she knew how to keep a straight face, and at the sight of the old man who on this morning looked even years older, she did so now. His cheeks were puffy with sleep and his blue eyes were dull. She spent a moment thinking that he had once been known and feared far and wide as the King of Storyville.

"Good morning, Mr. Tom." She made her voice cheerful. "You ready for some breakfast?"

He stared at her in a bleary way. "The telephone," he said.

"Yes, sir?"

"Was there another one?"

"I didn't want to wake—"

"Was there?"

"Yes, sir." She watched him sag into the closest chair. "A policeman this time."

"What was his name?" he said without looking up, his tone flat.

"Warren," Lucy said. "Captain Warren."

With a voice so low she could barely hear him, he said, "How did he die?"

"Poisoned. Someone got poison into his food. At a diner."

"Good God Almighty."

He sat unmoving for a disturbing half-minute. Finally, Lucy said, "Mr. Valentin called, too."

"What did he want?"

"He's sending someone out here. Fellow he called Each?"

"What for?"

"He didn't say."

He grumbled something she couldn't catch, but said nothing more.

"What about your breakfast?"

Now he did look up. "My... oh, just coffee. That's all." He began to push himself out of the chair and she leaned in to help him. His weight as he struggled to his feet was leaden, but she managed to get him up and moving into the dining room.

"I can call Doctor Calvert again," she asked once he was settled at the table.

"That won't be necessary."

"You want some brandy in your coffee?"

"No, Lucy, I don't want brandy in my coffee. I want whiskey in a teacup alongside of it."

"All right, yes, sir," she said and moved away, leaving him staring out the window.

On her way to the kitchen, she stepped into the bedroom to fetch his eyeglasses and saw on the night stand the little bottle marked **MORPHINE SULFATE**. She had never seen it before, but it explained his late rising. She left the glasses where they were.

Rebecca arrived back at the newsroom to find Reynard with his feet up on his desk, a copy of the morning paper and his hands folded across his stomach, and his head lolling back. She decided to have mercy and leave him to his nap, knowing that if another body had turned up, he'd be awake and waiting for her.

She was halfway to her desk when she heard him call her name and turned around. He was rising to his feet and yawning. He followed her to the corner. "So," he said. "Are you here through the afternoon?"

"I am," she said.

He noticed the cool way she was regarding him and said, "What is it?"

"You've been keeping things from me."

A tint of pink rose to the editor's cheeks. "What things?" he said.

"I met two charming ladies on my way in. You might recognize their names. They wrote letters to the editor. About me."

"Oh, those," he said, relieved she hadn't somehow learned of the more troubling discussions. "The letters. Yes. There were telephone calls, too. Most of them applauding you."

"Why didn't you tell me?" She waved a hand in the direction of Kassel's empty office. "Was it his idea?"

"It was, but I agreed." Her eyes flashed and he said, "You didn't need the distraction, Rebecca."

Her expression told him that she didn't quite buy the excuse. "May I see the letters?" she said.

"Now?"

"Yes, now." She was growing irked again. "Or you can hang onto them. And I'll keep what I have."

He caught the glint in her stare and said, "I'll be back."

Each rode the streetcar out St. Charles, stepped down at Fourth Street, walked the two blocks to the corner of Coliseum, and presented himself at Tom Anderson's front door.

Mr. Valentin had been correct; the woman who greeted him at the door was comely, with a sturdy figure and a wise and pleasant face that would have been all the prettier had it not been so stitched with worry. She looked him up and down. "You're Mr. Valentin's man?"

"Yes, ma'am," he said. "Each."

With a pronounced sigh, she waved him inside.

Reynard returned five minutes later with a handful of sheets in his hand. Holding them out to her, he said, "I left the nasty ones in his drawer."

This drew a sharp laugh. "How nasty?"

The editor's face resumed its previous shade of pink. "A couple offered to insert something between your legs," he said. "I think to remind you of a woman's place."

She hiked an amused eyebrow, reached into her bag, and produced the letter. Reynard read it twice. "So there's going to be another one delivered..."

"Before murder number five," she said.

"When? Today?"

"Or tonight."

"But how is that possible?"

"The same way as everything else has been," she said. "This is someone who's been very cunning."

"I can have a man watching out," he said. "One of the Pinkertons we use now and then."

"No, please don't," she said. "We want the letter to get here."

"Yes, all right," he said, marveling at how far she had come in five days.

She hefted the stack. "You can have these back as soon as I'm done." She sat down to read. "And, Reynard?" she said. "I'd love to see the nasty ones, too."

Justine was mollified when Valentin had sent her to Basin Street so she could confine her visits to the mansions, and then had not lectured on what questions to ask, trusting her to decide on her own.

Though she was ready, she lingered on the Bienville side of Anderson's Café, not yet willing to put a foot on the banquette of that notorious boulevard. She wondered if any one of the handful of men strolling by would see her alone and take her for what she had once been: a soiled dove or strumpet or any of another dozen sobriquets their minds might conjure. None would think to look at the simple gold band on her finger. Because she was on Basin Street.

She decided she didn't care. Though her husband kept circling back to the District, she'd never again find herself there for anything other than walking and talking. With this thought in mind, she stepped out.

She did not make her direct way to the first house on the line but passed them all, door after door, barely glancing up until she reached the far end of the street and stopping on the corner of Conti, with the wall of St. Louis Cemetery No. 1 directly before her. Eclipse Alley was only two streets away, close enough for her to feel it.

She made herself walk there, nursing only a faint memory of when it had carried a reputation as a place to be avoided. Even the filthy crib girls off of Robertson and Claiborne and the mattress whores who would lie down for any man anywhere stayed away. *Voodoo*, they whispered. She never learned why it had been dreaded so and wasn't in Storyville long enough to think much about it.

She crossed and stood at the mouth of the alley. Twenty feet back, it made a slight turn, and she imagined Valentin and McKinney in the shadows, standing over the bloody, mutilated body. She entertained a temptation to walk in, then thought better of it. There would be nothing to see. She had houses to visit. And Eclipse Alley frightened her. She turned back for Basin Street.

She learned nothing at the first four houses, nor the fifth and sixth. The madams—none of whom she knew—shook their heads in wonder at such foolishness. *Twenty years ago?* One laughed outright and another appeared on the verge of cursing over being bothered so early. She prepared herself for the same response at the remaining addresses.

She found her way to Antonia Gonzales' doorstep and stood for a moment on the gallery, drawing forth memories of the year she had spent there. It was in the parlor that she had first laid eyes on Valentin St. Cyr and in her upstairs room that she had first dropped her chippie and let him feast on her. The images were still fresh, because from that night on, her life was on a path that she could not have imagined. Now, nine years later, she raised her hand to pull the cord that rang the same cheery chimes.

She was relieved when the girl who came to the door announced that Miss Antonia was not in the house, but had gone to Corpus Christi for the funeral of her mother. Justine asked the girl to extend her condolences.

"Who shall I say?"

"Tell her Justine. It was Mancarre then. St. Cyr now."

"Oh, yes," the girl said. "She's talked about you in such a fond way."

Justine thanked her, descended the steps to the banquette, and walked on. She passed Mahogany Hall, again without looking up.

Lulu White knew that Justine St. Cyr was in Storyville ten minutes after that young lady knocked on the first door. The madam made two quick telephone calls and learned of a tall, ginger-haired man doing the same thing on Franklin Street. That would be Detective McKinney. They were both asking after a trick baby who would now be a young lady.

Standing in the middle of her grand parlor, she confessed to herself that she likely could have helped with a few words in Valentin St. Cyr's ear. Instead, she had kept quiet, leaving it for him to finish, as he had always done before.

Now she understood that he might fail. If that happened and he realized what she had done—which he would—their friendship would end while Storyville suffered yet another mortal wound. But it was too late now for her to do anything but wait.

So she beckoned her day girl and told her that if anyone came to the door looking for the madam of the house, she was not in.

Justine had heard the story dozens of times. The mansion had first been the infamous Josie Arlington's and then was managed by Gertude Dix, until she took up with her next-door neighbor Tom Anderson and seduced him into leaving his second wife in order to become his third.

The spouses had both engaged in illicit affairs until he got too tired and she too rich. At which point she took all of her money and a good chunk of his and rode away to parts unknown. Some said San Francisco, others New York. Those who knew weren't saying. Miss Gertrude did not want to be found. Tom Anderson proclaimed himself happy to be rid of her.

Now the landlady was a woman who had come up from Franklin Street named Kate Markley. She stepped into her parlor to greet Justine, a tall woman in a dressing gown, on the thin side, pale, and with hair a shade of blonde that could only come from a bottle. Her gaze was just shy of hard. Justine was not surprised; the gentle and regal madams had been drifting away for some time. Still, Miss Markley was courteous as she offered her a seat on her ornate sofa.

"You used to be with Antonia Gonzales?" she said. "Do I have that right?"

It was the question Justine had been dreading. She had no interest in any history there, unless it was about a certain trick baby and definitely none of hers. She also knew that this might not be the last time she'd hear the question this day. So she said, "I was. A long time ago."

"And now?"

"Now I'm married. And I'm helping my husband. His name is—"

"Valentin St. Cyr," the madam said. "The detective."

"That's correct."

"He's after this murdering bastard who killed the priest and those others."

"That's right."

"So what do you want here?"

"I'm visiting all the landladies on Basin Street. We're looking for any trace of a woman who would have had a baby nineteen or twenty years ago."

"What?" The madam was perplexed. "Who would remember?"

"She might still be around," Justine said. "If she stayed in the life, I mean."

"I'm sorry, Miss..."

"Justine."

"Justine. *I* would have been twenty years old or thereabouts. And I wasn't in New Orleans at all. Kansas City."

"Do you know anything about a landlady named Ruby Stein?"

Miss Markley frowned. "Ruby Stein? Oh, yes. Her house was a couple doors down from the one I was in at the time. She had been there a while. But she left out after about a year. Never heard anything from her again."

Again, Justine was not surprised. Too much time had passed and she'd be hearing more of the same as she continued on. Hadn't her husband warned her about the tedium of investigative work? Hours and days and weeks to find a single thread that might lead somewhere. The problem was they didn't even have the hours.

"I'm sorry," Miss Kate said.

Justine got to her feet. "It's all right. Thank you for your time."

The madam saw her to the door with a promise to ask her ladies if anyone came to mind. Justine had just started down the stone steps when a young dove, barefoot and wrapped in a kimono, opened the door. Her not unpretty face showed traces of makeup and her red curls were an early-morning mess.

"Miss?" She stepped closer on bare feet. "My name is Camille. I heard you talking to Miss Kate. You said the name Ruby Stein?"

Justine came to attention. "I did, yes."

"Then the one you're looking for? I think she's my sister."

Valentin pulled to the corner and saw the shape hunched beneath the same tree, a hat pulled low. Before he could climb out, Dolores had stepped to the Ford, swung the door open, and stepped up and settled in the seat.

"Every time I see you, it's raining," she said in greeting. She pushed the hat back. "That ain't a good sign."

"It's New Orleans."

"Yes, it is," she said, sounding forlorn.

He drove to the next cross street, rounded the corner, and pulled to the curb, leaving the engine running. After a pause, he said, "I came here because I believe there's more, Dolores. I think you have information that will help me. Do you?"

She studied the drops on the windshield. "You know, it still sounds strange to me sometimes. *Dolores*. After all those years being someone else." Valentin waited a long ten seconds. "He found her," she said at last. "That's what I didn't tell you. But it was actually *she* found *him*. She left a letter on our doorstep."

"When was this?"

"Last Monday."

*The day after the photograph appeared.* "Did you see it?"

She shook her head. "I didn't. I only know because Mr. Herbert asked if I knew anything about it. And I told him no."

"What happened then?"

"He went out the next night," she said. "But before he left, he called me into the library and asked what I knew about Eclipse Alley. I said I remembered it, but I hadn't never been there."

"And that's where he went."

She said, "Well, it's where he ended up, ain't it?"

Valentin felt a flush of anger and sat back, letting it cool. "Why didn't you tell me before?" he said.

She returned his ire. "Because of his son. Herbert, Junior. That's why. This past Thursday, he took me aside. First he told me not to talk to anyone about his father. Not to you or the coppers and not to the news people. Then he asked what did I know that he didn't. And I told him."

"And?"

"He said if I ever said a word about it, he'd tell his mother about Storyville and have me sent back. He said he could do it. Put me someplace I couldn't get away from. And the way he said it, I believed him. People who have money, they can do anything."

Now it was his turn to watch the rain. "So why are you telling me now?"

"Because I can't take it anymore. I'll leave the city if I have to. But I won't ever go back to Storyville. Can't nobody force me."

"I wouldn't let that happen," Valentin said.

She turned to him, tears welling in her eyes. "I'm sorry, Mr. Valentin." Her voice broke. "I wish I'd said something when you came 'round on Friday. Maybe I could have stopped what happened to them other two."

"No," he said. "They were dead the minute that photograph came out." He let her ponder that for a few seconds while he reached into his vest coat pocket. "Here's my card," he said, and placed it in her hand. "Use it if you need to." He put the machine in gear. "I'll drive you back."

She reached for the door handle. "No, thank you, sir," she said. "I'd like to walk."

By the time James McKinney reached the fifth house on the street, the rain was coming down in a steady drizzle, splashing off the banquettes and filling the gutters. When he reached the corner of Conti, he climbed the steps to Louisa Miller's establishment, slapping droplets from his shoulders and shaking out his hat.

The girl who came to the door gaped at him with bleary hungover eyes. Her voice was dry when she told him the madam and all the other women had gone to church at Blood of the Lamb Baptist on Touro Street. He was about to ask about the trick baby when she closed the door in his face.

Directly across Franklin Street was the house managed by a madam who called herself Princess Joy and was known to be crazier than Lulu White by a mile. How she kept a business going was anyone's guess, but she had managed to do that, in one place or another, all the way back to before Alderman Story's ordinance. He didn't expect to learn anything worthwhile at her address, but he wanted to be thorough.

She met him at the door, broad-faced, loose-eyed, in a Mother Hubbard and a hat that defied description, other than being round and flowered. She invited him inside before she knew what he wanted. Once he told her and mentioned Ruby Stein, she fixed him with a smile that would have suited a vaudeville clown.

He wasn't sure she had understood him and was about to repeat the question when she said, "Trick baby?" Her voice was a broken flute. "I've known quite a few of those."

"This would have been—"

"Some twenty years ago. Yes, I heard you." She tilted her head at an odd angle and said, "You're quite an attractive young man."

The lieutenant didn't know whether to laugh or turn heel and run for the door. He was still deciding when she said. "I do remember Ruby. But her true name was Roberta." Princess Joy paused, her stare shifting, and James sensed that he was no longer an object of interest. "And, yes, there was a trick baby. No, two. One's name was Camille." Her peculiar eyes came back to him. "Did you want to hear about them?"

*It could have been a trail of crumbs but instead it was bodies, one after the other. What happens when no sees it coming. Just walking about in Storyville, there's the quadroon and the police detective looking for something that's in plain sight. Good.*

*Keep them someplace else. Keep them busy.*

---

Each had been in the Fourth Street house for an hour, lounging at the kitchen table and admiring Lucy as she bent over him with fresh coffee and moved here and there, her hips swaying under the fabric of her shift, though she barely glanced at his face and said next to nothing. Her husband George, a dark stalk of a man, ambled in for coffee and ambled back out, nodding to him in an absent way.

He heard Mr. Tom before he saw him. First a door squeaked, then came the thuds of heavy steps. Next was a cough and a mumble of words he couldn't make out. After a half-minute of this, Tom Anderson was standing in the doorway.

"Haven't seen you in a good while," he said as he made his slow way to the table.

"That's true, sir," Each said, trying to connect the robust lion of Storyville with this aging sack, affecting a smile as the old man took a seat and Lucy went about fetching his coffee.

"So," he grumbled. "Mr. Valentin St. Cyr wants you here for what reason?"

"All the men in the photograph are getting someone as an escort," Each said, just as the Creole detective had instructed him. "He figured you'd rather have somebody you know already."

"You mean all the men who aren't already dead."

Each didn't know what to say to that. Lucy had been bringing his coffee to the table. Now she stopped and shook her head in dismay.

"Yes, sir, Mr. Tom," Each said. "I suppose."

The old man said, "That's all right. I guess he's telling me what to do now." He glanced at Lucy. "Well, don't just stand there." She stepped up, placed the cup at his elbow, and backed away. He took a sip and said, "You forgot something."

Lucy opened the cabinet and reached for the brandy bottle.

Valentin arrived in Storyville, parked on St. Louis Street at Liberty, and crossed over into the District, passing Eclipse Alley once again. During the drive back, and now as he walked the wet streets wearing the workman's hat he always kept in the machine, he revisited what Dolores had told him.

It had to be the trick baby who had left a letter on the doorstep, just as she was leaving missives for Rebecca Marcus and pieces of Herbert Waltham at the scenes of her crimes. Before she murdered them.

The thought of his wife roaming from house to house with no way for him to know whether or not she was being tracked quickened his steps, so he spent the next thirty minutes criss-crossing the District, only to miss her twice when he knocked on a door only to find out that she had been and gone. He saw no sign of James, either, and for a few brief seconds imagined both of them being stalked and—

He stopped on the corner of Bienville to take hold of himself. It was still almost a half-hour before their meeting at the Café. There was no point in rambling, so he decided to make one more walk down Basin Street, keeping his eyes peeled, and then wait for them to arrive.

But when he came in sight of the façade and its overhang, he saw the two familiar figures looking his way. Justine left the lieutenant's side and hurried to meet him with the words, "We found something."

Valentin still had enough friends and one of them was the Sunday maitre'd at Anderson's Café, a gentleman named Arthur who worked only the one day because of the special service. In fact, Sundays at the Café were quite ordinary: it was only unique in contrast to the music and gambling and carousing that went on every night of the week.

The dinner had always been something of an affair, a place for those in the news to be seen and for certain individuals representing both sides of the law to wrangle over money and power. Though the big room was showing the signs of age and neglect, the diners could still enjoy a meal from a well-known chef, also only brought in for that weekly occasion.

The trio at the door weren't there to dine and so Arthur whisked them into one of the private salons where they settled at a table. A waiter brought coffee and left, closing the door behind him.

Justine said, "Did you find out anything?"

"I did," Valentin said. "But I want to hear what you have first."

James bowed his head to the lady at the table. "You go ahead," he said.

She explained about visiting the house just two doors away, speaking to the madam, and then being stopped by one of the girls as she left.

"She had heard me talking to Miss Kate and she said the one we're looking for was her sister."

Valentin was stunned. "Her sister..."

"Her younger sister. Younger *half*-sister. The same mother. Two different fathers. Both tricks. This was at Ruby Stein's. The one I spoke to—her name is Camille—followed her mother into the life when she came of age."

Valentin said, "What about–"

"Wait," Justine said. "The younger one wanted nothing to do with Storyville. Camille said she was smart and pretty and did well at school. And then..."

Valentin sat forward. "What?"

"And then one night she heard all this awful screaming and crying downstairs. She came out of her room to ask what had happened and her mother chased her back and told her to stay there. A little while later, she heard a man's voice and peeked out the door and saw the doctor with his bag." She paused for a sip of coffee. "They wouldn't talk about it and wouldn't let Camille see her, even though she begged. A few days later, the sister was gone. Camille was told that she was very ill and had to be moved to a sanitarium. But when she asked to visit–"

"There was always an excuse why she couldn't." Valentin had recalled another such incident.

"That's right," she said. "She didn't see her again for about a year. James can tell that part."

When the lieutenant mentioned Princess Joy, Valentin rolled his eyes. "I know, I know," he said. "But Miss Ruby's house was close by and she knew both girls. She remembered how bright the younger one was, too. 'Brightest child I've ever seen.' That's what she said. But she also said that there was something wrong with her."

"What kind of wrong?" Valentin said.

"She didn't explain." He raised a finger to his temple. "She just tapped her head. So maybe six months after all this happened, she went to visit one of her girls at a private hospital for nervous ailments over in Algiers. And while she was there, she saw someone familiar."

"The younger sister from Ruby Stein's."

James nodded and then gestured for Justine to resume the story.

"So the next day, Camille rode the ferry over there and found her. She said it was clear that she was still in a bad state, all closed up, and she wouldn't say what had happened to her. They talked for a little while and Camille said she would come back to visit. Which she did, a week later."

"And her sister was gone."

Justine said, "How did you know?"

"I didn't. It seems to follow."

"Camille never spoke to her again," Justine said. "Except every now and then, she thought she'd spotted her at a distance, but when she went to find her..." She raised her hands, palms up.

"Well, we know that feeling," Valentin said. He looked between them. "So?" he said. "What's her name?"

Justine paused to let the drama build, something else she had learned from him. Then she said, "Her name is Arcelle."

# TWENTY-TWO

They stood beneath the colonnade, watching a train roll out of Union Station. The smoke from the engine billowed over the rails and drifted across Rampart Street, and for a few moments enveloped a small piece of the French Quarter in a cloud of steam, a peaceful image for such a hard day.

"She could be anywhere," Justine said and the spell was broken. "She could be right behind us. That's true, isn't it?"

Valentin said, "I doubt it."

"All right, what happens now?" Her voice was muted.

"We find her and stop her," Valentin said.

"Just like that?"

Valentin stared at her. She stared back. The lieutenant spoke up. "What are the chances she won't go after Tom Anderson?"

Valentin looked away. "Small. But I suppose it could be one of the others."

"You're still guessing?" Justine said.

Valentin decided it would be best to stay quiet. He couldn't blame her. The days had been long, she was on edge, and they were floundering.

The lieutenant came to the rescue again. "All the others have happened after dark."

Valentin said, "And I suspect this one will, too. So we have a little time."

"Then I need to look in on Evangeline," Justine said.

———

Valentin told her to take the Ford, which brought a look of surprise. Then he realized that she had never driven in the rain and now would be doing it alone.

They climbed into the lieutenant's Dodge and he carried them to St. Louis Street. Justine addressed her husband without turning around. "What will you be doing now?"

"I'll telephone Rebecca Marcus," he said and saw her stiffen. The lieutenant kept his eyes fastened on the street ahead. "Or Reynard. I want to know if they've gotten any more letters."

"And if they have?"

"Then we'll go by the paper and have a look."

"Or maybe she could meet you somewhere," Justine said.

"We'll see," Valentin said and issued a silent prayer of thanks that it was only a five-block ride.

James pulled the Dodge in behind the Ford and Valentin stepped down and helped his wife to the banquette. The lieutenant glanced at Justine, then at Valentin, mouthing the words *good luck* as the Creole detective closed the door.

She was already behind the wheel. After he cranked the engine, she took a few seconds practicing with the windshield wipers.

"All right?" he said.

"I'll be fine."

"I can call you in an hour or so and we'll make our plan from there."

"Give Miss Marcus my regards," she said and dropped the shifter into gear. "And watch yourself with that woman."

Valentin watched her pull onto the wet street then turned around and walked back to the Dodge, where he found the lieutenant gazing pointedly at the clouds. "We need to find a phone," he said.

*Well, of course,* Rebecca scolded the woman in the mirror. *What did you think would happen? Your friend was carrying the last letter, too, and followed you to the building. Maybe followed you right through the door.*

She stood back from the glass and laughed in exasperation at the gall. The lobby had been quiet when she passed through, as it always was on Sunday, with the lone guard on duty and Miriam, the part-time girl who took calls and sold copies of the Sunday at the desk. There had been gossip about the pair for months and so when no one was about, the guard spirited her into the hall and was crooning his sweet nothings in her tender ear when someone entered the lobby and stepped to the counter to lay the last envelope precisely at its center, then rang the little bell before fading back onto the street like a vagrant breeze.

"Coming!" Miriam had called when she heard the *ding-ding*. She dabbed at her lipstick, stepped out into the lobby, and received a surprise.

Rebecca now turned around, leaned against the sink, and read the letter over again.

"'So here we are at the end with one final act and then it will be over. The last one waits. Knows who I am. Knows that I'm coming. So it ends. Good-bye, Rebecca Marcus.'"

When she returned to the newsroom, Reynard was looking for her. "Mr. Valentin called," he said.

"Did you tell him?"

"I did. He and McKinney are on their way."

She sat down in the chair next to his desk. "I wonder what will happen now," she said.

Lucy called Each to the telephone set in the foyer. "It's Mr. Valentin," she whispered.

Each took the handset. "Where are you?"

"At Parish Precinct with the lieutenant," Valentin said. "How are things on Fourth Street?"

"Dull," Each said.

"I'm coming. Give me an hour."

"Why?" Each did not sound pleased. "There's nothing to do. I'm all right."

"This is no time to be foolish," Valentin said. "She's been beating us at every turn. She's ready to do violence. I believe she's heading your way."

"You sure about that?"

"About what?"

"*She.*"

"As sure as I can be."

"Doesn't seem possible," Each said. "I mean, a woman doing all this."

But they both knew that it was. Arcelle—whoever she was—could well have committed the raw bloodshed. Anyone could do what she had done and worse, murdering while wearing a smile, if the circumstances were right. As they were at this time and place.

"I'll see you in an hour," Valentin said and hung up.

By the time Justine arrived back at the house, the rain had settled into mist, though the low-hanging clouds threatened another storm. Once she shut off the engine, the street was silent. She saw no lights on inside the house when she reached the gallery and heard no sounds, either. She unlocked the door and pushed it open. "Evangeline?" she called.

She saw the older woman's wrap and her brocade purse on the sofa. She called twice more, but there was no answer, so she pushed inside, crossing to the kitchen, and then stepping out onto the back gallery.

Evangeline was standing by the satsuma tree, pulling the ripe fruit in a slow and absent motion, looking like a painting as she placed them in the basket she carried. Justine didn't want to startle her or, worse, break her reverie, so she made a quiet retreat to the kitchen and started the coffee pot.

Ten minutes later, she stepped into the kitchen. Her dreamy smile brightened when the older woman saw Justine at the sink. "How long have you been here?" she said.

"Not long." She reached for the basket. "May I?"

"Oh, yes, of course." She handed it over.

Justine began plucking leaves and laying them aside. "How was your lunch?"

"Just fine. We went to Le Porte Bleu on Decatur Street. Do you know it? There were a half-dozen people from the church. It was very nice."

Justine was about to ask about the gentlemen guests when she said, "I ran into someone who knows you and Valentin."

"Oh?" Justine said. "Who was that?"

"I'm sorry, she said her name, but I didn't catch it. She was outside the restaurant when we were leaving. She asked me to tell Mr. and Mrs. St. Cyr that she said hello."

"I wonder who—" Justine stopped and laid aside the satsuma she was holding. "How old was she?"

"How old?" Evangeline considered. "Maybe twenty, I'm not—"

"And what did she look like?"

"Very pretty," Evangeline said. "Sweet-faced. But I didn't get too good of a look. She stepped up, spoke to me, and then she was gone." She saw the frown on Justine's face. "Why, is something wrong?" she said. "Justine?"

When they reached the precinct, Lieutenant McKinney ushered Valentin into one of anterooms off the lobby and pointed him to the telephone that was sitting on the side table. Reynard Vernel came on the line. When the call was finished, Valentin turned to the lieutenant to explain about the letters. "So now we know. Today. Tonight. If she can pull it off."

"So she would have seen us, too." McKinney said. "My God. How does she do it?"

"She's very smart and not a bit afraid," Valentin said. "What was it Princess Joy told you?"

"'Brightest child she'd ever seen.'"

Valentin picked up the phone again and asked the operator for his home number and listened to Justine whisper about the stranger who had approached Evangeline.

"I'm coming back out," she said. "And I'm bringing her with me."

On the ride to the *Times-Picayune* building, Valentin opined that it could have been anyone who had approached Evangeline on the banquette. "I know she's clever. But that would have been some feat. How many places could she be at one time?" The lieutenant did not appear convinced of this. "It's got Justine worried, so she's carrying her into town."

The lieutenant steered the Dodge to the Tulane Avenue curb. Valentin leaned to the windshield. A fellow in a dark suit was standing by the lobby doors. "Is that...?"

The man, blade thin and handsome in a cool and slick way, crossed the banquette as the two detectives climbed from the machine. "Mr. Valentin," he said.

"Ridley Parker. I'll be damned. How long has it been?"

"Six or seven years, at least," Parker said.

"This is James McKinney." The two men shook hands.

"I remember you," McKinney said. "You were one of Major Deveaux's detectives. But then you..."

"Got caught with Mrs. Deveaux." He smiled like a shark. "We were both unclothed. And that was the end of my police career. At least in New Orleans."

"And now?" Valentin said.

"Now it's mostly with the Jefferson Parish Sheriff. Some work for Pinkerton. And this and that."

"So what are you doing here?" Valentin said. "Wait. Are you working?"

"Probably not anymore." Parker explained that he had been the one dallying with the front desk girl when the letter was dropped inside. "I've been reading about this," he said. "God damn. Did I let a murderer slip away?"

Valentin said, "I doubt it. This one wouldn't have let you lay a hand on her."

"Her?" Parker said.

"Yes, her," Valentin said and made for the lobby doors.

Valentin had Miriam, who sat pale with shame, call upstairs and in a few minutes, Rebecca and Reynard appeared from the elevator. The reporter was holding the two letters and they moved to a corner of the lobby so the detectives could read them.

Valentin finished and handed them back. "Well, now you have something for tomorrow's paper," he said.

"And what do you have for me?" Rebecca looked first at him, then at the lieutenant.

"I'll let you know when I know," McKinney said.

She was about to blurt something unkind when Reynard said, "One of us will be in the newsroom. Can you...?"

"We'll contact you when something happens," McKinney said.

They made their escape. When Rebecca and Reynard reached the newsroom, she turned to him and said, "Tom Anderson."

"What about him?"

"I need to find out where he lives."

A half-hour later, James pulled the Dodge into the alley that ran between Third and Fourth streets. Each was waiting at the back gate, ducking his head under the raindrops falling from the leaves of the tall oaks.

"You're going to the precinct?" Valentin asked.

"I need to get the word out that she's on the streets," the lieutenant said. "Even if we don't know where she'll be."

"I do," Valentin said. "But I understand."

"You can reach me there."

Valentin opened the door and climbed down to the gravel. After a grinding of gears the Dodge rolled away.

Each was holding the gate open. "Any news?"

"No, nothing," Valentin said as they started up the walk. "How's Mr. Tom?"

"Been asleep almost the whole time, that's how." They climbed the steps to the back gallery. When they reached the door, Each laid a hand on the knob then stopped. "He's got help. The kind that comes in a *little* bottle."

"You're sure about that?" Valentin had never known Mr. Tom to touch narcotics.

"Oh, I'm sure," Each said and pushed the door open. "I guess he's in pain."

Lucy was standing at the stove as it filled the kitchen with the aroma of baking bread. She nodded to Valentin as the two men passed through and to the door of the downstairs bedroom where Mr. Tom was on his back, asleep. It crossed Valentin's mind that in such a posture, he could just as well be dead.

They returned to the kitchen and took seats at the table. Lucy made to leave them alone.

"Stay, please." Valentin waved her to a chair. "Is he all right?" he asked her.

"No better, no worse," the maid said.

Each said, "He's sure acting worried. I can tell you that."

"But he didn't ask anything else about why you're here."

"No, sir."

Valentin looked at the maid. "Well, Lucy?"

"He's been in a state ever since these murders started."

He noticed her furtive look and said, "What?"

"Something I saw, sir. I feel like I should tell you."

Valentin said, "Go ahead."

She related seeing a mysterious figure near the house not once but twice, though she did admit that she wasn't sure about the second time, just the night before.

When she was through, Each said, "That's kind of what I saw. Couldn't make out no features."

"That's right," Lucy said. "Like some kind of..." She shook her head.

"So whoever it was knows where Mr. Tom lives."

Rebecca had stalked the newsroom for two hours, waiting for nothing. She kept casting sharp glances at Reynard, who had made it clear that he wasn't going anywhere until they heard something from Mr. Valentin. She busied herself with writing various news stories. One had the perpetrator captured by the police; a second, shot down in the street; and the third, escaping without a trace. All she needed were the facts.

She walked to the river-side windows and peered across at the newsroom of the *Sun*. It was mostly dark, with only a few lights burning, and she wondered if there was a reporter at a desk who was, like her, on edge waiting for word of a murderer nabbed, killed, or gone. Or would he have already done what a man would do, which was go out and chase the story?

She turned around and saw Reynard in what was during these trying days and nights was his favorite posture, slouched back, feet up, arms crossed, and eyes closed. When she passed his desk on the way back to hers, he didn't move.

# TWENTY-THREE

An afternoon sky already bloated with charcoal clouds was turning toward evening-dark as Justine piloted the Ford over a St. Charles Avenue still slick with rain. She turned onto Fourth Street and drove south under a canopy of oaks that formed a deep green shroud.

"This reminds me of when we came back from Our Lady of Sorrows down on the bayou," Evangeline said and Justine smiled because she had been thinking the same thing.

She slowed to a stop at Prytania. After looking both ways, she pushed the accelerator handle. On the other side of the intersection, she slid the Ford to a sudden halt.

"What is it?" Evangeline said.

"Did you see that?"

"See what?"

"Someone standing at the corner."

Evangeline turned in her seat. "Where?"

"She was..."

"Was what? Are you all right?"

"Yes, I'm fine," Justine said, and pulled out.

This time, it was Valentin waiting at the back gate and with one of Mr. Tom's umbrellas. He helped the ladies from the machine and held it high as they made their way into the house. They got Evangeline settled at the table with coffee. Each took one of the chairs while Lucy hovered over her. The commotion roused the King of Storyville and he made his slow way into the kitchen. He stopped to survey the five faces gazing back at him.

"Did I forget it was my birthday?" he said. "Or my wake?" There were no smiles.

Justine beckoned Valentin into the pantry to tell her about what she had seen—or thought she had—on the street.

"Lucy saw someone, too. Twice."

"Is it her?" When he didn't answer directly, she eyed him. "I did see someone."

"I believe you," he said. "And Lucy, too."

"So she could be outside right now."

"She could be, yes."

"But she can't get to him."

"I'd say that would be true if it was anyone else."

He stepped into the hallway and looked from one end of the house to the other.

"What are you doing?"

"Checking off all the ways in."

"What if it's too late for that?"

Valentin stared at her for a long few seconds. "Jesus, let's hope not," he said.

To be sure, he collected Each and the three of them covered every room in the house. In ten minutes they were back in the kitchen.

Valentin knew Mr. Tom would ask, so he sat down to explain that he had reason to expect that the person who had murdered the four men—the young woman they believed to be the trick baby they had been trying to find—would try do the same to him.

"Probably tonight."

"Tonight?" Anderson said. Valentin noticed how his face had paled. "And you say it's a woman?"

"Her name is Arcelle. I think you know her."

The old man said, "Know her? How would I?"

"Please tell me what you have to do with this," Valentin said.

"Nothing," Anderson said, his voice was starting to break.

"Why is she after you?"

"I don't *know*."

"That's not true."

The heads turned. Lucy had risen from her chair. "You tell him, Mr. Tom," she said. "Tell him or I will."

For what was only a few seconds but seemed to stretch on for minutes, no one spoke. The old man stared at the maid as if he could not believe what she had just done. She didn't flinch; indeed, she seemed to grow larger as he shrank into his chair. Finally, he said, "All right, then. All right."

The moment lingered until Lucy said, "I'll get you your brandy," and turned away.

Valentin said, "Well?"

Reynard was jerked awake by the clattering of his telephone and he all but tumbled from his chair scrambling to snatch it up.

"Vernel," he croaked.

"Reynard?" It was Rolf Kassel. "What's wrong? Are you drunk?"

"No, no." Reynard found his voice. "Dozing."

"Still quiet?"

"So far, yes."

"What's our Miss Marcus doing?"

Reynard stood up and peered into the corner. "She's..."

"She's what?"

"No," he said. "She wouldn't."

"Reynard? Wouldn't what? What's—"

"God *damn*." He grabbed his jacket from the back of his chair. "I'll call you back." He slammed the handset into the cradle and headed for the door.

Rebecca's mechanic wouldn't allow her to drive any of his customers' machines, but he did let her practice behind the wheel of the old Model T he used for shop errands. So that after she made her way to the lot where they garaged the newspaper's vehicles and beguiled the attendant into cranking one of the Ford roadsters, she found herself making her shaky way west through the city.

The Garden District was quiet under the rain and darkening skies.

Though her hands were tight on the wheel and her eyes fastened on Prytania Street, she stole glances at the grand houses she passed and wondered if she would ever live in one. She knew that she'd have a better chance of meeting a gentleman of means if she went back to the Society pages. It didn't matter; she'd forego that life if she kept having adventures like this one.

She made a slow turn at Third Street and crept along the block to Coliseum, where she turned again, then steered to the curb. After pulling her hat down tight, she climbed out.

Tom Anderson's mansion stood staunch on the corner, three stories with a gallery that stretched on both street sides. Such grandeur from all those women spending all those years on their backs. That and the Café that had been his other goldmine. But now...

She slowed her steps as she drew closer, realizing that she had only a vague plan, something about talking her way inside and then being there when St. Cyr brought down the murderer. *If.*

The iron gate on the corner of the property was standing halfway open, which struck her as odd. Wouldn't it more likely be latched and even locked at a time like this? She stood looking up at the front windows, all dark except for one that was lit by a single lamp.

It occurred to her that she hadn't expected to get this far and mulled going back. And do what? Sit and wait? Anyway, she was already in all kinds of trouble for taking the roadster and the only thing that might help her was to be an eyewitness to something remarkable.

She decided to find a spot on the gallery where she couldn't be seen and lurk there. If nothing happened, she'd slip away and deal with the consequences later. She could always try charming Reynard into forgiving her.

She pushed the gate open a few more inches and heard it creak. At the sound, something moved at the corner of her vision and in the next instant, a dark figure came rushing down the gallery steps. She let out a shriek and jumped to the side as the shape all but ran her down and then made a sharp turn on the banquette and was gone.

The front door flew open and St. Cyr was stepping onto the gallery with his wife and the fellow from the cemetery right behind him. He stared at her with eyes so terrible she could feel their heat even from that distance.

"What did you do?" he said.

Reynard's guess that she had pulled a galling trick was confirmed when he reached the garage and heard how she had convinced the attendant to let her take a vehicle. He was not the sort to berate anyone, but when he climbed into another of the sedans, the attendant was standing with his mouth agape at the scolding the editor had rained down on him. He steered the machine into the street knowing exactly where he was going.

Valentin called James McKinney to report what had happened. Then he returned to the kitchen where Rebecca was seated at the table with her head and eyes cast down. And yet when Valentin spoke to her, she looked up in defiance, a woman who did not wish to be corrected.

"So you didn't see a face," Valentin said.

"I told you, it happened too fast," she said. "There's nothing else I can tell you. You can stop asking." In the next moment, she realized it had come out with too hard an edge and retreated. "Am I going to be arrested?" Now her voice was subdued.

"That's not for me to decide," Valentin said. "You will be facing your editors, though. I called the newsroom. Reynard wasn't there. I'll try—"

Bells chimed, interrupting him. "Well, I wonder who that is?" he said and nodded for Each to get the door.

Reynard and Valentin spent a few minutes in the parlor before the editor stepped into the kitchen and escorted Rebecca out of the house without a word. The detective stood at the front window watching as an automobile pulled away and was lost in the darkness.

The mood in the kitchen was muted. A distraught Lucy sat next to Evangeline, who was patting her hand. Justine leaned at the counter, her arms crossed, staring at nothing, as if she was miles away. Tom Anderson looked tired but immensely relieved at the weight being lifted from his shoulders. And Each appeared befuddled by the wild minutes that had just passed.

Valentin took it upon himself to collect glasses from the cabinet and filled five glasses from the bottle Lucy had left out. They sipped in silence, barely moving until the telephone in the foyer shrilled.

Lucy said, "I'll get it," and rose to her feet.

Valentin guessed that it was McKinney calling, but when the maid returned, she fixed wide eyes on him and said, "I believe you better take this, sir."

Her voice was deliberate, beyond calm. But what had he expected from someone who coolly murdered four men in five days? She talked and he listened and when he did speak, it was the word, "Yes," until she told him what she wanted and he responded, "All right."

She broke the connection. He got the operator on the line and asked to be connected to Parish Precinct.

The three women and two men looked up when he reappeared in the kitchen.

"Was it?" Justine said. Valentin nodded. "Now what?"

"Lucy wants me to come to her."

"Come to her where?"

"Where do you think?" he said.

Ten minutes later, Justine and Each and he were ready to go out the door. Evangeline would stay at the house with Lucy. Tom Anderson rose without a word and shuffled his way to the downstairs bedroom, where the maid tucked him in. Lucy then went to find George, who now stood within reach of the William Read shotgun that was leaning in the corner. He looked none too pleased, but Valentin told him not to expect trouble.

It was time to leave.

"You'll be all right?" Justine asked Evangeline.

"I'll be fine," Evangeline said. "We'll be fine." She turned as Lucy settled into a chair. "Won't we?"

———

Leaving the house, Justine was pulling up her skirt and happened to see the package down the gallery and tipped on its side, likely kicked away in a moment of panic. She said, "What's...?" then: "Oh, my."

Valentin lifted it into Each's hands. "Carry it back inside and put it in the icebox," he said. "Don't say anything."

"What if they see?"

"It doesn't matter anymore," Valentin said.


Reynard and Rebecca arrived back at the newsroom and she crossed directly to her desk, dropped her bag, and slumped into her chair. She sat with her elbows on her blotter, leaning her forehead into her clasped hands and stayed so still and silent that Reynard wondered if she was praying.

He walked into Kassel's dark office and found his bottle of Scotch and two glasses. He poured both half-full and carried them to the corner. Rebecca shifted her eyes but did not straighten when he placed one next to her Underwood. When she made no move to pick it up, he tapped it with his glass and said, "I hate drinking alone."

She leaned back, and with an empty smile, hoisted the glass and sipped. After gazing at the liquid for a few moments, she said, "You don't have any hemlock, do you?"

"No hemlock," he said. "Sorry."

"What will happen to me?"

"I don't know," he said. "That's going to be up to Rolf."

"And the police."

"Yes. And the police."

"And I didn't even get a good look."

He had no reply to that, so he said, "Enjoy your drink," and headed back to his desk.

"You don't mind if I stay a while, do you?" she called after him. "I'd like to know how things turn out."

He said, "As long as you want," choosing not to mention that it might be the last time she'd get the chance.

———

They approached Parish Precinct to find McKinney standing by his Dodge. Two police sedans, both with dark shapes inside were waiting at the curb. Valentin put on the brakes and the lieutenant tossed the Omar he had been smoking into the gutter and stepped to the Ford.

"I'll ride with you," he said, and climbed into the back seat with Each.

During the seven-block drive, he explained the preparations that had been made to finally catch their prey in a net. "She'll be trapped," he said. "Unless she can fly."

Valentin said, "I would not be surprised." No one laughed.

# Twenty-Four

Valentin pulled the Ford to the curb a block from Eclipse Alley and directly across from Rachel Norman's bordello. It was Sunday, it was late, and it had been raining, so only a single lamp was burning in Miss Rachel's front window.

The headlights of the police sedans closed in behind. They sat for a moment. "What if she's not there?" Justine said.

"Then we might never see her again." Valentin studied the street. "Is everyone in place?"

"Four men at the other end," the lieutenant said. "And we'll close this side as soon as you're in."

When Valentin didn't make a move to get out, Justine said, "What is it?"

He laid his hands on the steering wheel. "I was just thinking that I'd be tempted to let her go if she just tells me why."

"I would prefer that you didn't," McKinney said.

Valentin said, "Then I won't," and opened the door.

For the first few seconds, he thought she had decided not to come. She could have easily gotten lost, disappeared into the dark lands beyond the city, gone to some other place to remain invisible. He doubted she'd finish with another try for Mr. Tom. With the men McKinney had placed inside and outside the house it would be too risky. Unless she didn't care what happened anymore.

He moved a dozen steps past the spot where Herbert Waltham's butchered body had fallen, farther from the street and deeper into the darkness than he'd gone before. All the doors and windows of the abandoned storefronts were boarded-up and he could hear only the faintest street noise from ahead and behind. Only a hundred feet and he'd be seeing the lights where the alley opened onto Marais Street and if she wasn't in sight, his question would be answered. A few more steps and he began to wonder if he had played a bad hand and she had—

"I'm here."

He stopped in a smooth motion that hid his surprise. A few seconds and one of the shadows took on form and then wavered to the center of the alley, where it was still lit enough for him to see.

She was perhaps a half-head shorter than he and didn't carry much extra weight. He studied her face and found it striking, an oval with soft cheekbones on either side of a nose that was neither sharp nor round over lips that were full. Instead of light coffee, her skin tone was a shade of copper. Her lids were slightly slanted, but the eyes themselves were wide and black. While the shadows were being kind, he expected that she'd be no less of a beauty under the full light of day.

Only one other murderer that he had encountered came close to matching the fine features displayed in that alley. And that one had been possessed of a fierce and furious fire, while Arcelle remained as calm as a creature deep in the forest.

There was more. She was sending out waves of the same kind of wicked allure Justine possessed, transmitting that same electricity, along with something else, the jagged shreds of whatever madness had driven her to commit her crimes

All this passed through his mind in the ten seconds she stood without speaking, watching him intently, yet not like a stranger; indeed, she had seen him at least a half-dozen times, a reminder of the cunning that had brought them both back to Eclipse Alley.

"Arcelle," he said.

The vaguest hint of a smile tilted her mouth and she looked past him. "You got police waiting out there?"

"I do. At both ends. How would you like this to go?"

Instead of answering, she said, "I was close. If it wasn't for that woman, the reporter. I could have..." She raised a hand and rubbed her forehead in an absent motion. "What did he tell you?"

"That something happened to you. And that he did nothing."

"So now he thinks he got away with it."

"He doesn't. He asked forgiveness. It was the first thing he said."

"Forgiveness from who?"

"You. God."

Her laugh was jagged. "I can't help him. Maybe God can. I don't really believe in forgiveness."

"So I saw." Now she produced a faraway smile and he said, "You know we don't have a lot of time."

"I know."

"Tell me why all this happened."

Her attention came back to him. "You couldn't figure it for yourself? I read that you were a master detective."

"I don't think that's true," he said. "I could only pick up pieces. You moved so fast."

"I had to."

"Because?"

"Once I saw the photograph in the newspaper. Mr. Waltham. The priest. That lawyer. The police captain. Mr. Anderson. I couldn't give anyone time to catch me. So I went on the hunt. And murdered four men. I mean executed." She shifted, studying him. "What *do* you know?"

Valentin said, "I told you. Pieces. That you were here and then something happened and you went away. You came back and committed all this..."

"Mayhem?"

"Yes. All that's pretty much all. I need you to tell me the rest."

A random noise echoed down the alley from Marais Street and she tensed in a way that made him fear she was about to bolt and take her chances. Then she settled again.

"I had seen him before," she said. "Waltham. He came to the house. His eyes were always on me when I was around. Watching me. Then he started asking about me. He spoke to my mother and she said, *Not for sale.* That should have been the end of it."

Valentin felt himself wince. *But it wasn't.*

"So he went to French Emma Johnson. He must have paid her a lot of money. Because she arranged to have me taken." She pointed back toward Liberty Street. "From there. A man grabbed me and carried me through here and to the other side." She stopped and her eyes swept the cobblestones. "They had a car waiting. And they took me to French Emma's."

For all his years spent in the dirtiest corners of the District, Valentin had rarely felt his skin crawl. Sensing what was coming, he did now.

Arcelle's tone remained matter-of-fact. "Mr. Waltham had paid that witch to have someone grab me up for him. So he could break me in. And he did. They made me drink whiskey before it started, but I knew what was happening." Her eyes hardened. "They took me to this bedroom. Someone stripped off my clothes. He was a big man. Heavy. Rough. I was bleeding. He held his hand over my mouth. He..." Now the words came slower. "He didn't just break me in. He broke me. Like I was made of sticks. At the end, my mind wasn't there anymore. It was gone. And I wasn't me." She drew a long breath. "After, they carried me back to Miss Ruby's. The driver tried to give my mother money. She threw it in his face."

Valentin kept silent, feeling a shadow of heartbreak coming over him.

"She stayed up with me all night. I thought I was going to die." She didn't speak for a dark moment. Then she continued. "I lost my mind over it and they took me to that place across the river." She made a faint gesture to the south.

"You ran away."

"It wasn't like that. After my sister came to visit, I asked to be taken somewhere else. I couldn't stand for her to see me like that." She smiled in a melancholy way. "So I made up a story. They found a place for me outside Biloxi and contacted my mother and she paid. All those years, she paid with the money she made right here. In Storyville. She did that and then she was dead." She looked at him. "What happened to me killed her. I believe that."

Valentin did, too. "So, then?"

"I got through their school and I decided I wanted to be a nurse. Like the ones who were so kind to me in those places. I took the training and I got my license. Twelve of us went to France to work in field hospitals. What I saw there..." She shook her head. "After I came back, I found a position in Savannah."

Valentin considered first what a wonder it was that she had accomplished so much and second, that it explained the ease with the drugs she had used. There wasn't time to dwell on either part. "Why did you come here?"

"Because I wanted to find Camille. But she wasn't at the house anymore. And her name wasn't in the..."

"*Blue Book?*"

"Yes. I was only here a day and I knew I couldn't stay. This place..."

Valentin was about to speak up about her sister, then thought better of it and let her continue.

"I was at the station, ready to leave, and I saw a newspaper lying open. And there was the photograph." She was quiet for a long moment. "I sat on the bench for an hour and then went to find a telephone book and a shop to buy paper and an envelope. I wrote a letter and carried it to the address in the book."

She noticed the way he was studying her and said, "I surprise you."

"Yes. It's all you've done so far."

"I surprise me, too," she said. "I never thought I could ever do these awful things. But then there they were, standing all proud, smiling like they owned the world. Like they would do their parts all over again if they could. I thought about what it had done to me. And my mother. And I just..." She let the sentence hang.

Valentin sensed nothing moving behind or ahead of him, but the minutes were going by and he knew James would not wait all night. When he turned back, she was becoming animated, her hands moving about and her features turning feral. "I left a letter for Waltham. I threatened to tell everyone what he'd done. Get someone to listen. Start it all over again." She smiled. "I'm sure he thought I was going to ask for money. That's how they all think. Money."

"So you lured him."

"Yes. After I went by the apothecary and purchased the supplies I needed." The smile turned cold. "He had no idea of what I was going to do."

"You mean cut him up like that?"

"Yes. That's what I did. While he was still breathing. Staring up at me." "She looked over her shoulder at the spot where she had done the deed. I think he quite deserved it."

Valentin drew a long breath. "Why Father O'Brien?"

She faced him again. "The church owned the house. Waltham went to mass there. The day after it happened, Miss Ruby told the Father. But he already knew. Waltham had run to him to confess. The Father said that his sin was forgiven. And that was the end of it."

Valentin sighed and shook his head.

"So I pulled myself together and rode the streetcars to the church to talk to him. I walked right into the confessional. And as soon as he understood who I was, he left and had a man come and take me away. His name was..."

"Terrell," Valentin said. "The deacon."

"He grabbed me by the arm so hard I thought he was going to break it. I asked why he was treating me that way and he said that Mr. Waltham gave more money to the church than anyone in New Orleans. And that's what mattered. Then he said to stop or he'd have my mother and everyone else put out on the street." Her voice had gone brittle. "And they were supposed to be Christian men."

Valentin allowed a moment for her to calm herself. "What about Barry? The attorney."

"He was responsible for prosecuting crimes. My mother went and asked him to have that man and Emma Johnson arrested. Put in jail. Shamed. But he wouldn't. I guess he wished he had."

"You did that all alone?"

"All alone. You don't believe it?"

"No, I do." There wasn't time to explain. "Captain Warren. He was the officer in charge of the District."

"We never asked him for anything," she said. "But he came to the house and told my mama that if she and I didn't stop making trouble, he'd have the both us locked up."

"What was in his dinner?"

"Cyanide. To stop his heart."

"It did."

"Yes, sir, it did, didn't it?" She raised her arms in a vague plea. "But you understand I had to do it. To all of them."

"And what about Tom Anderson?" he asked.

"Him?" she said. "He was my last chance. He knew what happened. He was 'the King of Storyville.' He could have done something. He did nothing. Some king."

"He got rid of Emma Johnson. Ran her out of town."

"Is that what happened? I was coming for her, too. Is she dead or alive?"

"I don't know," he said. "Either way, she's bound for hell."

She turned his way, her face composed in sadness, a lovely young woman who had been brutalized. "Too late for me."

Valentin was at a loss. He had come face to face with a dozen murderers. Half had taken more than a single life and what marked them all was the lunacy that seethed in their eyes and in their guts, a black rage that drove them on until he finished their careers. Or made it possible for someone else to. Arcelle was nothing like any of them. Though behind her eyes, he saw the same flat, empty light. But she was guilty in any case and would pay for her crimes.

She said, "So, Mr. Valentin?"

It was the first time she had spoken his name. It was strange though not unpleasant. He knew it was time to end it. But instead he said, "Buddy Bolden."

She cocked her head, puzzled. "Buddy Bolden, did you say? Who is that?"

"You didn't..."

"Didn't what?"

"Never mind," he said. Then: "I'm sorry for what happened to you. For what's going to happen now."

"You don't think I could make them believe it was all the doing of a madwoman?"

"You want to make up a story?" he said, bringing a smile. "I don't think that would work this time."

"No, probably not." She was quiet for a few seconds, then said, "All right, then. You go out ahead and I'll follow."

A moment of concern niggled at the back of his mind and he took a step closer. She didn't flinch, instead meeting his gaze, her eyes still ponds. He entertained another a flicker of doubt, but then nodded and said, "All right... all right."

"Let them know I'm coming. I don't want to get shot. Not after all this."

"Just make sure you come out this way," he told her. "I can't say what those others will do."

She said, "I understand."

He backed away from her and did not turn around until he reached the bend in the alley. When he was within a dozen paces of the street, he looked over his shoulder into the darkness. Two more steps and he stopped and grasped his head in his hands, aghast at his own stupidity, and let out a raw shout.

In a dozen quick strides, he was back to where he had found her. Another twenty and he was staring out at Liberty Street and the two detectives and two uniformed coppers who had been posted there. He whispered, "How did you..." and began a hard walk back the way he had come.

In the darkness, the fourth door looked exactly like the others, but when he laid a hand on its surface, it swung in on silent hinges. He pushed it the rest of the way open and saw darkness and a faint gleam on the far end. And he laughed out loud.

Lieutenant McKinney was on the verge of following Valentin into the alley when he saw the Creole detective appear and race down the banquette in the direction of St. Louis Street. He did leap out then, and followed behind.

He reached the corner. "Valentin? What the hell? Where is she? What happened?"

Valentin caught his breath. "What happened? What happened was she told me a story." And he laughed again, this time in resignation.

———

It developed into a bizarre night. What seemed every police officer in New Orleans, from the lowest recruit to the Chief, showed up at one time or another, and each one at least glanced at the Creole detective. Police vehicles rolled this way and that. Eclipse Alley—and especially the storefront with the loose door—were examined once and again. Uniformed coppers spread out through all the streets and alleys for ten blocks in an attempt to pick up any trace of her. The bordellos from Marais to Basin all got visits and even the crib whores on Robertson and Claiborne were rousted.

Valentin and James McKinney stood in the midst of it, watching and speaking little. The only mention of Arcelle, in fact, was the lieutenant saying, "I wish I could have seen her." Valentine considered that it was probably best that he hadn't.

Reporters from all the newspapers arrived, with Reynard Vernel representing the *Times-Picayune*. Valentin waved him over. The lieutenant told him he'd give him something for the Monday evening edition, not before. For now, he could report that the search for the murderer of the four men was ongoing. No one mentioned Rebecca Marcus.

Valentin left the lieutenant with his officers. As he walked back to the car, he felt the throb of an ancient sadness that reappeared every time he reached the end of a trail. How deep in his flesh and blood was the anguish buried? He couldn't say. He knew only that it would never quite leave him, but that he was kept from being dragged into its dark clutches by the joys that he had been so lucky to find.

He saw one waiting for him next to the Ford, her face so full of concern that he could make out every detail from fifty paces. He saw it soften as she realized that he was unharmed and it stopped him in his tracks. Then he kept walking until he reached her arms.

# TWENTY-FIVE

The last of the rain and most of the clouds passed overnight and Monday morning dawned under the odd orange light that only falls on certain places at certain times.

Though he had been up half the night, Valentin was awake to witness it, sitting on the top step of the back gallery with a cup of coffee that tasted of bitter chicory. The day's first birds were twittering in the branches and he thought about how their songs never ended, passed on one generation to the next, an endless melody. Even as it reminded him of Bolden, the clopping of hooves and the creaking wheels of the milkman's hack, one of the few vestiges left from horse-drawn days, a fond memory.

He was surprised that he felt so at peace after allowing a murderer to weave a spell and escape his clutches. Oh, there would be hell to pay. The fingers would point at both McKinney and him, but wasn't he the one who had stood mere feet from her in that narrow alley and let her slip away into the night? For the first time in his history of working the red-light district he had failed to take down his quarry, a defeat he never would have imagined. The great Valentin St. Cyr had finally been beaten. And yet it felt like any other Monday morning.

He sat for the better part of an hour, thinking random thoughts. As the sun shifted to soft yellow, he became aware of a presence and turned his head to see Evangeline standing in the doorway in one of her worn Mother Hubbards. She studied his face, her eyes curious and at the same time deep with sympathy for his plight.

He said, "It's all right."

She nodded and after a vague moment, turned her attention to the sounds and the colors of the garden, breathing it in as if downing an elixir. They waited there, not speaking for long minutes, until Evangeline came out of her reverie and said, "Valentin? She's calling you."

He stood up and as he passed her, she stopped him with a gentle palm over his heart, as if to feel its beat.

Justine was in the kitchen, standing in the middle of the floor with her hands at her sides. "Did you sleep at all?" she said.

"Some. Did you?"

"Not really."

He sighed and said, "I'm sorry."

"Are you feeling bad?"

He said, "I should be, but I'm not."

"Do you think there's any chance she'll be caught?"

"I doubt it," he said.

"What will happen today?"

"I don't know, except that James will be coming by."

"He already called," she said. "He's on his way."

"So he didn't sleep either."

"I'll make coffee," she said.

"No, I'll do it." He poured what was left in his cup into the sink. "You can..." He waved toward the back garden.

The women appeared ten minutes later. Valentin joined them at the table and they talked about nothing for the half-hour it took the lieutenant to arrive. When Valentin opened the door, he saw the morning paper still on the gallery, but decided to leave it. There would be time for that.

James sat down with his coffee. Turning to Valentin, he said, "How much do you need to know?"

"You can leave out the parts that don't matter."

"There's been no trace of her," the lieutenant began. "The search is continuing, but they're not expecting results, even with your description. They're figuring that if she could completely evade the police in a city this small, she's gone."

"I suspect that's right," Valentin said. He caught an uneasy glance and said, "Go ahead, James."

"The weight for this is going to land on you."

"I guessed as much," Valentin said. "What about your situation?"

"I'll be fine."

"Because they can't afford to lose a good detective," Valentin said.

"But they want us both downtown. To report to the brass."

Valentin said, "When?"

"Today."

"Can it wait until this afternoon?"

"I'm sure it can. I'll call and make arrangements."

"After we eat," Valentin said and mused on how much he had just sounded like Frank Mangetta.

Evangeline began to rise, then sat back down. She had said nothing all the way back from Tom Anderson's and when they reached the house, excused herself and went directly to bed. Now she was watching Valentin with her steady, knowing eyes.

"Tell me about Eclipse Alley," she said.

He tried to explain, but found himself struggling. What had happened? Did she bewitch him into letting down his guard, as Rebecca Marcus had tried but failed to do? Did he once again fall prey to the mystery of a woman? Or was he in that moment unable to continue with Storyville's bizarre dramas and, like its one-time king Tom Anderson, had at long last left it behind?

"I don't know what else to say," he murmured after several starts and stops. "I'll need time to think about it."

"Are you going to tell anyone what happened to her?" Justine said. "You're the only one she told."

Valentin said, "Like who?"

"The newspapers," she said.

"I might," Valentin said. "But it's over. Four men are dead. They all took part in a horrible abuse, but..."

"None of them committed murder," James said.

"So maybe it's best to let it rest." He looked at the lieutenant, who shrugged.

Evangeline said, "Do you think you'll ever see her again?"

Valentin sat back. The notion had not occurred to him. "Somehow I think I will," he said at last. "It's just a feeling."

Evangeline pondered this and then said, "Well, that means something, doesn't it?" She didn't wait for a reply before rising from the table to begin cooking.

After a musing silence, the lieutenant said, "What will you do now?"

"I'm going to find out about Bolden," Valentin said. "And that recording. The whole matter has me baffled. Other than that, I have no idea." He turned to his wife. "What will we do now?"

Justine said, "We'll live our lives." She laid her hand on his. "We'll be fine. We'll all be fine."

They spoke of small matters until Evangeline turned from the stove to say, "It's time."

# Thanks are due.

To my publishers Joe Phillips and Susan Wood, cover artist Kerrie Kemperman, and editor emeritus Michael Allen Zell.

To Sansanee Sermprungsuk, who brought first-rate skills as editor of this work and to typesetter extraordinaire Geoff Munsterman. Both did their parts to right the book whenever it ran astray and carry it to completion as true professionals. Any and all errors are mine.

And to all those who offered the little kindnesses that made all the difference.

**DAVID FULMER** is the author of eleven critically acclaimed and award-winning novels. *Chasing the Devil's Tail* was nominated for a *Los Angeles Times* Book Prize, a Barry Award, and a Falcon Award, was on Borders' "Best of 2003 List," and won the 2002 Shamus Award. *Jass* was nominated for the "Best of 2005" lists by *Library Journal, Deadly Pleasures Magazine,* and *The St. Louis Post-Dispatch. Rampart Street* was rated *New York Magazine's* "Best Novels You've Never Read" and the audiobook won a Benjamin Franklin Award. *The Dying Crapshooter's Blues* received the BookPage "Ice Pick of the Month Award" among other plaudits and *The Blue Door* was nominated for the Shamus Award for Best Novel. His books have received superlative reviews from *The Times Picayune, The New York Times, Publishers Weekly, The San Francisco Chronicle, The Washington Post, The St. Louis Post-Dispatch, BookList, Kirkus Reviews, The Baltimore Sun, Mystery Review, The Detroit News, The Telegraph (UK), The Plain Dealer, Crime Spree Magazine, The Boston Globe, Crimetime UK, The Tennessean, Library Journal, Jazz Review, The Christian Science Monitor,* and numerous other publications and book websites. His novels have been released in audiobook and have been translated into Italian, French, Japanese, and Turkish. A native of central Pennsylvania, David Fulmer lives in Atlanta with his wife Sansanee Sermprungsuk

CRESCENT CITY BOOKS
New Orleans, LA
www.blackwidowpress.com

*The Sound of Building Coffins* by Louis Maistros (2018)

THE VALENTIN ST. CYR MYSTERIES by David Fulmer

*Chasing the Devil's Tail*

*Jass*

*Rampart Street*

*Lost River*

*The Iron Angel*

*Eclipse Alley*